Maybe her withdrawal had been a form of punishment,

Becca thought, a subconscious attempt to atone for the heinous crime of allowing her child to be stolen. Of course, her self-imposed sentence had ended up punishing Ryan, as well.

Ryan was and always would be the father of her child. For that reason alone, Becca owed him.

The least she could do was *pretend* being close to him didn't arouse all sorts of treacherous desires she had no intention of giving in to.

So she agreed to his suggestion that they give their daughter a stable, loving environment.

A smile crossed Ryan's face, a smile Becca didn't trust. "Now that we have that settled," he said lazily, skimming his warm hand along her bare arm, "I think we should get married."

Dear Reader,

Welcome to Silhouette Special Edition...welcome to romance.

That telltale sign of falling leaves signals that autumn has arrived and so have heartwarming books to take you into the season.

Two exciting series from veteran authors continue in the month of September. Christine Rimmer's THE JONES GANG returns with *A Home for the Hunter*. And the Rogue River is once again the exciting setting for Laurie Paige's WILD RIVER series in *A River To Cross*.

This month, our THAT SPECIAL WOMAN! is Anna Louise Perkins, a courageous woman who rises to the challenge of bringing love and happiness to the man of her dreams. You'll meet her in award-winning author Sherryl Woods's *The Parson's Waiting*.

Also in September, don't miss *Rancher's Heaven* from Robin Elliott, *Miracle Child* by Kayla Daniels and *Family Connections,* a debut book in Silhouette Special Edition by author Judith Yates.

I hope you enjoy this book, and all of the stories to come!

Sincerely,

Tara Gavin
Senior Editor

Please address questions and book requests to:
Silhouette Reader Service
U.S.: 3010 Walden Ave., P.O. Box 1325, Buffalo, NY 14269
Canadian: P.O. Box 609, Fort Erie, Ont. L2A 5X3

KAYLA DANIELS
MIRACLE CHILD

Silhouette ®

SPECIAL EDITION ®

Published by Silhouette Books

America's Publisher of Contemporary Romance

To my adorable niece Amanda,
and to Kirsti and Bill,
who let me share the miracle.

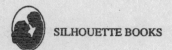 SILHOUETTE BOOKS

ISBN 0-373-09911-8

MIRACLE CHILD

Copyright © 1994 by Karin Hofland

This edition published by arrangement with Harlequin Enterprises B. V.

Printed in U.S.A.

Books by Kayla Daniels

Silhouette Special Edition

Spitting Image #474
Father Knows Best #578
Hot Prospect #654
Rebel to the Rescue #707
From Father to Son #790
Heiress Apparent #814
Miracle Child #911

KAYLA DANIELS

is a former computer programmer who enjoys travel, ballroom dancing and playing with her nieces and nephews. She grew up in Southern California and has lived in Alaska, Norway, Minnesota, Alabama and Louisiana. Currently she makes her home in Grass Valley, California.

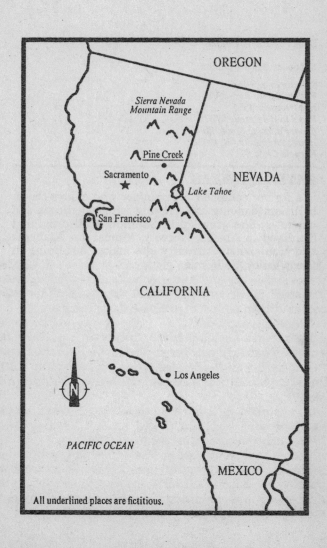

OREGON

Sierra Nevada
Mountain Range

⋀ Pine Creek

Sacramento
★

NEVADA

Lake Tahoe

San Francisco

CALIFORNIA

N

Los Angeles

PACIFIC OCEAN

MEXICO

All underlined places are fictitious.

Prologue

The lights of the midway glittered like a rainbow of gemstones strewn across the velvety backdrop of the night sky. The smell of popcorn and gleeful screams from the roller coaster drifted out over the county fairgrounds.

"Mommy, see! See!"

Becca Slater knelt beside the stroller, her eyes lifting upward in the direction of her small daughter's excited wave. "Ooh, such a big Ferris wheel, Amy! When you're a little bit older, Mommy and Daddy will take you to ride on it, okay?"

As she tilted back her head to watch the Ferris wheel's slow, dizzying pirouette, Becca amended her promise. "Well, maybe *Daddy* will take you."

She glanced down just in time to see Amy produce an enormous yawn. "Poor little angel." Becca adjusted the position of her child's favorite toy so that Amy could use the raggedy, one-eared teddy bear as a pillow. "You're so tired you can barely keep your eyes open, aren't you?"

Becca pushed herself to her feet and studied her drowsy daughter with unabashed adoration. "I guess even a two-year-old has to run out of energy sometime, huh?" She bent down to whisk a stray blond curl from Amy's half-closed eyes. "Tell you the truth, I'm kind of tuckered out myself, sweetie."

Amy's head drooped slowly to one side like a wilting sunflower, then jerked abruptly upright. Becca smiled at her little girl's stubborn refusal to surrender to sleep. "How 'bout we sit down on that nice bench over there while we wait for the fireworks to start?"

Amy clutched her beloved teddy bear closer and let her head plop down on top of his.

"Then after the fireworks, we can go home and tell Daddy how much fun we had today." Becca batted aside the red helium balloon tied to the stroller's handle and began to push. "Of course, we'd have had a lot more fun if he'd been with us, but we won't tell him that. Daddy already feels bad enough that he couldn't come with us."

Amy's only response was a soft gurgling sound.

Becca steered her way through the crowd and sank gratefully onto the empty bench in front of the livestock nursery. Behind her she could hear the peaceful bleating of lambs and the indignant snorting of piglets as the baby animals rustled in their pens, jostling for a closer position to their mothers.

She maneuvered the stroller so Amy was facing her, and saw that her exhausted toddler had finally lost her battle with the sandman. Without warning, a nearly overwhelming tide of love swelled up in Becca's chest and for a moment she could hardly breathe.

Asleep, Amy looked like a little angel—though a slightly grubby angel at the moment. Her silky eyelashes dusted cheeks that were sticky-pink from cotton candy. Becca pried a corn dog wrapper from her daughter's chubby fingers and brushed back a lock of the wispy, pale gold hair that was so like her own.

"My sweet little ray of sunshine," she murmured tenderly, using the tip of her finger to wipe a dab of mustard from the corner of Amy's puckered, Cupid's-bow mouth. Amy inhaled sharply, just once, then settled back into dreamland without opening her eyes. She smacked her rosy lips as if she could smell the cinnamon rolls being sold from a booth across the way.

Scattered throughout the fairgrounds, tall Douglas firs arrowed up like tent poles to prop up the black canopy of the sky. Becca leaned her head against the back of the wooden bench, gazed contentedly up at the stars, and thought what a fine thing it was to be at the county fair on a balmy summer evening, to be young and madly in love with her handsome husband, to have the most adorable, perfect child in the entire world.

The only thing that could have made this glorious day any better was if Ryan had been able to come with them. But a last-minute crisis at the building site had disrupted their plans. As general contractor for the project, Ryan was responsible for overseeing any problems that arose. He couldn't bear to disappoint Amy, though, and so had insisted that Becca and Amy go to the fair without him.

Well, never mind, Becca consoled herself. *There'll be plenty of other county fairs. After all, we have our whole lives ahead of us, and—*

"Maggie, no!"

A sudden commotion distracted Becca from her thoughts. Ten yards away, a girl of eleven or twelve was wrestling awkwardly with a brown-and-white calf that had apparently decided it didn't want to go back to the 4-H barn.

"Come on, Maggie, please!"

Becca glanced around, saw that none of the other fairgoers had yet noticed the girl's predicament. The poor kid looked about ready to cry, and the calf was making piteous, half-panicked noises as it strained against the rope tied around its neck.

Becca had always had a way with animals, and the situation seemed to be veering rapidly toward disaster. When no one else rushed to the rescue, she hopped up, checked to make sure Amy was still sound asleep, then jogged the short distance to where the girl and the calf were engaged in a desperate tug-of-war.

"Easy," Becca crooned to the struggling calf. "Easy there, sweetheart...everything's going to be just fine...."

The calf regarded her with huge, terrified eyes at first, but the soothing tone of Becca's voice combined with the gentle, reassuring touch of her hand soon calmed the poor animal down.

"Gee, thanks, ma'am," the girl said breathlessly when her charge finally stopped trying to escape. Red-faced and obviously embarrassed, she surreptitiously knuckled tears from her eyes.

"Can you make it back to the barn by yourself?" Becca asked. *Ma'am?* she thought in amazement. *That's it. Twenty-six years old and already I'm over the hill.* She bit her lip to short-circuit a grin as the calf nuzzled her palm.

"I think so," the girl replied. "Maggie just got scared by all the screaming, I guess." She gestured at the carnival rides, then pulled cautiously on the rope. Maggie appeared ready to follow her owner docilely this time. "Well, thanks again. I sure appreciate your help." Turning, the girl waved goodbye over her shoulder.

"Good luck!" Becca returned her wave with an amused smile, then headed back to the bench. The stroller was facing away from her as she approached, and it wasn't until she got close to it that she realized something was wrong.

Becca's smile faded. She practically flew the last several steps, propelled by a rush of adrenaline.

The stroller was empty.

Becca's long hair streamed through the air as she whirled her head back and forth, anxiously seeking a glimpse of her missing child. "Amy?" Her voice was a thin quaver. "Amy?" she called again, more loudly this time.

Her toe nudged a soft object on the ground. Looking down, she saw that it was Amy's bedraggled teddy bear. Becca's heart congealed into a cold lump of fear. She stooped to retrieve the bear, then dropped it into the stroller with trembling hands.

"No," she whispered through lips gone dry as paper. "Oh, no."

She ran a few steps in one direction, scanned the surrounding area, then dashed back the other way. Her heart was slamming so loudly against her ribs she could barely hear her own voice. "Amy?"

Becca plunged her fingers through her hair. Dear God, she'd only turned her back for a minute ... Amy had been sound asleep ... how could she have climbed out of the stroller and wandered off in such a short time?

She rushed back to the stroller, hoping against hope that she was either hallucinating or losing her mind—that Amy was, after all, still where Becca had left her.

But the stroller's only occupant was the one-eared teddy bear. The red balloon tied to the handle bobbed in the faint breeze.

Now Becca's initial alarm clawed its way toward terror. Black spots peppered her vision and she swayed for a moment, certain she was about to faint. She clenched her jaws together and dug her nails viciously into her palms. "Don't pass out now," she muttered through gritted teeth. "You've got to find Amy."

The stabbing pain restored Becca to full consciousness, but did nothing to banish her light-headedness or the nausea churning in her stomach, threatening to rise up inside her and explode. She retraced her steps again, frantically searching the shadows for the figure of a little lost girl.

"Amy?" she shouted, her voice rising nearly to a shriek. "Amy?"

Passersby were starting to stare at her, some embarrassed, others sympathetic. Becca clutched at their arms. "Have you seen a little girl? A little, two-year-old, blond girl wandering around by herself?"

She tried in vain to staunch the flood of panic pouring through her as she received nothing but helpless shrugs and shakes of the head. Deep inside Becca a little voice was whispering ominously that Amy couldn't have just crawled out of the stroller and wandered off. She'd been sound asleep...there hadn't been enough time for her to vanish from the immediate vicinity all by herself...and she would never have left her teddy bear behind.

Someone must have taken her.

"No, no, no," Becca chanted over and over, trying to ignore that sinister voice and the unthinkable implications of Amy's abrupt disappearance. Her terrified denials echoed the horrible throbbing at her temples. Her entire body shook as if she suffered from life-threatening fever. The fairgrounds seemed to waver and tilt, as if she were staggering past the distorted mirrors in the fun house. She stumbled and nearly fell.

Panicked gulps of air ripped in and out of her lungs. With pain searing her insides, Becca dashed back to the stroller one last time. At the sight of that abandoned teddy bear staring blindly up at her from the otherwise empty seat, fear and despair and hysteria all collided and came crashing down around her like an avalanche. She jammed her fists to the sides of her head and started to scream. "Amy! Amy!"

Overhead a colorful explosion blossomed across the night sky. For a moment at least, Becca's anguished cries were drowned out by the first deafening burst of fireworks.

"*A-A-m-m-y-y...*"

Chapter One

Ryan Slater came to a screeching stop beside the curb and swore.

Damn. He was too late.

Already reporters were gathering like vultures in front of Becca's Sacramento home, and no doubt there'd be plenty more lying in wait at the airport.

He gripped the steering wheel in frustration, then noticed his hands were shaking.

Well, nothing remarkable about that. His hands had been shaking ever since the Florida cops had called him this morning.

Might as well get this over with. Heaving his six-foot frame out of the pickup, Ryan slammed the door reading Slater Construction. Then he lowered his head and strode determinedly up Becca's front walk like a wide receiver heading for the end zone.

Someone yelled, "Hey, it's the father!"

In two seconds flat they were swarming all over him, sticking their microphones into his face, bombarding him with questions.

"How do you feel, Mr. Slater, to find out your daughter's still alive?"

"What's the first thing you're going to say to Amy when you see her?"

"Any chance of a reconciliation between you and Mrs. Slater?"

"Idiots," Ryan muttered under his breath. How did he *feel?* For Christ's sake, how the hell would any father feel when the child he'd given up for dead was suddenly, miraculously found alive? He wanted to holler with joy, to hurl himself down on his knees and give thanks, to slam his fists into a wall with rage over the four long years that had been stolen from all their lives.

He elbowed a particularly aggressive reporter out of his way. "No *com*ment," he replied, punctuating his statement with a strategic stomp on the man's instep.

The press trailed him up the front steps like a herd of pesky sheep. Ryan pounded on the door. "Becca, it's me!" He had to shout to be heard over the commotion. "Open up!"

The door instantly cracked an inch as if she'd been hovering right on the other side of it. It closed again while she fiddled with the chain latch, then reopened a scant foot or so.

Ryan squeezed through the narrow opening, resisting the urge to yell, "Back! Back!" as if holding a pack of slavering rottweilers at bay.

He banged the door shut, shot home three dead bolts, and turned to face Becca.

Becca. The woman he'd married . . . the woman who'd borne his child . . . the woman he'd once sworn to love for the rest of his life.

He hadn't stood this close to her for nearly three years.

"Becca," he said. It came out sounding like a croak, yet somehow that one word managed to convey both the plaintive echo of everything they'd suffered, and wondrous awe at this incredible miracle they'd been granted.

"Hello, Ryan." She spoke so quietly he practically had to read her lips.

Instinctively he moved forward, needing to share this moment with her, to hold her in his arms and feel her heart beating against his.

Becca recoiled with an upraised hand, as if he'd threatened to strike her. With lightning-quick reflexes Ryan halted in midstride, while they could both still pretend it hadn't happened. Almost.

He couldn't see Becca too well in the darkened living room, but it was pretty darn obvious she didn't share this crazy need of his to hold each other close.

Clearing his throat, Ryan flicked a thumb over his shoulder. "How long have they been out there?" Inane question. Yet what words could possibly be adequate at a time like this?

Becca rubbed her upper arms as if she were chilly, even though it was mid-July and the temperature in the house had to be at least eighty degrees. "Since early this evening." Her voice sounded rusty, as if she hadn't used it much lately. Or as if she'd spent the six hours since Ryan's phone call crying.

"I'd hoped we could at least get her home before the press descended on us, but I guess that wasn't too realistic."

She made a sound that might have been agreement. After the bright glare of the cameras, it had taken a while for Ryan's vision to adjust to the house's dim interior. Now he noticed things he hadn't before. Like the red puffiness around Becca's blue eyes. Like her new, shorter haircut. Like the fact that she must have dropped ten pounds since she'd left Pine Creek three years ago—pounds she couldn't afford to lose.

Her hands were knotted tightly together, as if she were afraid they would fly off if she didn't hold on to them. After an awkward pause, she sprang into motion with abrupt, jerky movements, grabbing her purse from the couch and hoisting the suitcase that waited nearby. "I'm ready," she announced. "Let's go."

"Becca, her flight won't land for nearly two hours. Wouldn't you be more comfortable—"

"Ryan, *please*." She swallowed, looking abashed by the faintly hysterical note in her voice. "I—I've been climbing the walls ever since you called this afternoon. I can't stay here another minute. Please." She blinked very rapidly, as if trying to hold back tears. "I feel like I'm under siege here. I want to get to the airport. We could get held up in traffic, or her plane could be early, or... or—"

"All right." Now Ryan was approaching the verge of tears himself. The strain of the past twelve hours—hell, the strain of the past four *years*—had definitely taken its toll. All day long, watching the minutes tick by with infinite slowness... knowing that a full sixty of them would have to drag by before he was even one hour closer to seeing his beautiful baby girl again....

He could certainly sympathize with Becca's eagerness to get going. "Here, let me carry that for you." He reached for her suitcase, his fingers brushing hers. Becca snatched her hand back as if he'd scorched her. Ryan glanced at her sharply.

She twisted her fingers together and mustered a nervous little laugh. "Guess I'm kind of on edge just now."

"Understandable."

"I really appreciate your picking me up like this. I could have met you at the airport, you know."

"Don't be ridiculous. I wouldn't let you go through all this by yourself." *And I certainly wouldn't let you drive yourself anywhere in this condition.* Tactfully, Ryan kept his thoughts to himself. Becca looked like a woman ready to come apart at the seams. Not that he blamed her. He felt a little frayed around the edges himself. "Ready?"

She nodded decisively, a hint of her old spunk showing through. Ryan felt better. Then, as he undid the locks, the expectant hubbub from outside crescendoed sharply.

Becca froze. Her limbs simply stopped moving, like the Tin Man's in *The Wizard of Oz.*

How can I go out there? she thought. *How can I face all those people after . . . after—*

Her mind refused to travel any farther down that path. Fortunately her heart took over. *Amy. My sweet, darling, precious Amy is coming home to me at last. Nothing else matters compared to that.*

"Becca, we could sneak out the back way, or—"

"No, I'm fine." Ha! She was a long way from fine. She managed to stab on a pair of dark glasses, even though her hands were shaking like someone coming down off a week-long bender.

"You sure you're all right?"

"I'm sure." Another lie. "Come on. Let's get this over with." She had to consciously order her limbs to perform, like a marionette's. *Reach for doorknob. Turn doorknob. Pull door open. Step out onto porch.*

The mob of jostling reporters surged forward. Flash-bulbs popped like firecrackers and the spotlights from TV Minicams nearly blinded her, even with sunglasses on. A thicket of microphones was suddenly thrust into her face like a magician's bouquet.

The jumbled barrage of curious faces and shouted questions paralyzed her. Then, with a shock, Becca felt Ryan's hand plant itself firmly in the small of her back. He propelled her forward through the crowd, using her suitcase as a battering ram to shove people aside.

"Let us through, please. Hey! Out of our way, if you don't mind."

Becca ducked her head, letting her hair fall forward to shield her face. Ryan's steady breathing was hot on the back of her neck. She kept setting one foot in front of the other, trusting him to somehow see her safely through this dreadful chaos.

He reached around her and opened a door. "Hop in," he shouted in her ear. Suddenly she was inside, the door was shut, the noise level muffled. It rose and fell again briefly when he opened the driver's door and leapt inside.

"You okay?"

She nodded.

"I can't believe this circus. Look at that guy!" Ryan revved the engine. "If he doesn't get out of the way, I'm going to flatten him."

Becca stared straight ahead through the windshield, her hands plucking nervously at the folds of her skirt. "I hate this," she said with a fierce intensity that surprised Ryan as well as herself.

He spared her a sympathetic look. "You and me both, honey."

She wished he wouldn't call her that. And she wished these reporters would vanish from the face of the earth. She couldn't bear all their attention, all those inquisitive eyes and accusing fingers. It was just like when Amy had first disappeared. Becca had felt violated, stripped bare, her innermost self probed and laid open for public scrutiny by their questions and their cameras.

How do you feel, Mrs. Slater? How do you feel? How do you feel?

On the surface it was such a stupid, obvious question. But the strange answer was that Becca couldn't seem to get a grip on her feelings at all. People spoke of being numb with grief. Could you also be numb with happiness?

She felt stunned, disoriented, afraid to believe this could all be real. What if she suddenly woke up and had to face yet another day in hell, another day of not knowing what had happened to her baby?

Of its own volition, her hand shot out and latched on to Ryan's shoulder like a claw. He whipped his head around to stare straight into her eyes. "Tell me this is real, Ryan," she whispered through stiff, frozen lips. "Tell me this is really happening."

"Becca . . . honey . . ." Ryan's face mirrored her own torment, but also an uneasy overlay of anxiety.

His obvious concern for her mental well-being burned through the mental fog clouding her mind. From some faraway pocket of cool reason she heard a stern voice. *Better get a grip, Becca. After everything you've already survived, this would be a fine time to get packed off to the funny farm.*

She detached her fingernails from Ryan's shoulder, forcing herself to settle back against the seat. "Sorry," she said in a not-quite-level voice with a not-quite-casual shrug. "It's just so hard to believe this is happening, that Amy's finally coming home." Her voice broke on the last word.

Ryan swallowed so hard, Becca heard him. After a pause, he said softly, "I know. I keep worrying I'm going to wake up, too."

Becca shot him a startled glance, surprised to hear the eerie echo of her own fears. "You *do* understand, don't you?" she said slowly.

The corners of his mouth tightened as if he'd bitten into something sour. This time when he spoke, his voice was hard. "I've *always* understood, Becca." With a vicious wrench, he released the emergency brake.

Guilt lashed through her as Ryan began to nose the truck through the surrounding crowd of reporters, but Becca ignored it. One thing she had learned during the past four years was how to live with guilt. Guilt was her old friend, her constant companion. Sometimes she couldn't even remember what it was like to live without it.

Once they'd left the reporters behind, Becca pulled off her dark glasses. From the corner of her eye she could make out Ryan's rugged, handsome profile in the pale glow of the dashboard lights. Her heart gave a painful little spasm, like an engine that was trying to turn over but just couldn't quite make it.

As they passed briefly through the beam of a streetlight, she noticed his sandy brown hair was a bit shaggier than she remembered it, curling an inch or so over his collar. Hard to tell in the dark, but was that a touch of silver at his temples? Gray hairs Becca herself had no doubt helped to put there.

His jaw was set at a rigid angle, his mouth compressed into a straight line resembling a high-tension wire. His last words seemed to hover in the truck cab like the lingering reverberation of a rifle shot.

I've always understood, Becca.

"I'm sorry," she said.

Ryan checked the rearview mirror. "For what?"

"For... for not being there for you. For turning away from you." Her burden of guilt nestled more heavily on her shoulders, making itself comfortable. "I'm sorry I couldn't help you cope with what happened, Ryan, but frankly, it was all I could do just to hold *myself* together."

Silence.

Then, "God knows I never wanted to lean on you, Becca. But maybe, if we'd both leaned on each other, dealing with our loss might have been just a little bit easier."

"Maybe. I don't know." She brushed a weary hand across her forehead. "I never meant to hurt you, Ryan. But I was in so much pain myself—"

"I know."

"Yes, of course you do."

"Look, let's put all that behind us, okay? It's ancient history. Through some incredible, wonderful twist of fate, we've got a second chance now." He braked at a stoplight, reached over and folded his hand over hers. "What's past is past, Becca. None of that matters anymore."

But Becca knew that it still did.

As soon as the light turned green, she extricated her hand from his. "Do you mind if I open the window? It's awfully warm in here."

"Be my guest."

She cranked down the window. As the truck accelerated up the freeway ramp, a hot, dry Central Valley wind blew through the cab, ruffling their hair, mingling rich, earthy agricultural scents with the city smells of asphalt and exhaust fumes.

Becca tilted her head back against the seat, as bone-deep exhausted as she'd ever been in her life, yet so pumped up by adrenaline she wondered if she would ever be able to sleep again.

Despite the warm breeze, Becca shuddered as her mind inevitably clicked back to this afternoon when she'd unsuspectingly picked up the phone and heard the words that would be engraved on her heart and soul forever...

"Becca?"

Though it had been three years since she'd heard his voice, she recognized it immediately.

"Ryan. Hello." Her own voice had come out sounding thick, breathless, as if someone had dropped an anvil onto her chest.

"Becca...there's news about Amy."

No. Oh, no. For a moment Becca had thought her heart would simply explode with anguish and she would die, because after four long years, what kind of news could there be but bad?

She'd always believed nothing could be worse than the uncertainty—that she would gladly sacrifice what little remained of her sanity just to know what had happened to her child. But in that one devastating split second Becca realized the folly of that assumption, saw with brutal clarity that hope was the most precious thing in the world—only now Ryan was about to kill that hope forever and then how could she possibly bear to go on living?

Becca's knees turned to slush and she felt herself sagging to the floor, sliding into a deep, dark tunnel where she would at least find merciful oblivion.

She must have made some kind of sound, perhaps uttered an incoherent moan of bleak, total despair, because all of a sudden the phone was squawking into her ear with what seemed like panic-ridden noises.

Becca struggled to ignore them, to put off hearing the words that would finally destroy her, but their urgent repetition finally penetrated her murky consciousness.

"It's *good* news, Becca! *Good* news, do you hear me? It's what we've prayed and hoped for all these years! Do you hear me, Becca? Amy's alive! Our little girl is alive and well and she's coming home to us! Becca, are you still there? Can you hear me? Honey, please say something if you're all right."

Afterward, Becca could have sworn Ryan was crying by that point, but that was ridiculous. Ryan didn't cry. Becca had never seen him cry, not even during those first terrible days after Amy was stolen from them.

"Damn! I shouldn't have broken the news like that, I should have done it more gently…Becca, are you still there? Do you understand what I'm saying?"

It was then that the full impact of Ryan's words had slammed into her, like a meteorite hitting the earth. Becca had waited for the joy to surge through her, to raise her up and send her soaring to the heavens. But the shock had somehow flipped an emotional Off switch within her, like a circuit breaker that protectively snaps off when the circuit is overloaded.

Even now, finally on the way to the airport to meet the plane bringing Amy home, Becca didn't feel the way she'd always imagined she would feel on the rare occasions when she'd dared to envision this miraculous outcome. Instead she felt incredibly brittle, as if she were made of fragile spun glass and would shatter into a million pieces if anyone so much as touched her.

Ryan had touched her, though. And she hadn't splintered into smithereens. Still, Becca intended to steer clear of any further physical contact with him. Some sixth sense warned her that letting Ryan touch her again would be a very bad mistake.

She rolled the window up a ways to lessen the roar of the wind. "Tell me again how they found her," she said.

Ryan rubbed the nape of his neck, exhaling a stream of air through his lips. "The woman who...who took her—"

"*Kidnapped* her, you mean."

The bitter edge to Becca's voice drew a sideways glance from Ryan. "Yes, kidnapped her. Anyway, she took Amy to Florida. The social worker who's bringing Amy back assured me on the phone that the woman took very good care of her—"

"Did they catch her? That horrible woman? Is she in jail?"

Ryan slanted her an odd look, then cleared his throat. When he resumed speaking his tone was soothing—the same tone you'd use to talk a person off a ledge. "The woman's dead, Becca."

Her jaw dropped. "Dead?"

"I explained all this when I called this afternoon, remember?"

Becca massaged her temples with shaky fingertips. "Not...not really. I was sort of in shock, I guess. After you told me Amy was alive, I—well, I'm afraid I didn't hear much of what you said after that."

Ryan gave a forced sort of chuckle. "I know what you mean. When that detective called me from Florida this morning, I had to ask him to repeat himself about half a dozen times before it finally sank—"

"*What* did you say?"

Ryan frowned. "I said, I had to ask him to repeat himself half a dozen—"

"No, not that. I mean about this morning."

"This morning?"

At last an emotion struggled forth, nearly breaking free of the shell around Becca's heart. But it wasn't happiness. It was fury. "You're telling me they called and told you about Amy this *morning?*"

"Yes..." There was that down-off-the-ledge tone again.

"And you didn't call me till this *afternoon?* Ryan Slater, how could you not call me the instant you got off the phone? How could you let me suffer even one extra *minute* of torture? Don't you understand what I—"

"I understand." His reply slashed through her protest. "Don't you ever accuse me of not understanding what it was like to lose our child, Becca."

She heard an element in Ryan's voice she'd never heard before—an element that silenced her.

"As I *also* explained to you this afternoon, I *did* try to call you as soon as I heard." A muscle twitched along his jaw, as if he were battling to keep his temper under control. His brown eyes smoldered in the dim light like carefully banked embers. "I spent half the day dialing your number every ten minutes, in fact. You didn't answer."

"Oh, God." Becca slumped back against her seat. "I— I was working. I had to deliver some papers to one of my clients, then stay for a meeting."

But that wasn't all of it. One of the major advantages of working as a freelance bookkeeper was that Becca could bring her work home with her, so she never had to be far from the phone for long.

For some reason, though, she'd awakened this morning unusually depressed. Her bleak mood had persisted through her meeting with the client, gathering force and gloom like an approaching storm front. Desperate for some distraction, no matter how temporary, she'd sought refuge in the darkness and solitude of an early matinee.

It figured. She'd spent the past four years practically glued to the telephone, ready to pounce on it. And when the long-awaited call finally came, she was at the movies.

"I'm sorry." She seemed to be apologizing a lot lately. "I should have known you'd call the second you heard."

A descending jet on final approach to Metro Airport passed overhead, making conversation impossible for a brief interval. As the whine of the engines died away, Ryan said, "The woman's name was Dolores Mayfield."

Becca took a moment to absorb that. Such an ordinary-sounding name. *Well, what did you expect her to be named? Lucrezia Borgia?*

"Apparently she was passing Amy off as her orphaned granddaughter," Ryan went on.

"Her *granddaughter?*" Somehow Becca had never pictured her baby's kidnapper as the grandmotherly type.

"She was in her seventies. Died suddenly of a stroke. The social worker who came to take custody of Amy was searching the house for Amy's birth certificate when she found some old newspaper clippings about the kidnapping."

"Gee, she actually kept a scrapbook? How touching."

"Yeah, well, it's a good thing she did, because that's how the authorities managed to put two and two together." The pickup coasted down the airport exit-ramp. Once they were off the freeway, Ryan mentioned almost offhandedly, "The detective said they also found a journal that more or less explains why the woman took her."

Becca stiffened as if someone had applied a high-voltage current to the base of her spine. All these years she'd been frantic for the tiniest clue, for the least little scrap of information about her baby's disappearance and subsequent fate.

Now, apparently, all was to be revealed. But for some odd reason her mind seemed to shy away from the truth, as if by remaining ignorant of the facts she could somehow pretend the whole thing had never happened.

Well, she might have turned out to be a washout as a wife and a poor excuse for a mother, but one thing Becca Slater wasn't, was a coward.

"Tell me," she said, sounding as if she had lockjaw.

Ryan pulled the truck into a parking lot, found an empty space and killed the engine. "Look, we've probably got about thirty seconds before some loyal minion of the Fourth Estate spots our license plate and gets a fix on us, so I'm going to make this fast."

"Fine."

He unhitched his seat belt, shifting position to face her. "It's a tragic story, Becca. It may not be easy to hear."

She would have laughed if she hadn't felt so much like crying. "A tragic story, Ryan? I doubt it could be as tragic as what you and I have experienced firsthand."

He sighed, dragging a hand over his face. "Okay. Here goes. Dolores Mayfield once had family in Pine Creek—her son and his wife, several grandchildren. They lived about four blocks from us, in fact." He peered at Becca as if trying to judge how well she was bearing up so far.

She made a rolling, let's-get-on-with-it motion with her hand.

"A few days before Amy disappeared, the whole family was wiped out in a terrible car accident just outside of town."

Shock obliterated Becca's impatience. She flinched in spite of herself.

"When the detective mentioned the accident, it vaguely rang a bell," Ryan continued. "I'd pretty much forgotten about it, since Amy was kidnapped shortly afterward."

"No... I don't really remember it, either."

"Anyway, Dolores Mayfield came to Pine Creek for the funeral. The detective speculates that she just happened to be wandering around the fairgrounds that night, in a daze. She'd buried her entire family that morning."

"Oh, my God." Becca pressed trembling fingers to her mouth.

"Then she spotted Amy."

"Whom I'd left all alone, unprotected." Tears smeared her vision.

Ryan gripped her shoulders and shook her gently. "Becca, we've been through that over and over. The kidnapping wasn't your fault."

She wrenched herself from his grasp. "I shouldn't have left her all by herself, Ryan! She was so defenseless, so...so vulnerable!"

"You stepped away for one minute to help out some poor kid! Pine Creek's hardly a major crime center. Any reasonable person would have assumed Amy would be safe for one lousy minute."

"But she wasn't." Becca dashed tears of self-recrimination from her eyes.

Ryan probed his cheek with his tongue, apparently assessing the futility of rehashing this old argument. Abruptly, he resumed his narrative where he'd left off. "It seems Amy bears a striking resemblance to Dolores Mayfield's dead granddaughter."

"Oh, no." Becca stared at him in dawning horror.

"Probably something just snapped in her mind. The woman had to have been an emotional basket case after the unimaginable tragedy she'd suffered, and so..." Ryan lifted his hands helplessly.

"And so she just took Amy. Our child." Becca's brain reeled as if she'd taken a blow from a two-by-four. She wanted to hate the woman who'd stolen her baby—knew she should feel cheated that the woman was dead and would never be punished.

But what that poor woman must have gone through, losing her entire family like that....

Reluctantly, Becca came to the realization that what she actually felt was no longer hatred or a burning desire for vengeance, but something that was trying to twist itself into compassion.

Maybe because, in a weird kind of way, she could almost identify with the woman. God knows, Becca certainly understood what being an emotional basket case was like.

"Come on, we're pressing our luck. Let's get out of here before the great galloping hordes show up." Ryan was out of the truck and around to her side before Becca even had a chance to unbuckle her seat belt.

"What are you bringing my suitcase along for?"

"Because we're not coming back to the truck." He hustled her through the sea of parked cars.

"We're not?"

"Tyler McCoy's going to fly us back to Pine Creek in his Cessna."

"That's awfully nice of him, but why?"

"First off, we'll beat the press back to Pine Creek and have a chance to get Amy settled in before they start hounding us."

"Good idea."

"Second, we might be able to avoid bringing Amy through the airport terminal if we can rendezvous with Tyler out on the tarmac."

Becca cringed, envisioning Amy subjected to that frightening gauntlet of cameras and shouted questions. A warm feeling toward Ryan, which she hastily chalked up as gratitude, swept through her.

Then the press descended upon them and the next few minutes raced by in a blur of confusion and lights as a representative from the airline escorted them through the madhouse to the relative peace and privacy of the VIP lounge.

"Can I get either of you some coffee? A soft drink? Something to eat?" The attendant was the picture of efficient concern in her tailored, navy blue suit with its snazzy red bow at the collar.

Becca shook her head.

"No, thanks." Ryan answered for both of them. "We appreciate your letting us wait in here."

"The airline is anxious to make sure you're as comfortable as possible. And the airport management is only allowing ticketed passengers into the gate area, so that should keep the press away for the time being."

"Until one of them gets the bright idea of buying a plane ticket." Ryan folded his arms and settled onto the arm of an overstuffed chair.

The woman sighed. "Unfortunately, that's true. But we have security guards stationed outside this lounge, so at least they can't get in here to bother you."

"Well, thank you for all the special arrangements you've made."

"Glad to be of help. I'll be right outside, in case you need anything."

"Becca?"

She managed to paste a polite smile on for the woman, who, after all, was doing her best to be helpful. "I'm fine. Thanks."

"Please let me know if you need anything." The woman paused in the doorway. Her professional demeanor slipped a couple of notches. "I just want to tell you how... how happy I am for both of you." Her eyes glistened with suspicious moisture.

Ryan squeezed her hand as if she were the one in need of emotional support, not he. "Thank you. We appreciate that."

Then the woman straightened her shoulders, resuming her calm, capable persona, and left Ryan and Becca alone together. To wait.

The next hour dragged by in excruciating slow motion. Under the bright lights of the lounge, Ryan got his first really good look at Becca this evening. He studied her over the top of an open magazine that he couldn't have concentrated on if his life depended on it.

What he saw dismayed him. Becca had definitely lost weight since the last time he'd seen her. Pronounced hollows dipped beneath her cheekbones, and the skin stretched taut across her delicate features, giving her a strained, haunted look.

In startling contrast to her pale complexion, her eyes burned feverishly like two blue flames. Over the past few years Becca's healthy, vibrant good looks had faded to a sort of ethereal beauty, like the dying heroine in some two-hankie tearjerker movie.

As she paced nervously across the plush carpet of the lounge, her blouse and skirt hung loosely on her fragile frame like a shapeless bundle of scarecrow rags. Ryan was prodded by an urge to whisk her out to an all-you-can-eat restaurant for a huge meal, then ply her with hot-fudge sundaes for dessert.

Only problem was, he figured neither one of them could possibly force down even a bite of food just now—not judging by the way his gut was churning with a nauseating blend of apprehension and anticipation.

Not to mention anxiety. For Becca.

Ryan's inner turbulence kicked into high gear all at once as the lounge door swung open. He tossed aside the magazine and rose to his feet.

The woman from the airline stepped into the room.

Becca's head snapped up like a deer's caught in a car's headlights.

"Mr. and Mrs. Slater?"

Ryan's fists clenched convulsively. Becca made a funny little sound in her throat.

"I just got word from the control tower." A tremulous smile broke across the woman's face. "Amy's flight has landed."

Chapter Two

Becca couldn't remember taking Ryan's hand, yet there it was, wrapped possessively around hers as if it would take surgery to separate them.

He kept her pulled close to his side as they made their way to the arrival gate, surrounded by a phalanx of security guards who plowed through the terminal in a protective wedge formation.

This time Becca was only peripherally aware of the press, quite a few of whom had resourcefully found a way to circumvent the airport management's protective measures. Their eager questions bounced off her without registering. All she could hear was the high-pitched thrum of blood rushing through her veins...the frantic thumping of her heart...the quick-step beat of footsteps carrying her closer and closer to her long-lost child.

At the entrance to the boarding ramp the security guards held the crowd back. "The other passengers on the flight have already deplaned," the airline representative told Ryan and Becca as she led them down the sloping tunnel, carrying Becca's suitcase. "And your friend—Mr. McCoy, is it?—has his plane waiting close by. There's a staircase at the end of this ramp that leads directly down onto the tarmac, so you won't have to go back through the terminal."

"Thank you," Ryan said. Even though a rush of excitement filled her ears like the scream of a jet engine, Becca noticed that Ryan's voice sounded peculiar, as if he was having trouble breathing.

Boy, not her. Becca's lungs were pumping air in and out so fast she felt as if she was about to keel over with hyperventilation.

Then three figures appeared at the far end of the ramp.

Becca halted as if she'd run into a brick wall. Some still-functioning circuit in her brain immediately identified two of the figures as the social worker and a stewardess.

But it was the third, smaller figure that every jagged nerve, every maternal cell in Becca's body instantly homed in on with laser-beam intensity.

The little girl was small, yes, but taller than Becca had expected. For one agonizing second, doubt clawed at her mind. Could some horrible mistake have been made? What if that sleepy six-year-old shuffling up the ramp, clutching the social worker with one hand and a doll with the other, wasn't Amy at all?

Next to Becca, Ryan went rigid. He squeezed her hand nearly hard enough to break her fingers. The unexpected bolt of pain restored some of her reason, and she reminded herself that Amy had only been a baby when she was stolen, that, of course, she would look much different now.

Becca remained rooted to the floor, still staring at the somehow forlorn figure coming slowly toward her. In her mind's eye she suddenly recalled a toddler's tipsy, bowlegged walk... the drowsy droop of a familiar blond head....

And all at once Becca knew with the soul-deep certainty of a mother's heart that—miracle of glorious miracles!—this sad, confused-looking waif *was* their own darling little girl come home at last.

In that breathtaking moment, the bands of steel that had imprisoned Becca's heart for the past four years fell away. The icy shell that had encased her emotions ever since she'd heard the news this afternoon finally shattered.

Pure, undiluted, indescribable joy surged through her in a torrent of feeling that nearly swept her off her feet. With a glad cry she stumbled forward, managed to get her wobbly legs under control, then flew down the ramp.

She'd taken barely a dozen steps when Ryan seized her wrist and dragged her to an unwilling halt.

"Let go of me," she gasped. "That's Amy...my baby...I have to go to her." She flailed against his grip, spots sifting before her eyes like confetti.

"Becca." Something in Ryan's hoarse, insistent tone managed to get through to her.

She ceased her struggling long enough to stare at him and choke out, "Ryan, it's really Amy! Our little girl!"

"I know." Though Ryan was obviously straining to keep his emotions under control, his eyes were wild, his skin flushed. Tiny veins throbbed at his temples and the planes of his face shifted briefly, giving Becca a glimpse of his inner turmoil. "Honey, we don't want to scare her."

"What?" She twisted around to look over her shoulder. The three figures had paused, now waiting uncertainly at a distance. The social worker knelt and spoke softly into Amy's ear.

"Becca, for God's sake!" Ryan rasped in a harsh, low voice. He captured her other wrist and forced her to meet his tortured gaze. "Don't you think I want to grab her up in my arms, spin her around and smother her with kisses? My God, it's all I've thought about for the last four years!" The cords in his neck stood out as he gulped back the rising agitation in his voice. "But the poor little kid's got to be frightened enough as it is by everything that's happened to her in the past few days. The last thing she needs is to be rushed at and manhandled by a couple of strangers."

"*Strangers?*" Becca echoed in amazement. But the urgency of Ryan's words was gradually sinking in, and she made a heroic effort to gather up the scattered remains of her common sense.

Though it nearly killed her to admit it, what Ryan said was probably true. Very likely, Amy *wouldn't* know them. She'd only been two years old when she was stolen, had spent the last two-thirds of her life with a woman who'd filled her innocent head with a pack of lies.

"Dear heaven, it never occurred to me..." Becca closed her eyes. It was starting to dawn on her that Amy's return didn't necessarily mean the nightmare was behind them.

"Are we agreed?" Ryan arched his eyebrows questioningly.

Becca nodded, too overwhelmed to speak for a moment. With what felt like the last gasp of air in her lungs, she said, "You're right. We'd better go slow with her."

Ryan's mouth tightened in grim consensus. He released his manacle hold on her wrists, then gently wiped her cheeks with the pads of his thumbs.

It was only then Becca realized her face was streaked with hot, sticky tears.

"Come on," Ryan said softly, tilting her chin up with the crook of his finger. "Let's go meet our daughter."

Becca squeezed her eyes shut, let herself sway toward him just a little. Then she remembered herself and drew back. Ryan linked her arm through his, and even though Becca had vowed to keep a good, safe distance between them, she had to admit she was grateful for his support while they continued down the ramp.

Becca couldn't keep her eyes off Amy. She drank in the changes in her child like a woman dying of thirst. Amy was so tall, so thin! All her baby fat had melted away. Her blond hair fell nearly to her waist, and the soft baby skin Becca had always taken such pains to protect was now tanned by the Florida sun.

She leaned against the social worker with her head lowered shyly, golden curls tumbling forward to conceal her face.

The social worker held out her hand. "I'm Melissa Carpenter," she said. "You must be Mr. and Mrs. Slater. We spoke on the phone earlier today, Mr. Slater."

Ryan stuck out his hand in automatic response, but he was barely aware of the young woman. Beside him he could feel Becca trembling, while in front of him stood the little girl he'd have given his life to get back.

Melissa Carpenter gently brushed Amy's hair back from her cheek. "Can you say hello to these people, Amy?"

Amy clung tighter to the woman's leg.

"Sweetie, these are the people I told you about, remember? The ones who are going to be your mommy and daddy from now on."

Her words startled Ryan until he recalled their earlier conversation. In the social worker's opinion, it would be less traumatic for Amy if they let her get used to living with them first, before trying to explain that they *were* her real mommy and daddy.

Becca knelt so she was eye level with their daughter. "Is this your doll?" she asked, touching its arm.

Amy hesitated, then nodded once.

"She's pretty. What's her name?"

Amy mumbled something Ryan couldn't understand.

"Jessica?" Becca repeated.

Amy nodded again. Ryan marveled at the serene, soothing melody of Becca's voice. He knew she was as stunned, as shaken by this amazing reunion as he was, but you'd never know it now. It was as if her maternal instincts had come charging to the forefront, determined to protect her child from any sign of emotional turmoil that might upset her further.

Never had Ryan admired his former wife more than at this very moment.

As he watched the two blond heads bent close together, an exhilarating whirl of emotions swept through him. He was dizzy with joy, drunk with gratitude, seized by the urge to throw back his head and shout "Hallelujah!"

Instead he lowered himself next to Becca and spoke to his little girl for the first time in four years. "Did you like riding on a plane, Amy?" There, he thought, he'd done a pretty good job of keeping his voice from shaking.

Amy raised her head just a little, to peer at him curiously through her eyelashes. One finger crept toward her mouth.

Melissa Carpenter rustled Amy's hair. "She sure did, didn't you, sweetie? We looked out the window and saw lots of lights way, way down below us."

Now Amy's finger was hooked snugly in the corner of her mouth. When she opened her droopy eyelids wider to study Ryan, something almost painful snagged in his chest. Looking into his daughter's wary, chocolate brown eyes was like looking into a mirror.

It took every last scrap of Ryan's self-restraint not to touch his daughter, not to bundle her into his arms and plaster her sweet face with kisses. But the last thing he wanted was to terrify her. "How would you like to come for another airplane ride with your mo—with Becca and me?"

At this, Amy's long-lashed eyes flew open with alarm. She burrowed her face into Melissa Carpenter's side again, shaking her head wildly.

Becca exchanged a glance of despair with Ryan, but when she spoke to Amy, her voice was calm and cajoling. "I know you must be awful tired, sweetheart, but this won't be a very long plane ride. And when we get home, you can have a room of your very own with a nice soft bed to sleep in, okay?''

Amy shook her head.

The social worker sent Becca and Ryan a crooked smile of apology. She bent over and gently tried to detach Amy from her hip. ''Sweetie, remember what we talked about on the plane? You're going to go home and live with Becca and Ryan. They like little girls *very* much, and they're going to take very good care of you from now on.''

''But I wanna stay with you, 'Lissa!'' Amy wailed.

Becca's battered heart went out to her child with a silent cry of anguish. Never in her wildest imaginings had she considered the possibility that Amy wouldn't be glad to see them.

Yet despite her helplessness, her empathy with her little girl's sorrow, once again Becca felt that triumphant surge of happiness wash over her. She caught her breath, blinked back tears. All that really mattered now was that Amy was back, she was alive and well and close enough for her parents to touch.

Surely, given time, Amy would eventually come to love them, to call them Mommy and Daddy again.

Wouldn't she?

Like any mother, Becca knew it was better to rip a bandage off quickly from a skinned knee rather than prolong the agony. It was time to step in and quickly end this tearful scene, this painful moment of parting. With gentle yet firm hands she managed to pry the now-sobbing Amy from the social worker's side.

Lifting her little girl in her arms for the first time in four years, Becca nearly swooned with happiness.

Amy, however, was another story. Her grief-stricken wails filled the air as she struggled in Becca's arms, straining to clutch at her new friend Melissa. ''I think we'd better make this fast,'' Becca said loudly.

The social worker nodded, obviously close to tears herself. "Goodbye, Amy. Be a good girl, now."

"This way, Mrs. Slater." The stewardess swung open a door leading to an outside staircase, and Becca carried her weeping daughter out into the night.

A warm wind whipped her hair about her face as she cautiously descended the stairs. The smell of jet fuel and the roar of an aircraft taking off assaulted her senses. Amy's body shook with sobs.

And then Ryan's best friend, Tyler McCoy, was there, a broad smile of welcome splitting his handsome face. "Want me to carry her?" he shouted at Becca.

She shook her head.

"Where's Ry— Oh, here he comes. Come on, follow me." He wrapped a sheltering arm around the two of them and guided Becca over to his small plane.

Ryan caught up with them at the Cessna. "Had to sign some papers for the social worker." He set down Becca's suitcase, which she'd completely forgotten about. "Here, I'll hold her while you climb inside."

But by now Amy had attached herself to her mother like a limpet to a rock. "I'll hold her," Becca said. "Can the two of you help me?" Each man grabbed an elbow and hoisted Becca and her precious cargo into the plane.

Ryan stowed the suitcase and climbed into the front seat while Tyler ran through his preflight checklist. Within minutes, they were taxiing toward the runway.

Ryan looked back to check on Becca and Amy. "All buckled in?" Amy's face was buried against Becca's shoulder, her heartbreaking sobs now reduced to the occasional hiccup. With an expression of disbelieving wonder, Ryan reached out, brushing Amy's hair with a featherlight caress.

His Adam's apple bobbed up and down in a convulsive swallow. Becca met his glance over the top of their daughter's head and gave him a shaky smile. Ryan had never been much for sloppy public displays of emotion, preferring to express his feelings in more private ways. But the deep love blazing in his eyes came through loud and clear, startling Becca with its power.

This profound expression of love was directed solely toward Amy, of course. How could Ryan retain even the slightest residue of affection for Becca after all she'd put him through?

Still, at that moment, Becca felt closer to Ryan than she had since the day Amy disappeared. How could she help it, when Ryan was the one person on earth who'd shared her nightmare, who now rejoiced in this miracle with her?

"Just got clearance from the control tower," Tyler said. "Here we go."

As the sound of the Cessna's engines grew louder and the runway lights slid by faster and faster, Becca hugged her little girl close. Amy's heartbeat fluttered against her breast. Becca marveled at the feel of her child's warm, velvety-soft skin, inhaled the wonderfully sweet scent of her hair. All blessedly familiar, yet so strange, so different.

With a slight bump, the landing gear parted company with the ground. As the Cessna lifted upward into the star-filled night, heading for the Sierra foothills, Becca's heart soared along with it.

Home. At long last they were bringing Amy home.

Becca tilted her head to rest it gently on top of her daughter's. With a little jolt it occurred to her that she, too, was on her way home for the first time in a long, long while.

"Thanks for the lift, buddy." Ryan took Becca's suitcase from the trunk and extended his hand. "Well, for both of them, actually." Tyler had also given them a ride to their house from the small Pine Creek airfield.

"Don't mention it." Tyler grabbed Ryan's hand in both of his, hesitating as if he wanted to hug his old pal but sensed that such an overt physical display would only embarrass both of them.

He settled for whapping Ryan on the back. "Listen, if there's anything else Gretchen or I can do..."

Ryan sighed, massaging the back of his neck. "Actually, sooner or later I'm gonna need a lift back to Sacramento so I can pick up my truck."

"Just say the word. I've got a couple of charter flights down to Metro scheduled for later this week, and you're more than welcome to tag along on either one."

Becca shifted the sleeping child in her arms. "How can we ever repay you for all your help, Tyler?"

He staggered backward, clamping a hand to his chest. "Becca, I'm crushed! Old friends don't have to pay each other back."

Becca blushed. Well, it was nice to know Tyler still considered her a friend after everything that had happened.

"Besides, seeing the three of you together again—" He cleared his throat ostentatiously and made a big production out of slamming the trunk closed. "That's all the thanks I need, believe me."

Becca quickly lowered her gaze. She hoped the rest of her hometown wasn't jumping to the same erroneous conclusion that Tyler seemed to be hinting at. She and Ryan might have Amy back, but their marriage was long past reviving, buried under the ashes of their tragedy along with those four lost years.

"I'm sure Gretchen will be anxious to stop by and see you...should I tell her you'll call?"

Tyler's question was cautious, and with good reason. Gretchen had been Becca's best friend since grade school, maid of honor at her wedding, and closer than any sister could be. But Becca had severed that tie at the same time she'd fled Pine Creek and its torture chamber of painful memories.

How could she bear to face Gretchen again? Caring, understanding, loyal Gretchen. She'd done everything a best friend could to help Becca survive the agonizing ordeal of Amy's mysterious disappearance. She'd even stood by her when Becca decided her marriage to Ryan was over, although it had been written all over Gretchen's face that she'd thought it a terrible mistake.

"Sure. Tell her I'll call her when—um, when things settle down a little."

Tyler nodded, obviously pleased and relieved. "Okay, then. Well, I'd better stop yakking and let you guys go inside. Let me know if you need anything."

"Will do. Thanks again." As they proceeded up the path to the two-story Victorian house they'd purchased as newlyweds, Ryan draped his arm around Becca's shoulder. She wanted to shrug it off—odd things seemed to happen to her nervous system whenever Ryan touched her—but didn't want to risk disturbing Amy's restless slumber.

"Shoot. I forgot the porch light was burned out." Ryan held her even more protectively as they carefully climbed the front steps. "Sorry about that. I should have thought to replace it."

"For heaven's sake, don't apologize," Becca murmured. "I'm amazed at how well you've thought everything out. Frankly, I could barely think clearly enough to pack a suitcase—oops!" She stumbled on a loose step, and clutched Amy more securely.

Ryan instantly steadied her with a firmer grip on her shoulders. "Rats! I meant to fix that. I'm sorry, honey. Are you all right?"

She *was* breathing a little harder, but not from fright. Did he really have to stand so darn close, now that they were safely at the front door?

"I'm fine. Just my arms are a little tired, that's all." Becca would gladly have carried Amy all the way across the

Sahara desert, but she was anxious to put a little distance between herself and Ryan.

He obligingly moved forward to rummage through his pockets, then slot the key into the lock. He stepped inside first to turn on a light. Becca followed, automatically heading upstairs to the baby's room.

Actually, she would have to stop thinking of it as the baby's room from now on. The nursery-rhyme wallpaper and brightly colored mobiles would definitely have to go.

Hmm. What would a six-year-old prefer instead? Pink ruffles? The Little Mermaid? No, that was passé, Becca decided. If she wasn't mistaken, Beauty and the Beast was the latest rage among preteen girls.

Reaching the top of the stairs, Becca shivered with delight. What a happy chore—redecorating Amy's room! Ryan stepped past and preceded her into the nursery to switch on the light. Becca braked to an astonished halt as soon as she got a good look at her surroundings. "Ryan...what on earth?"

Except for the child-size bed they'd bought to replace Amy's crib shortly before the kidnapping, the room was completely empty. No toys, no pictures, no furniture. The walls had been painted a stark, chilly white. The place looked like a monk's cell, not a little girl's bedroom.

Oblivious to Becca's surprise, Ryan crossed the room to draw back the bed covers. Still in a mild state of shock, Becca laid her precious burden down, pulled up the quilt and tucked it under her sleeping child's chin. Amy stirred, whimpering. Becca smoothed her forehead and made soft shushing noises till she quieted down.

Meanwhile Ryan hovered at Becca's shoulder, enveloping her in the warmth emanating from his body, rustling her hair with his breath...so close she could smell that disturbingly pleasant blend of sawdust and sweat and denim she would always associate with him.

Becca could happily have stood there for hours gazing down at their little girl, at peace for the first time in four years—except for that vivid awareness of Ryan's presence. She was sensing vibrations from him that worried her.

Just because Amy was back where she belonged didn't mean that her parents could simply pick up right where they'd left off. Becca had no intention of trying to sew the tattered remnants of their marriage back together. She and Ryan were divorced now, and there was no way to turn back the clock and relive the past—thank God.

But the cozy intimacy of this scene was unsettling. Becca found it uncomfortable standing so close to Ryan in this eerie replay of the past . . . of all those nights they'd stood in this room together, watching over their sleeping baby and whispering to each other how lucky they were.

And then their luck had run out.

Becca bent down and touched her lips to Amy's forehead. How odd that a little girl who was virtually a stranger should be dearer to her than anyone else on earth! It was going to take a while to superimpose this new image of Amy over the memory that had been imprinted on Becca's heart for so long. If only she and Ryan had been able to watch their child growing day by day, to take note of the gradual changes in her development like other parents . . .

If only . . . if only. Two little words that had taunted Becca mercilessly ever since the night she'd left Amy all alone, easy prey for a kidnapper.

Abruptly she averted her face from the sad, bewildered child huddled beneath the bed covers—the child whose life Becca had ruined. *If it takes me the rest of my life,* she vowed silently, *I'll make it up to her. Somehow.*

Amy's hands curled over the top edge of the quilt, as if her little fingers were clutching the only lifeline she could find in this scary new topsy-turvy world of hers. Ryan barely brushed his finger along the ridge of her small knuckles, as if he were afraid she might evaporate if he touched her too hard. With one last, backward glance, he finally followed Becca out into the hall.

When he started to close the door, she stopped him. "Leave it open a little. We can leave on this light in the hallway, so she won't be scared if she wakes up during the night."

As they tiptoed back downstairs to the living room, Becca whispered, "If we still had her old Winnie the Pooh night-light we could plug that in, but I suppose you threw it away along with all the rest of her things."

"Threw—? What are you talking about?"

When they reached the living room, Becca's voice climbed back to a normal volume. Normal, that is, for when she was furious. "I'm talking about Amy's room, Ryan. My God, did you think I wouldn't notice? You've stripped it completely bare!"

His brows tugged together in a pair of dark slashes. For a minute or so his jaw shifted back and forth as if he were sampling the taste of several possible responses. Finally he said, "I'm going to have a beer. Want one?"

Becca trailed him into the kitchen. "No, I don't want a beer—it's two o'clock in the morning! What I want is to know why you trashed Amy's room like that."

Ryan scowled at her as he opened the refrigerator. "You make it sound like I rampaged through it with a sledge-hammer."

Becca ticked off the evidence on her fingers. "You painted over the wallpaper, emptied the closet, took down the curtains and pictures on the walls, hauled away the furniture. And you tossed out all her toys!"

Ryan shoved the refrigerator door shut. "Wrong, Becca." He popped open a beer can. "All of Amy's things are stored up in the attic, just like her bed was before I brought it back down this morning."

"Oh." But Becca wasn't ready to let go of her anger yet. It was such a nice, safe refuge from other, more treacherous feelings. "Why, Ryan? What on earth possessed you to obliterate every single trace of our child from that room?"

He slammed his beer down on the nearby counter so hard that foam spumed over the sides. "What did you want me to do, preserve it as a shrine the way *you* tried to?"

Becca felt the color drain from her face. "I did no such—"

"The hell you didn't!" Ryan took a punch at the air, nearly knocking over the beer can. "You left her toys scattered all over the floor, just exactly where she'd been playing with them before you took her to the fair that day. You wouldn't even *hear* of giving away her baby clothes, even after a year had passed and she would have outgrown them anyway."

He knocked aside a kitchen chair blocking his path. "You spent hours alone in her room with the door shut, swaying back and forth in that rocking chair, humming lullabies to yourself..." He plowed his fingers through his hair like a man at the end of his rope. "Did you think I didn't know what was going on in there, Becca? Huh? Did you think I was deaf, dumb and blind?"

The blood rushed back into her face. "So what, Ryan? Was it such a crime, trying to find whatever small measure of comfort I could, the only way I knew how?"

He shook his head as if he couldn't believe how dense she was. "No, Becca. If torturing yourself with memories was the only way you could find comfort, I didn't mind." He braced his arms on the kitchen table and leaned across it, bringing his face close to hers. "What I minded was that you never let me in there with you. Not into that room, not into your head, not into your heart—"

Becca jammed her fists over her ears, as if she could shut out the sound of his accusation. "I told you before, Ryan, I'm sorry for that! Sorry it was all I could do just to keep from going out of my mind. Sorry I couldn't be strong for your sake, as well."

He dragged a hand over his jaw. "I wasn't asking you to bear my grief for me, Becca." He folded his hand into a fist and pounded softly on the table, punctuating his words. "All I wanted from you was some acknowledgment that I was in terrible pain, too."

There was a degree of awful truth in what he said—truth that Becca wasn't yet ready to confront. "So this was your way of punishing me," she retorted with a toss of her head. "Wiping out every trace of Amy that was left in that room."

Ryan jerked back as if he'd stepped on a rattlesnake, but then a dangerous gleam flickered in his eyes. "Is that what you think, Becca? That all this is about *you?*" He gave a harsh bark of laughter. "Well, think again."

"I don't know what you're talking about."

"No?" His face was a mask of sarcastic surprise. "Funny, I should think you would. After all, you're the one who ran away. You're the one who couldn't stand to stay here any longer, jumping every time the phone rang or someone knocked at the door or—"

"That isn't why I left! I ran away because...because—"

Fortunately, Ryan was in no mood to hear her confession. He aimed an accusing finger at her. "It's easy for *you* to say I should have kept her room exactly the way it was, when *you* were off in Sacramento, starting a new life with a new job, a new house—"

"Oh, right!" Becca cut him off with a bitter laugh. "The last three years have been an exciting new adventure for me. Nothing adds a little spice to your life like waking up every morning and wondering whether your child's alive or dead, whether today's the day you'll get word that they've finally found her body, or whether—"

"Shut up." Ryan dropped the words into the air quietly, almost casually. But their savage undercurrent warned

Becca that she was waltzing very close to the edge of an extremely dangerous cliff. She shut up.

The barely restrained violence carved on Ryan's features slowly seeped away, leaving him with a haggard look. "All I'm saying," he explained wearily, "is that you're in no position to judge me."

Judge *him?* Becca thought wildly. He had it backward, didn't he?

"You're not the one who had to walk past that room a dozen times a day," Ryan went on. "Who had to lie awake in bed at night knowing that just on the other side of the wall were all her clothes, all her toys, and that...that stupid purple crayon mark where she scribbled on the wallpaper that time—"

He broke off, averting his head and gripping the back of a chair with both hands. His knuckles turned white.

Becca stepped toward him. "Ryan, I—I'm sor—"

He turned his back on her, waving her away. Becca respected his wish to be left alone, even though right now she fairly ached to wrap her arms around him, to pull his head down onto her shoulder and whisper that everything was going to be all right—just the way she'd comforted Amy earlier.

A tremor racked his body, but when Ryan finally turned around, his eyes were dry. "I'm going to bed," he said. "You coming?"

His casual inquiry knocked the wind out of her. Was he literally asking her to share his bed, or...

"I'll sleep in the guest room," Becca replied.

Ryan shrugged, as if she could sleep up on the roof for all he cared. "Suit yourself. See you in the morning."

Then he was gone. Becca retrieved her suitcase from beside the front door, turned off the lights and went upstairs. A short while later when she opened the linen closet, she could hear the mattress springs groaning as Ryan lowered himself into the bed they'd once shared.

On her way back to the guest room with an armload of sheets and blankets, she couldn't help detouring for one last peek into Amy's room. A triangle of light shafting in from the hallway illuminated her daughter's uneasily sleeping features.

It was only natural, Becca decided, this urge to check up on her child, to make sure Amy was still safely tucked in bed asleep.

What wasn't natural, she admitted—and certainly not wise—was this crazy desire to check up on her former husband, too.

Chapter Three

The heavenly aroma of coffee teased Becca awake the next morning. For a few confused seconds she couldn't figure out where she was, or why. Then the fog lifted from her mind and blessed, blissful memory returned. Oh, glorious, happy day!

For the past thousand and some mornings Becca's memory had dealt her the same traumatic blow upon awakening. But not today! Never again would she wake up to the horrifying recollection that her child was missing, to the agonizing questions that might never be answered.

She flung off her blankets, jumped out of bed and spun around and around in the middle of the guest room, hugging her arms around her middle as if that could help her contain her happiness.

Either her giddy whirling or the delirious aftereffects of yesterday's events suddenly made her dizzy. She slowed, came to a stop, stood paralyzed. How many times had she rejoiced in this same dream, only to wake up and find—

No. Oh, no. That would be the ultimate cruelty, the one that might finally drive Becca right over the edge once and for all.

She clapped a hand to her mouth and stumbled down the hall to Amy's room, all at once sick with fear that last night had only been a dream, that Amy wasn't home, after all.

At the reassuring sight of her sleeping child, Becca splayed her hand over her heart, collapsing against the wall with relief. When the strength returned to her watery limbs, she tugged up the covers her little girl had kicked off during what had obviously been a restless night.

Amy's velvety-soft cheeks were smudged with tears. One arm was flung out as if to ward off some unseen danger. "My poor baby," Becca whispered. "You've been through so much already, and I'm afraid you still have a long way to go."

They all had a long way to go. So many adjustments, so many decisions to make . . .

But then Becca had to press her hands to her mouth to stifle a cry of joy. "Thank you, thank you for this miraculous second chance," she breathed. "I promise I won't blow it this time."

Delivering one final butterfly kiss to Amy's troubled brow, Becca tiptoed from the room.

In the bathroom she found the mirror fogged with shower steam. She rubbed the heel of her hand on it to make a clear circle in the glass, then nearly yelped at the gaunt stranger staring back at her.

Her shocking appearance went beyond the fact that Becca had gotten maybe ten minutes' sleep last night, or that she hadn't combed her hair since . . . well, she couldn't exactly remember the last time she'd combed it.

Back here in the home where she'd lived with her husband and child, in the house where she'd known her greatest happiness and greatest tragedy, Becca saw objectively for the first time what kind of toll the past four years had taken on her.

Her visual survey filled her with dismay. She pinched her sallow cheeks, leaving a red mark on each. "I look like a scarecrow," she mumbled, rubbing her skin. "Or a ghost." Her hair hung limp and lackluster to her shoulders, framing features that seemed all sharp points and angles. Her complexion was leeched of color, her skin stretched too taut over her bones. "No wonder Amy was scared to come home with me."

Unable to bear her own reflection any longer, Becca splashed cold water on her face, briskly scrubbing it dry with a towel. She hesitated, her hand hovering over Ryan's comb on the counter next to the sink. "What the heck." She jerked the comb through her tangled hair in quick, hopeless strokes, trying to ignore the intimacy implied by this use of his personal grooming equipment.

Then she padded down to the kitchen on bare feet, nearly turning back once she got downstairs. She'd always eaten breakfast in her nightgown, waiting until Ryan had kissed her goodbye and left for work before she got dressed.

"Old habits die hard," Becca murmured. A good thing to keep in mind during the days ahead. Now she wished she'd gotten dressed before coming downstairs, or had at least thought to grab a robe yesterday while she was madly flinging items into her suitcase. This flimsy summer nightgown was comfortable in hot weather, but not too suitable for breakfasting with one's former husband in what could only be called *un*comfortable circumstances.

Never mind. She doubted the sight of her skinny arms and legs would arouse Ryan to a fever pitch of uncontrollable lust. And going upstairs to get dressed would only postpone their inevitable meeting.

"Quit being such a chicken," she scolded herself. Head held high, a cheerful "good morning" poised on her lips, she entered the kitchen.

Whew! No sign of Ryan, though the automatic coffee-maker was full and steaming. Becca got a mug from the cupboard, poured herself some coffee and sat down at the table. Where could Ryan be, anyway?

Just as the mug touched her lips, the back door swung open, and Becca mentally braced herself for their first encounter of the day. But instead she encountered a flurry of wagging tail and panting pink tongue as a flash of coppery red fur slipped through the door and burst into the kitchen. "Southpaw!" she cried.

Becca hastily set her mug on the table and flung herself to her knees as the shaggy Irish setter launched himself at her face. He whimpered and slobbered all over her, interrupting his joyful attentions every so often to chase his tail around in a circle, as if needing a break from such overwhelming ecstasy.

Becca laughed. "Good boy!" She scratched briskly under his ears, eliciting a doggy howl of pleasure, then got a faceful of wildly wagging tail for her trouble. "I'm so glad to see you, fella! I wondered where you were last night."

The back door clicked shut. "I had Mrs. Guthrie from next door keep him overnight," Ryan said. "Figured the last thing we needed when we brought Amy home was a hyperactive Irish setter bouncing off the walls."

"Good idea." Becca had to admit, Ryan had certainly thought of everything. She recalled their shouting match last night, and was quickly awash in remorse. "Goodness, Southpaw, what a reception! Still remember how to shake hands?"

The handsome dog fell back on his haunches and proudly extended his left paw, just as he'd done ever since the day they had brought him home from the animal shelter.

"Atta boy!" Becca pumped his paw with enthusiasm, then scratched his head. When she sat down at the table again, Southpaw tried to jump up into her lap.

"Southpaw, down!" Ryan snapped his fingers, and instantly the dog bounded to his side. He proceeded to ricochet back and forth between the two humans, as if he couldn't make up his mind which one he was most delighted to see.

Ryan poured himself some coffee, turned one of the chairs around and straddled it, propping his elbows on the back. "I took the dog to the vet last week, hoping he could cure Southpaw's chronic low-energy problem, but as you can see..." He gave a long theatrical sigh that blew little wisps of steam off his coffee. Over the rim of his mug, his dark eyes twinkled at Becca.

She giggled. "We'll have to feed him some pep pills in his dog food, I guess."

"Speaking of food, how about bacon and eggs for breakfast?"

"I'm not hungry, but I'll be glad to fix some for you." She pushed back her chair.

"Sit down." Ryan's hand shot out and captured her wrist. "I didn't mean for you to cook them, silly."

"Oh." She sat down.

"And whether you're hungry or not, you're going to eat something." He went to the refrigerator and began transferring ingredients to the counter.

"But I'm really not—"

"Becca, you need to eat. I know your stomach's probably twisted up in knots—mine is, too." He turned and gave her a critical frown. "But you, especially, need to eat. You look like a famine victim."

"Thanks a lot."

He brandished a spatula at her. "I'm only concerned about your health. You need to put some meat on those skinny bones of yours."

"Well, maybe a piece of toast."

"Maybe *two* pieces of toast, to mop up the remains of your bacon and eggs. And here." He sloshed liquid into a glass, setting it down in front of her. "You can start with orange juice."

"Gee, thanks, mom." But when she took one sip to humor him, she discovered to her surprise that the juice *did* taste pretty good.

Southpaw's russet plume of a tail thumped eagerly against the floor as the sizzle and smell of bacon filled the air.

Becca watched Ryan break open eggs, grate cheese and flip bacon with a swift, competent economy of movement. Apparently he'd had plenty of practice cooking for himself since Becca had made him a bachelor.

Freshly shaven jaw...damp brown hair curling over his collar. Despite the evidence of his recent shower, Ryan looked like a man in need of some serious bed rest instead of one who'd just gotten up. Creases of exhaustion bracketed his mouth; dark circles rimmed his eyes. He used the back of his hand to stifle a yawn.

"How'd you sleep?" Becca asked with no conscious forethought. The words just slipped out of their own accord.

"Fine. And you?"

"Fine."

"Liar." He grinned over his shoulder.

She stuck out her tongue. "Liar, yourself, then."

Ryan turned his attention back to cooking—a welcome distraction from the sight of his former wife lounging at his kitchen table in a skimpy nightie that left little to the imagination. Not that it was brazenly sexy or anything—no strategically placed lace, no seductive little peekaboo openings here.

But the fabric itself was nothing but thin cotton, and when sunlight from the back door window fell just right, revealing outlines of the slender curves and secret hollows Ryan remembered so well—

He rapped the spatula sharply on the side of the frying pan. Darn it, he'd sworn he wouldn't let Becca get to him this way, had assured himself that he'd gotten her out of his system long ago. But the cozy domesticity of this setting, the familiar intimacy, not to mention the way her nightgown gapped open at the neck every time she leaned over to pet the dog...

Ryan dropped two slices of bread into the toaster and shoved down the lever with more force than necessary. He had to keep reminding himself why Becca was here, that it had nothing to do with him.

"Amy still asleep?" he asked over his shoulder.

"Last time I checked."

"She seemed kind of restless when I looked in on her a while ago."

"Mmm. Small wonder, considering all the upheaval she's gone through recently."

Ryan dished up their breakfast, setting the plates on the table. "I guess one of the first things we should do is have her examined by a doctor."

"What about Dr. Kirkwood? Is he still in practice, or has he finally retired? By the way, I can't possibly eat all this."

"Try. And yes, Doc Kirkwood's still got his same office over on Chestnut Street. Claims the only way he's gonna leave it for good is in a pine box."

"Ugh." Becca made a face—not at Ryan's cooking, presumably, but at the macabre image his words brought to mind. She'd always been quite fond of Doc Kirkwood. "Would, um, would you call him and make the appointment?"

"Sure." Ryan wiped his mouth with a napkin. He made no further comment, even though he saw right through Becca's seemingly innocent request.

He hadn't forgotten how Becca had gradually withdrawn into her own private hell after Amy disappeared. She'd begun avoiding people, even their best friends, closing herself off from the world until finally she hardly set foot outside the house anymore. The only reason she'd kept answering the phone and doorbell was in the desperate hope it might be someone with news of Amy.

On the rare occasions when Ryan could even persuade her to talk about it, she'd insisted that she couldn't stand the curious stares, the faces full of pity, the awkward conversations with people trying to comfort her.

Maybe all that was partially true. But Ryan knew that the main reason Becca had turned into a virtual hermit during the last year of their marriage was because of guilt, because whenever she went out in public she imagined people were pointing at her, accusing her, whispering about her behind her back. *There goes that woman who let her own child be stolen.*

Well, Ryan knew a thing or two about guilt himself. And he also knew that not a soul in Pine Creek blamed Becca for the tragedy that had befallen them.

Sooner or later she was going to have to confront her guilt, to overcome it or at least put it behind her. Asking Ryan to call the doctor was just a way for her to postpone contact with someone else who knew and cared about her.

No need to press the issue now, however. They had plenty of other emotional pitfalls to deal with first.

Ryan pushed his empty plate aside. "Becca, there are some things we need to discuss, some decisions we have to make."

She lowered her fork, though it was only halfway to her mouth. She swallowed. "I know."

"Like, for instance...are you going to move back in here?"

A flush of color blossomed across her cheeks.

"I mean, for the time being," Ryan added hastily. "Until Amy...well, until the three of us really have a chance to adjust to all this."

Becca nibbled her lower lip, tracing the rim of her coffee mug with the tip of her little finger. For some reason, Ryan found both gestures vaguely arousing.

Knock it off, he scolded himself. *We're discussing our daughter's future here, and all you can think about is getting that nightgown off your ex-wife.*

"I guess that would be best, don't you?"

Ryan nearly sloshed coffee on the table, he was so wrapped up in his tantalizing train of thought. "Uh... Oh. You mean moving back in here for a while?"

"Isn't that what we're talking about?" Becca's eyebrows feathered upward in confusion.

"Yeah, sure." Ryan coughed into his fist. "I mean, yes."

Her pretty blue eyes shone with sincere appeal. "After all, our most important priority now has to be Amy's well-being."

"Right."

"She's going through a very traumatic ordeal."

"Yes."

"You and I have to provide a stable, loving environment where Amy can feel secure. We've got to focus on Amy's needs, not our own."

"Absolutely."

"And that means putting aside our own differences, our own, um, personal history, and doing what's best for Amy." Becca leaned back in her chair, folding her hands in her lap. Speech finished.

Ryan wasn't fooled by her logical, dispassionate reasoning. From all the signs, Becca was having as difficult a time ignoring their "personal history" as he was.

He shifted forward to rest his elbows on the table, brushing his knee against Becca's. She pretended not to flinch, but managed to draw her knee aside without seeming to move.

Ryan tapped a spoon against the table and studied her thoughtfully. "Think we can really make this work?"

Becca blinked at him. "What do you mean? Of course we can." She spread her hands wide. "We have to, for Amy's sake."

"I agree." Then he shook his head. "But it's not going to be as simple as you make it sound, Becca. There's a lot of unfinished business between you and me, a lot of unresolved feelings."

She straightened her spine like a prim Victorian schoolmistress caught slouching. "Not as far as I'm concerned."

Ryan chuckled. "You always were a rotten liar."

"Listen to me, Ryan." A note of desperation crept into her voice. "What you and I once had together is a closed chapter—it's over and done with." She was staring sternly at some point just past Ryan's left ear. "I know that's mostly my fault, not yours, but regardless of who or what's to blame, our marriage is dead and buried."

Ryan leaned forward, adjusting the position of her chin so she was forced to look him straight in the eye. "Who are you trying to convince?" he asked softly. "Me? Or yourself?"

She jerked her chin away. "Don't be ridiculous."

"Then don't kid yourself."

"Ryan, please! If I'm going to stay here—"

The doorbell rang.

"Terrific." Ryan scraped back his chair. "One guess who that is."

"Who? Oh, the press?" Becca wrapped her arms around herself, clutching the thin folds of her nightgown as if suddenly aware there might be photographers lurking outside the window who could pop up at any moment and snap a shot of her in a state of dishabille. "Oh, gosh, I forgot all about them."

"I have a feeling we'll both be reminded of them constantly in the days ahead. I can't believe they actually waited till daylight to start pounding on our door." With a nimble swoop, Ryan snagged Southpaw by the collar just as the dog scurried past him. "You stay here with Becca, mutt. I might need you to be my secret weapon to chase those reporters away."

"Come here, Southpaw." Becca stroked the dog's quivering flanks while Ryan went to answer the front door. She was going to sneak him a slice of bacon to distract him, but then realized her plate was empty. Goodness, had she actually polished off that enormous breakfast?

An unruly chorus of voices filtered through the front of the house. Becca couldn't quite make out Ryan's entire response, but it ended with "No comment." More voices. Ryan's voice got louder. The other voices grew more insistent. Then Ryan hollered something about calling the cops. The door slammed shut and for the moment, at least, there was silence.

Ryan stomped back into the kitchen. "Damned vultures," he muttered, pouring himself another mug of coffee. He patted Southpaw on the head. "Too bad you're not an attack dog, fella."

"Do you think they'll go away?" Becca asked.

Ryan snorted. "Sure, they'll go away. As far as the front sidewalk."

"Isn't there anything we can do?"

Ryan leaned back against the counter and shrugged. "As one of them so smugly pointed out, they have a right to be on public property. And whether we like it or not, honey, we're news."

Becca sprang to her feet. "Haven't we been through enough already? Why can't they just leave us alone?"

"Hey, come on now. Don't get all worked up." Ryan captured her wrist, forcing her to stop pacing. "Just keep remembering the reason they're so interested in us. What do a bunch of nosy reporters matter, compared to the fact that we have Amy back?"

Becca bowed her head, burying her face in her free hand. "Oh, God. You're right."

Ryan tugged her toward him. Becca's skin flamed where he touched her. "Everything's going to be all right from now on, honey." He slid his arms around her, stroked her hair. "Everything's going to be fine."

Becca wished she could believe that. She wished Ryan wouldn't hold her so close. She also wished she was wearing something more substantial than this nightgown.

Through the thin layers of clothing that separated them she could feel the heat of his body, the steady thump of his heart. He smelled of shampoo and shaving lotion, and she knew he would taste like coffee if he—if she—if they—

Becca swallowed. Somehow the quality of their embrace was changing, shifting from one of comfort to something far more dangerous. Ryan's heartbeat tripped into higher gear; his hands slid down Becca's shoulders, blazing a trail of tingling heat along the curve of her waist, over the swell of her hips.

Something long dormant inside Becca flared into life. She fought to extinguish it, to smother it with the weight of all the emotional baggage she'd been hauling around for four years.

But it was too powerful, too seductive, to resist. She let her head fall back and found herself gazing into Ryan's compelling, coffee-colored eyes. In their hypnotic depths she recognized the same flame that burned so hot and bright inside her.

No, no! This was all wrong, a terrible mistake that could only end up hurting them both.

Becca was close enough now to see the tiny gold flecks in his eyes, to feel the moist warmth of his breath on her mouth—

Then a faint wail from upstairs split them apart like the clean stroke of an ax.

"Amy!" Becca's hands flew to her mouth. She bolted from the kitchen with Ryan hot on her heels.

"Southpaw, stay! I mean it, boy. Stay!"

Ryan caught up with her on the stairs, and they shouldered their way into Amy's room at the same time. To Becca's surprise, Amy's eyes were closed and she appeared to be sound asleep. Then as they cautiously drew closer, she flung her head from side to side and let out a moan that nearly broke Becca's heart.

"Nightmare," Ryan said softly.

"I'd better wake her." Becca dropped to her knees beside the bed and stroked Amy's sweat-dampened curls, desperate to draw her child from the clutches of her bad dream, yet not wanting to frighten her more by waking her too abruptly. "Sweetie-pie, it's okay. Come on, honey, wake up."

Amy thrashed around beneath the covers...her eyelashes fluttered...finally opened wide. From the scared look that leapt onto her face, she didn't find the vision that greeted her any more reassuring than the nightmare she'd left behind.

Becca clasped Amy's small hand between hers. "You were having a bad dream, sweetie. But you're safe with us now. Everything's going to be okay."

Amy's luminous brown eyes darted back and forth between Ryan and Becca like a terrified little animal's. Then all at once her face crumpled and her eyes squinched shut as she started to cry.

Anguish lanced through Ryan's chest like a white-hot spear. At that moment he would have paid any amount of money, crawled across burning coals on his hands and knees, slain an army of dragons just to dry his little girl's tears. A cage of helplessness descended to imprison him, bringing back the same sense of failure, the same impotent frustration he'd suffered when Amy had vanished, when Becca had walked out on him.

"Gramma!" Amy sobbed. "I want my gram-ma-a-a-a-a!"

"Her grandma?" Becca's forehead pleated with confusion.

Ryan automatically thought of Amy's only living grandparent. Becca's mother was a down-on-her-luck alcoholic, who'd remarried ten years ago and moved to Texas. She'd never even met Amy.

Then with a bolt of comprehension, the truth slammed into him. Judging by the stunned dismay on Becca's face, it must have hit her, too.

The woman Amy knew as "Grandma," the woman she now cried out for so pitifully, was none other than her kidnapper.

Bitterness rose in Ryan's throat like bile. He choked it back. No matter how much he and Becca might yearn to rail at the woman, to curse her name and shake their fists at her memory, they would never have that luxury. For Amy's sake, they would have to swallow their hatred, their rage. No matter how vile it tasted.

Ryan leaned over to smooth Amy's tangled hair back from her eyes, intending to wipe the tears from her glistening cheeks. But Amy rolled away, wrenching her hand from Becca's grasp and seeking refuge on the far side of the bed. Her frail little shoulders shook as she huddled in a fetal position, her face toward the wall.

Pain clawed at Ryan's insides, frantically seeking some kind of release. The tears that sprang to Becca's eyes, the despair etched across her lovely, haunted face, only added to his torment. Her helpless, hopeless murmurs of comfort were drowned out by Amy's sobs.

Then a faint whining noise intruded on Ryan's misery. He turned to find Southpaw pacing back and forth in the doorway, tail tucked guiltily between his legs as if ashamed of his disobedience in leaving the kitchen.

Ryan snapped his fingers and pointed sternly back toward the hallway, but for once Southpaw completely ignored his master's command. He sidled into the room, paws clicking on the hardwood floor, and nuzzled his way in next to Becca.

"What on—? Oh, Southpaw, it's you. You scared me. Come on, boy, get out of here."

Instead the dog propped his paws on the bed and stretched his muzzle toward Amy. Ryan grabbed for his collar as the setter began to explore Amy's neck with his tongue and make soft, inquisitive whimpers.

Amy cautiously rolled over.

Southpaw nuzzled her face with his wet nose, licked her ear. Amy hiccuped a couple of times, rubbing her puffy eyes. Then she sat up and threw her arms around Southpaw's neck. "Doggy!" she crooned happily.

The teary smile that lit up her face beat the most gorgeous sunrise by a mile. Becca pressed her fingertips to her mouth to cover the same goofy, surprised grin Ryan had on his face.

Southpaw's tail whipped back and forth like a windshield wiper. Becca pushed herself to her feet and stood next to Ryan. "Do you think she remembers him?" Her low voice was laced with wonder.

"I don't know. She might." Ryan stroked his chin. "She sure seems to have taken a shine to him, though."

"I'd say the feeling's mutual."

"Maybe *he* remembers *her.*" Without thinking, Ryan slipped his arm around Becca. Instantly her whole body tensed, as if his touch had turned her to stone.

He dropped his arm. His newly restored good mood dropped away, as well. Damn it, why did she have to react as if he had the plague or something? Every time he thought she was thawing a little toward him, something would make her freeze up again.

"You're going to have to get used to it, you know." He spoke with barely disguised irritation.

Becca looked up at him, puzzled. "Get used to what?"

"Touching me."

She took a step backward as wariness leapt into her eyes. "Ryan, I agreed to move back into this house, not back into your bed."

Annoyed with himself for having recently harbored exactly those thoughts, he took it out on Becca. "Don't flatter yourself. I wasn't issuing an invitation."

"Well, then, what . . . ?" Did he only imagine it, or had that actually been a slight glimmer of disappointment in her eyes?

"I'm talking about us living here under the same roof," he said. "We're going to be constantly bumping into each other—literally. I'm not going to creep sideways down the hallway with my back up against the wall just so I don't accidentally brush against you."

Either embarrassment or annoyance stained Becca's cheeks pink. "Don't be silly."

"We're going to be cooking meals in the same kitchen, using the same bathroom, playing together with our child, for Pete's sake. You can't keep jumping like a startled rabbit every time our bodies accidentally come in contact."

"It's not the 'accidental' contact I'm worried about," Becca retorted.

Ryan glanced at Amy, saw she was still happily involved with Southpaw, then dragged Becca across the room and spoke in muted tones. "What's the matter, afraid I'm going to sneak into the guest room in the middle of the night and ravish your body?"

She yanked her arm from his grip. "Don't be ridiculous."

"You're the one who's being ridiculous, Becca, if you think we can live here together while you play the role of Miss Touch-Me-Not. What kind of message does that send Amy? Do you want her to grow up thinking there's something wrong with physical affection, that men and women shouldn't express themselves by touching?"

"Ryan, for heaven's sake, she's only six years old! Don't you think it's a little soon to start worrying about how she's going to relate to the opposite sex?"

"Nope." He shook his head. "Amy's at a critical turning point in her life right now, a crucial stage in her development. Like it or not, Becca, you and I are going to be her role models for how men and women are supposed to behave toward each other."

Ryan could tell by the consternation furrowing her brow that he was getting through to her. "Don't forget how sensitive and smart kids are," he continued. "They've got some kind of built-in radar for tuning in to any kind of adult phoniness. No matter how you and I feel about each other, we're going to have to learn to treat each other with warmth, consideration and respect."

He tugged playfully on a lock of her hair to emphasize his point. "And it's got to be the real thing. No phonybaloney."

Becca chewed her lower lip. Ryan was right, of course. How could they expect Amy to make an emotional recovery if she was living in a house with two people constantly on guard against any kind of emotional or physical contact?

Her own words came back to haunt her. *You and I have to provide a stable, loving environment where Amy can feel secure. We've got to focus on Amy's needs, not our own.*

It had sounded simple enough when she'd said it. But now Becca was beginning to see all the complicated emotional undercurrents swirling beneath the surface, like some horrible sea monster with long tentacles trying to grab her and haul her down into the murky depths.

After Amy's kidnapping, Becca had turned away from everyone who cared about her—her friends, people she'd known all her life, even her husband. Especially her husband.

Maybe it had been a defense mechanism, this inward withdrawal. Maybe she'd known instinctively that the only way she could survive was to focus on her own suffering to the exclusion of everyone else's.

But maybe it had been a form of punishment, as well. Maybe, it now occurred to Becca, locking herself into an emotional prison with only her grief and guilt for company had been a subconscious attempt to atone for the heinous crime of allowing her child to be stolen.

Of course, her self-imposed sentence had ended up punishing Ryan, as well.

Becca knew she could never patch up the shattered ruins of their marriage, could never erase the way she'd added to Ryan's suffering during the most horrible time in his life.

The least she could do was *pretend* being close to him didn't disturb her, didn't arouse all sorts of treacherous desires she had no intention of giving in to. Ryan was and always would be the father of her child. For that reason alone, Becca owed him that much.

She summoned a smile, commanding her hand to move over and weave her fingers through his. "Agreed," she said. "No phony-baloney."

Ryan dipped a suspicious glance to their joined hands. Then a pleasant smile spread across his face, a smile Becca didn't trust for a minute. "Good." He lowered his head and brushed her lips briefly with his.

Becca forced herself to ignore the shock wave that careened through her whole body. Oh, God, she'd forgotten what his kisses could do to her....

Ryan drew back and studied her critically while Becca did her best to maintain a facade of casual composure. His eyes gleamed with amusement, his mouth quirking with satisfaction as if she'd passed some kind of test.

"Now that we've got that settled," he said lazily, skimming his warm, callused hand along the sensitive skin of her bare arm, "I think we should get married."

Chapter Four

"*Married?*" Becca's astonished voice echoed as if she couldn't possibly have heard him correctly.

One second after his impulsive proposal had popped out, Ryan wished he could snatch it back again. What secret streak of masochism could have prompted him to blurt out such an idiotic suggestion? Hadn't he suffered enough the first time Becca left him?

Apparently not, or he wouldn't have set himself up for another dose of rejection.

She was staring at him as if he'd suggested they go knock off a liquor store. "Ryan, I don't know what to say... I— I can't believe..." She closed her mouth, jerked up her chin. "I don't think that's necessary."

Necessary? He wasn't talking about re-roofing the house or buying a new car, for Pete's sake. Perversely, the curt, out-of-hand way Becca dismissed his proposal only drove Ryan to press his case further. "Being married to me wasn't so terrible, was it?"

Her eyebrows puckered together in dismay. "Of course not, Ryan, but that's hardly the point."

"No? Then tell me what the point is, Becca. Isn't the whole point, isn't our overriding concern, to provide a loving, stable family life for Amy?"

"Yes, but that doesn't mean we have to—"

Ryan shook his head sadly. "I don't know about you, Becca, but I'm committed to the long haul here." Ryan knew he wasn't exactly playing fair. It didn't stop him. "Once Amy's adjusted to being back home with us, are we going back to being divorced again? Living in separate houses? Dragging her back and forth as part of some custody arrangement?"

"No..." Doubt shimmered in her eyes. "That is, I—"

"Don't you see that our being married would be in Amy's best interest?"

Becca's gaze automatically slanted toward their child, who was still playing happily with her newfound canine friend. "Maybe... I don't know. I need time to think."

"Think about this, then." Ryan curved his hands around her bare shoulders. "How is Amy going to feel when she starts school in September, and the other kids tease her about how her mommy and daddy aren't married?"

Ouch! That was a low blow, Slater, his conscience protested. Knowing how sensitive Becca was to both the actual and imagined opinions of others, it was inexcusable of Ryan to take advantage of her vulnerability.

He didn't care. Some inner motive he didn't want to examine too closely was egging him on, urging him to use any means at his disposal to make Becca his legally wedded wife again.

Oops! Maybe he'd gone too far. Her eyes narrowed with suspicion. "In this day and age? Lots of children have parents who aren't married anymore."

"But not who are still living together under the same roof."

"I find it hard to believe that a bunch of first-graders—"

"Kids can be cruel, Becca." He squeezed her shoulders. "And don't forget that, like it or not, you and I are going to be the objects of plenty of speculation and gossip for a while."

She winced, and now Ryan did feel guilty for reminding her about the glare of public attention she so sought to avoid. He wanted to draw her into his arms, to comfort and protect her, as if to shield her with his body from the harsh circle of the spotlight.

But he didn't. Becca would only recoil from his touch, would cover her ears to shut out the sound of his comforting words.

Ryan brushed a quick kiss against her furrowed forehead, then dropped his hands from her shoulders. "Just think about it," he said.

Becca folded her arms and aimed her glance sideways. "I will."

A bright flame of hope flared in Ryan's chest.

Now if he could only get her to say "I do."

Just think about it.

Ryan's words lingered in Becca's mind like a haunting refrain. If it hadn't been for Amy, she would hardly have been able to think of anything *else*.

Fortunately, practicalities intruded. The morning of Amy's first day at home brought with it an assortment of problems Becca hadn't stopped to consider. Clothes, for example.

"She doesn't have anything else to wear, Ryan." Becca had slipped into the guest room and hastily thrown on a pair of slacks and a short-sleeved cotton blouse. "She *slept* in those clothes, for heaven's sake! I never thought to ask if she brought a suitcase or anything with her."

"I could call the airline and find out," Ryan said. They both stood in the doorway of Amy's room, unable to take their eyes off their little girl as she threw an old tennis ball for Southpaw to fetch.

"Even so, it'll take time to have it brought all the way from Sacramento." Becca twisted a lock of hair around her finger. "To tell you the truth, I don't think I want her wearing anything from...from her time in Florida anyway."

"You mean you don't want her wearing anything that woman bought her." Ryan kept his voice pitched low, so Amy couldn't overhear them.

Becca's mouth compressed into a tight line. "Frankly, no. Do you?"

Ryan sighed. "It's not what either of *us* wants that's important, honey. It's what would make Amy happy. She'd probably feel more comfortable wearing familiar clothes."

Becca rubbed her temple. "I know. You're right." Her fingers curled into a fist. "It's just that I wish I could blot out everything having to do with...with that woman, with Florida, with these last four years!"

"I know." Ryan circled his arm around Becca's waist, and for a moment she allowed herself the luxury of resting her head on his shoulder, lifting her hand to his chest. "We have to learn to accept that Amy's life wasn't on hold all those years, that she formed other attachments and other memories that you and I will never share." He propped his chin on top of Becca's head. "And thank God she did," he muttered fiercely. "Thank God, she was alive all that time..." His voice broke off with a strangled sound.

Becca felt Ryan's heart beating faster beneath her palm even as her own throat closed up. "You're right," she said, blinking rapidly. "How can we stand here wringing our hands over something as trivial as what she's going to wear?"

"We should be overjoyed that we even have to worry about it."

"Thrilled about buying her a whole new wardrobe."

Becca felt Ryan's jaw muscles shift as he grinned. "We'll take her to the most expensive department store in town and let her buy anything her heart desires."

"Oh, Ryan." Becca curled her arms around his neck, letting his warmth and comforting presence envelop her. "I *am* happy. So very, very happy."

He stroked her back, molding his hands around her ribs, her shoulder blades, finding that secret spot near the small of her back that felt like heaven when he massaged it.

Every muscle in her body seemed to dissolve; her knees turned to mush. Ryan's hands felt so *good,* so soothing.

Paradoxically, as he rubbed the tightness out of her muscles, Becca felt Ryan's own body growing tense, stiffening, as if he were absorbing all of her tension into himself.

A charming idea, but after about thirty seconds the meaning of his response finally penetrated Becca's dreamy haze. This wasn't some noble attempt to absorb her tension into himself, this was good old-fashioned arousal!

Startled, she wriggled out of his embrace and took a giant step backward. Now they were both breathing hard. Becca's cheeks felt flushed. Inadvertently, her gaze slipped to below Ryan's belt. Yup. Just as she'd suspected.

As usual, Ryan easily read her thoughts. His mouth quirked into a wry grimace and he flicked a stray lock of hair off his forehead. "Old habits die hard," he said, trying to sound casual but not really succeeding.

Hadn't Becca given herself that very same warning just this morning? Yet with a will of its own her body now responded instinctively to his, like a flower unfurling in the dawn's first rays of sunlight. For a moment it was all she could do not to hurl herself back into his arms, to leap headfirst into a frenzy of grasping hands and eagerly exploring mouths and the delightful friction of Ryan's naked skin against hers.

Then the tennis ball bumped against Becca's foot, nudging her back into reality. Absently she patted the dog on the head as he retrieved the ball. Dear Lord, what could she have been thinking just now?

She *hadn't* been thinking, that was the problem. For a moment desire and the seductive lure of memories had simply taken control, drawing her into the past as recklessly as her raging teenage hormones used to draw her into the back seat of Ryan's beat-up old Chevy.

Well, this wasn't high school anymore. Becca had learned a lot since then, including the fact that some happy endings came with a huge price tag.

She had her darling little girl back, though, and that was enough. Maybe she'd lost her marriage in the process, but she wasn't about to make the foolish mistake of hoping she could also get back the man she loved. *Had* loved, that is.

Hadn't Ryan as much as told her that his aroused response was purely automatic? Just a bad habit he hadn't managed to kick yet.

That was probably what her own rush of desire had been—habit. No problem. After all, Becca had survived four excruciating years of not knowing what had happened to her daughter. Mustering a little willpower to break the Ryan habit would be a snap in comparison.

A little insurance never hurt, however. "Would you mind running over to the mall and buying Amy something to wear?" Becca asked, hoping he wouldn't see through her scheme to get rid of him. "Just tell the salesperson you're shopping for a six-year-old girl. I'm sure whatever you buy will be close to the right size."

"Why don't all three of us go?" Ryan was scrutinizing her closely. "That way Amy can pick out something herself."

Becca thought of all the people she knew whom she might run into at the mall—people full of curious questions and openmouthed stares and congratulatory hugs and exclamations. Just imagining it gave her the chills. She simply couldn't deal with people yet.

Ironically, her biggest fear became her salvation. "Reporters," she said with near relief. "If we go out in public, the press will be swarming all over us."

"Mmm." Ryan moved down the hall to the window at the top of the stairs, parting the lace curtains with one finger. "They're still out there, all right. Like a bunch of coyotes waiting for a prairie dog to come out of its burrow."

"Maybe you could sneak out the back."

"You're forgetting I don't have my truck. I could never outrace them on foot." He let the curtain fall. "Why don't you call Gretchen? She's probably got some hand-me-downs of Sarah's that would fit Amy."

"Sarah?" Becca smiled at this typical example of male impracticality. "Sarah's only four years old. I doubt that her clothes would fit—"

"Sarah's eight now, Becca." Ryan's words were mild, but he might as well have dashed a bucket of ice water in Becca's face.

"Eight?" Even as she said it, she realized it must be true. While Becca had been trapped in her never-ending nightmare, frozen in a horrified state of suspended animation, time had stood still for her. It was a shock to discover that it hadn't for everyone else. "And Christopher?"

"He's five now. Plays softball in a little kids' league. You ought to hear Tyler and Gretchen holler from the stands whenever he actually manages to smack the ball with the bat."

"My gosh, Christopher was only a baby..."

"A lot's changed while you've been away, Becca." He turned slightly aside to look out the window again. She didn't quite catch what he mumbled next, but it sounded like "and some things haven't."

Then, with an impatient click of his tongue, Ryan dropped his hand from the curtain. "Call Gretchen," he said. "She's never stopped worrying about you, you know."

Maybe she was only imagining the note of accusation in Ryan's voice. Maybe it was simply her own guilt that instantly put Becca on the defensive. She hardly needed any reminders about what a lousy best friend she'd turned out to be. "No doubt the two of you have spent plenty of time discussing me behind my back."

Ryan's eyes narrowed as he considered his response for a moment. "You're upset, Becca."

"Don't patronize me."

"I know you must be upset," he continued as if she hadn't said anything, "because otherwise you wouldn't make such an unfair remark."

"Don't tell me you and Gretchen have never compared notes on me—how I cut you both out of my life, deserted you . . ."

Comprehension dawned in his face. All at once Becca realized she might have revealed too much. But all Ryan said was, "You should know better than anyone how loyal Gretchen is. She's not the type to go blabbing all over town about your friendship."

"You mean you and she never talked about me?"

"On a few occasions, sure we did. So what?" He spread his hands wide. "We both cared about you, Becca. You make it sound like we were conspiring against you."

She noted his use of the past tense—*cared*—with a pang of regret. "Sorry," she said, pulling a deep, trembling breath into her lungs. "It's just that I can't bear the idea of people talking about me, making judgments about me."

"No one's making any judgments, Becca." Ryan plowed a hand through his hair. "Anyone who hasn't suffered what

you've been through has no right to second-guess your behavior.''

"But it was my fault Amy was kidnapped in the first
place!" Becca clapped her hand over her mouth in alarm.
What if Amy had just overheard her outburst?

Ryan seized her wrist and dragged her down the hallway. "Knock it off," he said harshly. "How many times do
I have to tell you it wasn't your fault? It was an accident—
some terrible twist of fate.''

"If I hadn't left her alone—"

"Listen, Becca, if you want to keep up the sackcloth-
and-ashes routine, fine with me. I give up." Ryan tossed his
hands in the air, then brought a warning finger in front of
her nose. "But don't you dare dump any of that nonsense
on Amy. She's got enough to deal with as it is.''

Becca batted his hand aside. "You think I'd burden Amy
with my guilt? What kind of rotten, self-centered mother
do you think I am?''

Ryan gritted his teeth. "I think you're a wonderful
mother, Becca. That's my whole point.''

His words deflated her indignation like a pinprick to a
balloon. All at once she could barely remember what they
were arguing about. How on earth had her emotions veered
so wildly out of control?

She felt like an idiot, blowing things out of proportion
like that. From now on she would keep her guilt locked inside where it couldn't hurt other people. On the surface she
would be the old Becca Slater—competent, in control, un-
afraid to face the world.

No one need ever know that inside she was a quivering
mass of insecurities and guilt.

She didn't deserve an understanding husband like Ryan,
a loyal friend like Gretchen. But she would do her best to
live up to their expectations.

Becca straightened her spine, forced herself to meet
Ryan's wary eyes, and spoke with a confidence she was far

from feeling. "Would you mind watching Amy for a few minutes?" Her hand barely shook as she reached for the banister. "I need to make a phone call downstairs."

"Gretchen?"

A long pause stretched out at the other end of the line, finally broken by a sound that was half sob, half sigh. "Becca?"

She could barely hear her old friend's voice, but it brought back a flood of memories. Trading sack lunches every day in the third grade... listening to records after school while they both mooned over the cutest boy in algebra class... being maid of honor at each other's weddings.

"It's me," Becca said softly.

"Ohhh, boy." Gretchen's exclamation came out in a whoosh. "Um, just a second." The connection grew muffled as she apparently clamped her hand over the phone and called, "Sarah? Christopher? Could you play outside for a little while, kiddos?"

Abruptly Gretchen's voice came through loud and clear again, with only a hint of a wobble. "Summer vacation. Whoever invented it obviously didn't have to worry about keeping two whirling dervishes occupied all day."

"I suppose Christopher will be starting kindergarten this fall." *Goodness,* Becca thought, *what's wrong with my voice?*

"First grade, believe it or not. His birthday's next month."

Becca cleared her throat. "Um, Gretchen..."

"Becca, I'm so happy for you! I mean, happy doesn't even begin to describe it. Delirious, ecstatic! When I heard they'd found Amy—" Gretchen's stream of words choked off in a sob.

"I know." Becca sniffled. "I still can't believe it. It's like this wonderful dream...Gretchen, please stop crying or you'll have me blubbering, too!"

Too late.

A few minutes later Becca grabbed a paper towel from the holder above the sink and wiped her eyes. "Gretchen, there's so much I need to say to you..."

"I know. Me, too. By the way, do you think you can electrocute yourself by dripping tears into a telephone receiver?"

Becca laughed into the wadded-up paper towel. "You always were the practical one."

"Heck no, I was the gorgeous one, remember?"

"In your dreams, McCoy!"

Gretchen blew her nose and giggled at the same time. "Seriously, Becs, if there's anything I can do to help..."

"Well, now that you mention it..."

Ten minutes later, before the traces of Becca's tears even had a chance to dry, Gretchen was banging on the front door. She squeezed inside when Becca cautiously opened the door a crack. "Whew! You didn't warn me I'd have to run a gauntlet of reporters." She fanned her face with her free hand, stirring straggling wisps of her dark ponytail. "Think I could make a few bucks by agreeing to appear on one of those tabloid shows?"

Becca grinned. "'Family Friend Tells All'?"

Gretchen made a pistol with her thumb and forefinger and pointed at Becca. "You got it." Her gaze bounced up and down as she surveyed Becca from head to toe. Her jaw dropped, followed by the shopping bag stuffed with Sarah's outgrown clothes, which landed with a soft thud at her feet.

She propped her hands on her waist. "You," she said with a ferocious scowl, "are too darn skinny."

Becca rolled her eyes. "Good to see you, too, pal."

Gretchen's eyes misted with tears. She drew in a long, shaky breath. "Oh, Becs," she whispered, "you can say that again."

Then they fell into each other's arms.

"Amy, honey, I'm sorry, but Southpaw can't come to the doctor with us." Ryan finally managed to wrestle the squirming Irish setter into his bedroom and close the door. He hated to shut the dog up like this, but the excitable animal would only get in the way of their escape plan.

"Why not?" Amy asked in a tiny voice. Her lower lip trembled.

Ryan wanted to scoop her up into his arms and give her a big, reassuring bear hug. Unfortunately, it would probably have the opposite effect on his darling girl. "Because, sweetie, a doctor's office is no place for a dog." He hunkered down in front of Amy and gave her a teasing little poke in the tummy. "Why, with that big twitching tail of his, he might tickle someone under the nose and make 'em sneeze!"

His attempt to cheer Amy up failed miserably. "I don't want to go to the doctor," she said for about the dozenth time in the past hour, staring at him with those huge, pleading eyes.

"Dr. Kirkwood's just going to check you over, honey. He'll look into your eyes and ears and listen to your heart and probably tap your knee with a little hammer." At Amy's look of alarm, he said hastily, "It won't hurt a bit, I promise."

"Will he give me a shot?"

"Er…" Ryan's mind quickly scrolled through the list of childhood vaccinations. Were there any Amy might have missed? Would her kidnapper have bothered to take her in for regular checkups?

When suspicious dread crept over Amy's face, he assured her quickly. "No shots today. Cross my heart." He made the appropriate crisscross motion with his hand. A few more days wouldn't hurt, if a vaccination was necessary. The least they could do was give Amy some more time to adjust before they started poking her with needles.

"Ryan? Are you ready?" Becca called from downstairs where she'd been seeing Gretchen off. While the two women had been trying clothes on Amy, Ryan had phoned Doc Kirkwood, who'd been more than happy to fit them into his schedule today.

"Coming," he called back. He held out a hand to Amy.

She ignored it, lowering her head so her long blond curls screened her face, huddling against the newel at the top of the staircase.

Ryan's heart squeezed painfully. "Come on, princess. Dr. Kirkwood's a very nice man, and afterward we'll all go out for some ice cream, okay?" Maybe the child experts wouldn't approve of such blatant bribery, but to hell with them. Amy deserved to be spoiled a little.

Her curls rippled as she shook her head.

Ryan sighed. Looked like he was going to have to be the bad guy. With a twinge of foreboding in his gut, he took Amy's hand to lead her downstairs.

"No-oo!" Her terrified wail slashed through Ryan like a knife. Immediately he heard the rapid patter of Becca's ascending footsteps.

She shot him a look of understanding as she knelt on the top step beside their quaking daughter. "Amy? It's all right." She tucked a curtain of hair behind Amy's ear. "We'll both be right there while the doctor visits with you. I know it's a little scary meeting all these strangers, but Dr. Kirkwood's very nice. Gretchen was nice, wasn't she?"

Pause. Amy nodded once, reluctantly.

"And I know for a fact Dr. Kirkwood passes out lollipops to all the boys and girls who come to see him."

First ice cream, then lollipops. Ryan made a vow to make sure there were plenty of vegetables on tonight's dinner menu.

But Amy couldn't care less about sweets. She flung her arms around the newel and hung on for dear life when Becca tried to draw her down the stairs. "Gramma!" she sobbed. "I want my gramma!"

Sympathy and resentment lashed through Ryan, each battling for control. Amy's grief tore at his heart, but it was so unfair, damn it, that the woman who'd stolen their child had also managed to steal her love and her loyalty away from her real parents.

Becca worked her mouth as if working up the nerve to swallow something vile. "Your grandma's gone to Heaven, Amy." Her gaze flickered to Ryan, acknowledging this irony. Only yesterday they would both have gladly consigned Amy's kidnapper to the opposite direction. "I know you miss her, but it won't always hurt this much. I promise." She stroked Amy's hair. "Ryan and I love you very much, and pretty soon we'll all be a family together."

Her words pierced Ryan with a stab of powerful longing. For the first time he admitted to himself just exactly how much he wanted the three of them to be a real family again. Even if she remarried him for the wrong reasons, he still wanted Becca back as his wife. Maybe just going through the motions of being a normal family would somehow make it come true.

Then helplessness nearly overwhelmed him again in the face of his little girl's misery. Amy's chest heaved as tears cascaded down her cheeks. "Jessica," she choked out through her sobs. "I want Jessica-a-a."

Becca and Ryan exchanged puzzled frowns. Jessica? Becca mouthed the name at him.

Ryan scratched his head. Maybe some playmate she'd left behind in Florida? "Sweetie, who's Jess—"

Comprehension dawned on Becca's strained face. "Her doll!"

Ryan snapped his fingers. "The one she had last night."

"Is that who you mean, Amy? You want your doll?"

Amy rubbed her puffy red eyes with the back of her wrist as she bobbed her head up and down.

"Ryan, do you remember what happened to her doll?"

"Hmm." He fingered his chin. "Did she have it here at the house?"

Becca shook her head. "I don't remember seeing it except at the airport."

"She must have dropped it on the boarding ramp."

Becca chewed her lip. "Sweetie, we'll buy you a new doll after—"

"But I want Jessica! She's mine and I love her!" If Amy's lower lip was any barometer of her feelings, they were in for another storm of sobs.

"Don't you worry, princess. I'll get Jessica back for you."

Becca glanced up sharply. "Ryan, I don't think you should promise—"

"I'll drive down to Sacramento as soon as we're done at the doctor's. I'm sure Gretchen will lend me her car."

"But it's so far to drive, and the chances of finding the doll..." Becca let her voice trail off, jerking her head slightly toward Amy as if warning Ryan not to get her hopes up.

He looked at the small, forlorn figure of his daughter, clad in a borrowed T-shirt, shorts and sandals. She'd awakened this morning in a house she didn't remember, surrounded by people who were strangers as far as she was concerned. She didn't have one familiar object to cling to, not one single, solitary thing she could call her own.

He was going to get her doll back if he had to turn that airport upside down.

He grasped Amy's limp little fingers and patted her hand reassuringly. "I'll find Jessica, don't worry." He chucked her under the chin. "It may take me a little while, but I'll start looking as soon as we're through at the doctor's, okay?"

To his surprise and delight, Amy nodded, gripped his hand tighter and tugged him toward the stairs. "Let's hurry, okay?" she said in a breathless, tear-clogged voice.

"Okay."

"Ryan..." Becca sounded helpless, worried, pleased. "I hope you know what you're doing," she muttered into his ear as she followed the two of them downstairs.

So did he. Ryan was stumbling along on pure instinct here, just following his heart. Only trouble was, his heart wasn't always such a reliable navigator.

Example. Common sense warned him that asking Becca to remarry him was asking for trouble. Logic told him that pretending the three of them were a real family would be as futile as trying to put Humpty-Dumpty back together again.

And while his heart tugged him in one direction, every single ounce of Ryan's self-preservation cuffed him in the chest and hollered that he was a chump for giving Becca another chance to hurt him.

"We're going to play a little game now," he told Amy as he handed his daughter over to her mother.

"A game?" Amy tilted her head to one side.

"Yup." He gave one of her curls a playful tug. "After I go out the front door, you and Becca are going to sneak out the back and run toward the alley. Remember Gretchen? She's going to be waiting out there in her car for you."

"How come we have to run?"

"Well...it's sort of a race, sweetheart." He straightened and touched Becca's cheek. "All set?"

She gave him an uncertain half smile. "Do you really think this will work?"

"I think we'll give them a run for their money, that's for sure." Ryan hoped he sounded more confident than he felt.

"So... after you distract the reporters long enough for us to get away, how are you going to get over to Dr. Kirkwood's office without being seen?"

"Walk." Ryan shrugged. "After they harass me for a while, they'll lose interest. I figure none of them will stray too far from the house for fear of missing a glimpse of you and Amy."

Becca smiled again, only this time the corners of her mouth quirked with that hint of mischief Ryan remembered so well from the days when they were young and carefree and blissfully ignorant of how lucky they were. "Except Amy and I won't even be here."

"Nope."

"You missed your calling, you know that? You should have been a secret agent."

"Or an international jewel thief, huh?" He twirled an imaginary mustache.

Becca laughed. "You're certainly sneaky enough."

"Thanks. I think." He kissed Becca on the cheek, then dropped a kiss on top of Amy's head. "Ready, princess? Last one out to the car's a rotten egg."

"Good luck." Becca's beguiling blue eyes twinkled with what Ryan could have sworn was affection.

Maybe he wasn't such a fool to hope, after all.

"Shall we synchronize our watches?" he asked with a grin.

"I don't think that's necessary." Becca threw him a salute. "We'll see you at the rendezvous point, Captain."

Ryan returned her salute, then gave one to Amy.

After a moment's hesitation, she somberly returned it. Then she actually giggled.

At that moment Ryan felt like he'd just scored the touchdown that won his team the state championship. "Okay, here I go." He headed through the house with a spring in his step and happiness surging through his veins. He'd lead those reporters on a merry chase, all right. Right now anything seemed possible.

Even winning Becca's heart again.

Throwing caution to the winds, he opened the front door.

Chapter Five

"Amy, you're the picture of good health," the doctor pronounced in a booming voice. He tucked his dangling stethoscope into the pocket of his white coat. "Why, I'll bet you could run circles around your mommy and daddy."

Amy blinked up at him, swinging her thin, bare legs back and forth over the edge of the examining table. "My mommy and daddy are dead," she said matter-of-factly. "That's what Gramma told me."

Becca's heart dropped with a sickening swoop. Ryan looked like he wanted to punch someone.

"Ah, er, ahem." The doctor rubbed a hand over his white-fringed bald pate, sending Becca and Ryan an apologetic grimace. "Well, you're a very healthy six-year-old." He patted Amy's knee. "Nurse?" he called over his shoulder.

She bustled in immediately. "Would you help my friend Amy here get dressed," the doctor said with a wink, "and then see that she gets a lollipop while I talk to her—er, to the Slaters for a moment?''

"I'll get Amy dressed," Becca said hastily. "Ryan can tell me what you talked about." She wasn't about to let Amy out of her sight for a second.

"Becca..." Ryan touched her arm. She pulled away as she reached for Amy's clothing.

"Go ahead," she told him, avoiding his eyes. "Amy and I will meet you in the waiting room."

"Honey, I think the doc would like to talk to both of us."

Amy's head popped out through the neck of her T-shirt. "He just said Amy was fine," Becca observed. She helped Amy off the examining table. "Here, sweetie, can you put on your shorts?"

The nurse moved forward. "I'll do that."

"No!" Becca's cry startled everyone in the room. She covered her eyes with her hand. Dear heaven, she'd promised herself not to lose control like that, but the thought of handing Amy into someone else's care simply terrified her.

"Amy will be fine," Ryan said quietly but firmly. "Gretchen's out in the waiting room, remember? Amy can sit with her."

"My nurse will take very good care of her, I promise," Dr. Kirkwood said soothingly.

Becca glanced up just in time to see Ryan and the doctor exchange worried looks over her head. Resentment seeped in through the cracks in her emotional barricade. What right did they have to diagnose her as some kind of fragile, unstable, half-hysterical female who needed to be reasoned with like a three-year-old? How could they blame her for wanting to keep a close eye on her precious little girl, after the nightmare she'd been through?

Still, making a scene would only upset Amy. Though it went against every protective grain in her body, Becca forced herself to smile and say, "You go with the nurse and get your lollipop, sweetie. Ryan and I will be right there."

Obviously Amy didn't share either Becca's fears or her reluctance to be parted. She went willingly with the nurse without a backward glance.

Becca sighed. "Guess I'm being overprotective, huh?"

Ryan draped an arm around her shoulders and gave her a sympathetic squeeze.

"Quite understandable, all things considered," Dr. Kirkwood said in a kindly tone.

"But Amy *is* all right?" Becca's anxiety suddenly channeled itself in another direction.

"Hmm? Oh, yes, yes. I didn't mean to worry you." The doctor took off his horn-rimmed glasses and polished them on his sleeve. "No, the real reason I wanted to talk to you privately was so I could express my delight at your amazing good fortune." He poked his bifocals back on with a slightly unsteady hand. "After all, I delivered that little girl out there—not to mention her mother and half the other people in this town!" He shook his head sadly. "When I'd heard she'd been kidnapped..." The doctor suddenly looked older than his seventysome years. "Well, that was a bad business. A very bad business."

Becca's cheeks grew hot. Everyone in Pine Creek had hashed over the details of Amy's kidnapping for months. No doubt Dr. Kirkwood was recalling how Becca's negligence had led to the kidnapping in the first place.

Then the doctor's usual sunny demeanor reasserted itself. "All's well that ends well, thank the good Lord. Amy's home safe and sound, the two of you are back together..."

Ryan's arm began to feel like a yoke around Becca's shoulders. It seemed as though everyone in town was jumping to the same wrong conclusion.

The doctor peered at them over the top of his glasses. "I take it Amy doesn't realize you're her real parents?"

"The social worker who brought her back from Florida suggested we let her get used to us before trying to explain everything." As Ryan spoke, he slid his hand up and down Becca's arm.

This absent gesture of affection only increased the sensation that the walls were closing in on her. She felt pressured from all sides—Ryan, Gretchen and Tyler, and now even Doc Kirkwood—all seemed to be nudging Becca back into a marriage she'd vowed to put behind her forever. And Ryan's casually possessive air wasn't helping matters any.

She shrugged off his arm and moved a few steps away. "What about Amy's nightmares?" she asked the doctor. "She was tossing and turning all night long, poor baby."

"Perfectly natural, considering the trauma she's suffered." Doc Kirkwood's cheery, benevolent manner turned awkward all of a sudden. "Apparently Amy was quite attached to the woman who...who, uh—"

"Kidnapped her," Becca finished. "Who took her when I wasn't looking."

"Becca—"

She cut off Ryan's exasperated voice with another question. "Do you think we should take her to a psychologist, get her some kind of therapy?"

"Not at this point." Dr. Kirkwood picked up Amy's file and tucked it under his arm. "For now, let's wait and see." He chuckled. "Call me old-fashioned, but I'm not one of those doctors who think people need professional help to deal with every little upheaval in life." He ushered them out of the examining room. "Amy's young, she's in good health—let's give her a chance to bounce back on her own before we start calling in therapists, all right?"

"Sure, Doc." Ryan insisted on hovering at Becca's shoulder the whole way down the hall. "Whatever you say."

"Lots of tender loving care, that's my only prescription for Amy. But as for you, young woman..." He wagged a scolding finger at Becca. "You need to put on some weight. Don't skip meals, and get plenty of sleep at night."

Becca swallowed her irritation. It seemed everyone she ran into lately tried to tell her what to do. Even though she knew Dr. Kirkwood only had her best interests at heart, his unsolicited advice rubbed her the wrong way.

"Don't worry, Doc. I'll see that she eats." Ryan's proprietary assurance only annoyed Becca further. How dare he act as if she were some incompetent ninny unable to take responsibility for her own well-being?

Then they entered the waiting room and the sight of Amy curled up on the couch next to Gretchen blew away Becca's resentment like a brisk wind. She wondered if she would ever again get used to these unexpected glimpses of her daughter. Each time she caught sight of her little girl after even the briefest absence was like an incredibly precious gift. A gift Becca intended to protect and treasure.

Gretchen looked up from the children's magazine she was reading aloud and smiled. "Ready to go?" She rose to her feet and fished into the pocket of her slacks as she spoke. "I wish Tyler were here so he could fly you down to Sacramento, but he had to fly up to Portland at the crack of dawn and won't be back till late tonight. Here." She tossed Ryan her car keys.

He caught them in midair. "Thanks for letting me use your station wagon."

"Why don't you drop the rest of us off at my house? Becca and Amy can spend the afternoon with me and the kids until you get back."

"Actually, I was going to suggest Becca and Amy ride along to Sacramento with me."

"You were?" Becca asked. She was starting to feel invisible. Ryan and Gretchen were discussing arrangements as if she wasn't even there.

"Sure, why not?" He knelt beside Amy, who sat on the couch sucking a grape lollipop and listening to the conversation with wide-eyed interest. "We could stop and have a picnic along the way, get some fresh air instead of staying holed up inside the house hiding from the press.''

"That way Ryan could pick up his truck from the airport,'' Gretchen declared. "If you wouldn't mind driving my car back to Pine Creek, Becca?''

"How 'bout it, Amy?'' Ryan tugged on her sandal. "Would you like to go for a ride in the car?''

"Excuse me, but do I have anything to say about all this?'' Becca asked.

Ryan levered himself slowly to his feet. "Sure you do, honey.''

Always the peacemaker, Gretchen hastened to add, "What do you think of the idea, Becca?''

What could she say? That she'd rather spend the whole afternoon cowering indoors instead of enjoying the sunshine? Ryan and Gretchen's plan made perfect sense. Even if this wild-goose chase to find Amy's doll was unsuccessful, at least they could get Ryan's truck back. And escaping from all those reporters for a few hours would be a welcome respite.

So why did Becca feel as if everyone was ganging up on her? Put some weight on. Marry Ryan again. Go to Sacramento.

"Can we have peanut-butter-and-jelly sandwiches on our picnic?'' Amy piped up.

Becca knew when she was outnumbered. "You bet we can, sweetie.''

"And 'tato chips?''

"A whole big bagful.''

"I've got all the makings of a picnic at my house,'' Gretchen added.

"Everything's settled, then?'' Ryan's dark eyes held a triumphant gleam that Becca did her best to ignore.

She nodded. But even as Becca gave in, she knew everything was far from settled.

* * *

Ryan stretched his legs across the picnic blanket, leaned back on his elbows and contemplated blackmail.

Emotional blackmail, that is. He was having second thoughts about playing on Becca's guilt to get her to marry him. For cryin' out loud, she was carrying around a heavy enough load of the stuff as it was without him adding to it! He shouldn't have implied that Amy's happiness depended on having parents who were married to each other.

Overhead a red-tailed hawk coasted lazily around on air currents against a backdrop of blue, blue sky. Ryan dropped his head back and inhaled deeply, breathing in the scents of pine and clover.

He made a minor adjustment to his position so he could study Becca from beneath eyelids half-closed to the bright sunshine. She perched on the far edge of the plaid blanket, motionless, legs folded beneath her, staring across the roadside rest area to the rustic playground where Amy was swinging back and forth beneath the tall pines. There was a certain tension to her posture, as if she were on alert, ready to be on her feet and running in a split second should the situation require it.

"You haven't taken your eyes off her once in the last fifteen minutes," Ryan said.

Becca's back stiffened. Ryan could read her mind, her body language as well as his own. "She's perfectly safe over there," he said, reaching over to pluck another grape from the plastic sack that held the remains of their picnic. "There's no one else around." He swung his arm in a semicircle to indicate the surrounding grassy expanse, the parking area that was empty except for Gretchen's station wagon.

Becca's voice drifted back over her shoulder. "She could get hurt on the playground equipment or wander off somewhere. These mountains are full of steep ravines. She could fall or get lost or—"

"Becca." In one swift move, Ryan was across the blanket. His second move was to wrap his arms around her. "I know it's hard not to worry about her, but—"

"Let go of me, please."

"Not until you listen to what I have to say." After a brief wrestling match, Ryan pinned Becca to the ground by her wrists.

"Ryan, get off me. I mean it!"

"Honey, you've got to let Amy be a kid. And kids need independence. You can't watch over her like a hawk every waking moment."

"Yes, I can!" Becca's struggles took on a panicky quality. "I'm never going to let anything bad happen to her ever again."

Reluctantly, Ryan released her. She scooted away and sat up, hugging her knees to her chest.

Ryan sighed. "Much as we'd both like to, Becca, we can't stop bad things from happening to Amy. She's going to fall down and scrape her knees, and have best friends move away, and not get picked for the school play. We can't protect her from all the little hurts that come with childhood."

"You're a fine one to talk." Becca readjusted her sunglasses, which had gotten dislodged during their brief tussle. "Promising you'll get her doll back—what are you going to do if we can't find it?"

"Yeah, well, maybe that was a mistake." Ryan cracked a sheepish grin. "Okay, so I'm as bad as you. Maybe we both need a lecture."

"I don't need any lectures from you."

Ryan rolled over onto his stomach and clasped his hands in a beseeching gesture. "Don't be mad at me, Becs, please...."

Her lips twitched, then a reluctant smile broke across her face. "Don't use that wheedling tone with me, Ryan Slater. You sound just like you did back in high school, when I'd have to stop those roving hands of yours from getting too fresh.''

"Fresh?" His jaw clunked open. "I'll show you fresh." He lunged at her, capturing her in a big bear hug. They rolled over and over several times before coming to a stop.

"Ryan, cut it out." But she was giggling.

"Talk about fresh..." He nuzzled her neck. "How 'bout this, huh?"

"Stop! That tickles!"

"Does it? Not my intention, I assure you." He circled her narrow waist with his hands, positioning her more securely beneath him. He drew off her sunglasses and tossed them aside. Then he lowered his head to nibble on her earlobe.

"Um, Ryan..." Becca sounded a little out of breath.

"Yes?" He continued his teasing foray, planting a trail of kisses along her jaw, her exquisite cheekbones, her eyelids, rediscovering the textures, the tastes, the curves and hollows of the lovely face he knew so well.

"I, uh, really don't think we should be doing this..." Becca braced her hands against his shoulders.

"*Now* who sounds like she's back in high school?"

Ryan felt her breasts heaving beneath him, felt her skin grow warm under the thin cotton of her blouse. He undid the lowest button. He'd only meant to cajole Becca out of her irritable mood, but now he was startled to realize how aroused he was. Old memories, familiar sensations, long-buried emotions came back in a rush.

He slid his hand beneath her blouse, splayed his fingers across her bare ribs. He felt her stomach contract when she sucked in her breath. "Ryan, no..."

"Yes," he murmured against her lips. "Oh, yes..."

Her mouth was soft and warm, hesitant at first, but increasingly responsive as Ryan continued to kiss her, losing himself in her sweetness, aware of a longing ache that unfurled deep in his abdomen. Faint, breathless whimpers escaped from Becca's throat, only to be captured by his mouth. She was making him reckless, crazy, stirring up all sorts of desires he hadn't experienced for a long, long time.

That old familiar feeling of rightness descended upon Ryan, the certainty that this time, this place, this woman, were part of his destiny—that if he lived to be a hundred he would never find a woman who felt so right in his arms as Becca.

They both sensed Amy's presence at the same second. Their heads turned simultaneously to glimpse scuffed sandals, thin little legs and dirt-streaked shorts....

Quick as a wink, Ryan heaved himself off Becca, who scrambled into a sitting position and groped for her sunglasses. "Hi, sweetie. Did you have fun on the swings?" she inquired in a voice pitched higher than usual.

Amy's head was cocked to one side at an angle that made her look like a curious sparrow. But all she said was, "Can I have some more grapes?"

"Sure." Becca's cheeks felt sunburned, though they hadn't been sitting outside all that long. She handed Amy the bunch of grapes, thankful for the dark glasses that concealed her eyes. She was actually embarrassed in front of her own child, for heaven's sake!

She darted a quick glance at Ryan and saw that he was as beet red as she was, but only because he was trying so hard not to laugh. His eyes shimmered with mirth as he clamped his jaw shut and did his best to keep his face straight.

Becca didn't see the humor in the situation at all. If Amy had shown up a few minutes later, she might have gotten a lesson she was way too young for. "It isn't funny, Ryan," Becca whispered indignantly while they folded up the blanket. Amy was already meandering back toward the car with the bag holding the remains of their picnic.

"You should have seen the expression on your face." Ryan chuckled, shaking his head with amusement. "You'd think the school principal caught us making out in the broom closet or something."

"How can you make a joke out of it?" Becca snatched the blanket from his hands. "What if Amy had wandered off while you and I were rolling around on the ground, groping each other like a couple of sex-starved adolescents?"

Ryan's smile faded. He probed his cheek thoughtfully with his tongue. "And how can *you* make what we were doing sound so childish, so meaningless?"

"Don't make any more out of it than it was, Ryan." Becca held the folded blanket in front of her as if it were a protective barrier.

With a barely controlled movement he shoved a stray lock of hair out of his eyes. "What the hell is that supposed to mean?"

The dangerous expression on his face would have made a more cautious woman back off. But Becca already knew what it was like to lose everything. What could Ryan possibly dish out that was any worse?

"What it means is that we can't let our hormones run amok like that again. We can't get carried away by memories, or lose control just because it's been a long time since either one of us has..." Becca's nerve faltered. She swallowed. "You know."

Ryan folded his arms across his broad chest and looked as implacable as a brick wall. "No, I don't know, Becca. Why don't you enlighten me?"

"You know perfectly well what I'm talking about," she mumbled.

He continued to study her as if she were an interesting specimen in biology class. She felt like a butterfly pinned to a corkboard.

She tried to shrug off her self-consciousness. "I'm just saying that, sometimes, when people are deprived of ... certain physical needs for a long period of time ... well, sometimes they let those needs get the better of them. That's all."

Ryan scratched his chin. "Let me get this straight." On the surface, his voice sounded curious, as if he were truly interested in solving this puzzle. But Becca could detect the anger coiled just beneath the surface like a rattlesnake. "You think the only reason you and I were so hot for each other just now was because neither of us has gotten any for a long time?"

She cringed at his crude phrasing, even as annoyance flared inside her. "Well, I could never have put it so elegantly myself, but basically—yes."

"Uh-huh." Ryan shifted his weight to one leg and assumed what Becca took to be a deliberately arrogant pose. "Better check your assumptions, sweetheart." He brought his face close to hers. "Just because *you've* been leading a celibate existence doesn't mean *I* have."

He pivoted away from her, then turned back. "And by the way, your blouse is unbuttoned." With that, he stalked off across the grass toward the car.

Stunned, Becca stared after him with her mouth hanging open. How could he...? Surely he didn't mean...?

She snapped her mouth shut. Pain slashed through her like a knife. Sex had been the furthest thing from her mind for the past four years. It was only now, after being with Ryan again, that she'd felt that part of herself stir and begin to come alive.

Apparently Ryan hadn't suffered the same numbness, the same death of desire. He'd just come right out and told her he'd been with another woman, hadn't he?

Quit deluding yourself, a jealous voice taunted. *Why not make it plural? Other women.*

With clumsy, trembling fingers Becca refastened the button on her blouse. She hadn't exactly expected Ryan to carry a torch for her forever. In fact, the main reason she'd divorced him was that Ryan had deserved better than a cold, hollow shell of a woman for a wife. He'd deserved more than Becca had been capable of giving him during those hellish months after Amy was kidnapped.

But to discover that Ryan had actually made love to another woman while Becca's own emotions had been in the deep freeze...well, it hurt more than she would have thought possible. And Becca was something of an expert on pain.

"This is what happens when you let your guard down," she scolded herself as she trudged toward the car where Ryan and Amy were waiting. "Letting yourself care about anyone but Amy is bound be disastrous."

But as she slid into the front seat beside Ryan, carefully avoiding his gaze, Becca worried it was already too late. She'd opened that Pandora's box of emotions just a crack, but it was wide enough to remind her of how happy she'd once been with Ryan, of how glorious their lovemaking could be.

And everyone knew that once you started fooling around with Pandora's box, it wasn't so easy to reel back in whatever escaped.

"Are you going to get Jessica back?"

Amy's worried brown eyes made Ryan feel even more guilty. Why had he been stupid enough to make such a damn-fool promise? Now he was haunted by the fear of letting his little girl down.

Just as he was haunted by the hurt he'd put in Becca's eyes with his other stupid, thoughtless comment.

The ugly truth was, for a second he *had* wanted to hurt Becca, the same way she'd hurt him by shrugging off their passion as nothing but uncontrollable lust brought on by a long spell of abstinence. But for Ryan, at least, the intensity of his desire had sprung from his heart and soul, not his sex-starved hormones.

Wounded to the core, his instinctive response had been to strike back in the most juvenile, immature way possible—by implying that *he*, at least, hadn't suffered from any lack of companionship with the opposite sex.

How Becca would despise him if she found out he'd lied to her just to protect his injured male pride.

He could decipher the pain etched in every taut line of her profile as she stared straight through the windshield at the airport terminal. She sat as close to the opposite door of the parked station wagon as possible, knees drawn primly together, spine straight as a book's.

She hadn't spoken two words to Ryan since they'd left the picnic area an hour ago. He didn't blame her.

What a mess. Once again he cursed himself for lashing out at her like that. "I'm gonna do my best, princess," he told Amy, draping his arm along the front seat as he spoke over his shoulder. "But there's a chance some other little girl might have found Jessica and taken her home."

"But you promised!" Amy's eyes blurred with tears.

Nice going, Slater, he berated himself. *Now you've managed to hurt* both *people who matter more to you than anyone else in the world.*

Becca finally consented to look at him, but the I-told-you-so he saw written all over her unhappy face was no comfort at all.

"I'll be back," Ryan muttered, wrenching open the car door.

Inside the terminal, he checked the airport lost and found.

No doll.

He proceeded to the gate where Amy's plane had unloaded last night, but the airline employee who checked the boarding ramp reported no sign of Jessica.

He hurried back through the terminal to the airline ticket counter, wishing he could remember the name of the woman who had been so helpful last night.

No one at the ticket counter could help him.

He even ducked into the airport gift shop in hopes of finding a doll who *looked* like Jessica, even though he knew it wouldn't be the same.

But he hadn't the faintest recollection of what Jessica had looked like, and the gift shop didn't have any dolls in stock, anyway.

He was striding back through the terminal to double-check around the gate area when he spotted the office for airport maintenance. He halted, changed direction, then walked over and stuck his head inside the open doorway.

"Excuse me," he said to the beer-bellied worker slouched in a folding chair in front of a portable TV. "My daughter lost her doll here in the airport last night, and I was wondering—"

The man shushed Ryan with an impatient wave of his hand. "This here's the final round. If this guy comes up with the right answer...yes!" He clenched his fist in a victory salute. "Nearly eight thousand bucks that guy just won. Whoo-eee!" He turned down the volume, leaned back in his chair and scratched the roll of flesh peeking over the belt of his maintenance uniform. "Now, you was sayin'?"

"I was wondering if you or anyone else on the cleaning crew might have found a child's doll last night, maybe over in the gate area."

The man's eyes slid quickly sideways, then just as quickly back again. "Hmm. A doll, you say?"

Ryan followed the direction of the man's furtive glance. "Yeah. Like that doll right over there." Yellow hair and a plastic arm peeped out from behind a bunch of cleaning supplies on a shelf across the small room.

"Hey! Hold on a sec, now." The guy jumped up, knocking over a bucket of brooms and mops with a clatter. He moved his ponderous bulk faster than Ryan would have thought possible to intercept Ryan before he could reach the shelf.

He grabbed the doll just as Ryan's fingers brushed it. "How do I know this here's the same doll you're lookin' for?" He hitched up his pants and glowered at Ryan from beneath bushy gray eyebrows.

"That *is* my little girl's doll. Now if you don't mind—"

"Hold your horses, sonny." He clutched the doll like a possessive kid trying to keep a playmate from taking it away. Then a sly look oozed into his beady eyes. "See, I was gonna take this doll home for my little granddaughter. I figure, finders keepers, right? And since you ain't got no proof this here's even the doll you say you're lookin' for..." He shrugged expressively.

Ryan sighed. "How much?"

Triumph flickered through the man's eyes like a snake's tongue. Then he pasted on a dubious expression. "Well now, my little granddaughter's awful fond of dolls, and I know this one would really mean a lot to her...."

Ryan jammed his hand into his back pocket and pulled out his wallet. "I said, how *much?*"

"Lemme see, now..."

Ryan could practically hear the cold-blooded calculator whirring and clicking inside the guy's brain as he tried to figure out how much Ryan was good for.

"A hunnert bucks," he said.

"A *hundred*—?" Ryan gaped at him. "You've got to be kidding. Why, I could buy ten of those dolls at a toy store for that price!"

"Suit yourself." He shrugged one meaty shoulder. "I'd just as soon give the doll to my granddaughter, anyway."

Ryan doubted that, but what if he called the man's bluff and ended up walking away empty-handed? Amy's woeful eyes and tearstained cheeks came back to haunt him.

Aw, hell. He'd never been much of a poker player, anyway. Gritting his teeth, he opened his wallet and counted through the bills. "Here." He shoved them at the guy. "Eighty-nine dollars. That's all I've got." He showed him the empty wallet. "Take it or leave it."

"I'll take it." With one eager swoop Ryan was relieved of all his cash. "Here." He lobbed Jessica in Ryan's direction, immediately losing all interest in the doll.

Ryan caught her just before she hit the floor. "I'm sure you'll be able to buy your granddaughter a real nice present for eighty-nine dollars," he remarked, not bothering to hide the sarcasm in his voice.

"Huh? Oh, yeah, right, right." The guy licked his thumb again, greedily counting his spoils. "Shut the door on the way out, would ya?"

Ryan did. With a bang.

But then, back at the car, the joy on Amy's face when Ryan handed her the doll was worth every penny. "Jessica!" she cried. "You got found!" She bundled the wayward doll into her arms and hugged her for all she was worth. "Oh, thank you!" she said to Ryan in a voice that made him feel ten feet tall.

Even Becca was regarding him with wonder and admiration as she got out of the car and walked around to the driver's side. "How on earth did you—?"

"Long story." Ryan checked to make sure the key was still in the ignition. "You're okay about driving Gretchen's car back to Pine Creek, right?"

"Sure." The breeze blew wisps of blond hair across her troubled blue eyes. For a minute Becca looked like she wanted to say something, but she didn't.

"Well...see you at home, then." Ryan turned, started walking toward where he'd left the pickup truck last night. Then he thought of something and went back. "Um, I hate to ask, but...do you have a few dollars I could borrow?"

Becca's brows curved questioningly. "Of course." She reached inside for her purse, rummaging through it. "Is ten dollars enough?"

"Great. I just need enough to pay the parking fee on the way out." He folded the bill into his shirt pocket. "Thanks."

He was starting to walk away again when Becca touched his shoulder. "Ryan," she said with a puzzled expression, "did you have to *pay* someone for Jessica?"

For some reason, he was embarrassed. "Er, let's just call it sort of a finder's fee."

Suspicion flitted through her eyes. "How *much* of a finder's fee?"

"It was worth it." Ryan dismissed the subject with a flip of his hand. "Look how happy Amy is."

"Yes, but—"

He cut off Becca's inquisition with a brief, hard kiss. "I'll pick you up at Gretchen's."

"All right." His kiss had left Becca looking stunned, bruised—like an accident victim.

He ducked his head to peer through the rolled-down window. "Bye, princess. See you when we get home."

"Bye." Amy wiggled the doll's arm so Jessica waved at him. Ryan grinned. "Goodbye to you, too, Jessica."

As he made his way through the parking lot, taking a wrong turn or two while he tried to remember where he'd left the truck, Ryan decided it definitely *had* been worth it. Eighty-nine dollars was a small price to pay for Amy's happiness.

If only he could buy Becca's happiness so easily.

Chapter Six

Amy was still hugging her beloved Jessica when Becca tucked her exhausted daughter into bed that night. "Did you have fun playing with Sarah and Christopher today?" she asked, smoothing Amy's hair off her forehead.

"Mmm-hmm." Amy nodded sleepily. Gretchen had insisted the Slaters stay for dinner after they got back from Sacramento. Though much more interested in playing alone with Jessica at first, Amy had gradually warmed up to the McCoy children. By the time her parents were ready to go, Amy was running around the backyard squealing with the other two, caught up in a rousing game of tag.

Becca pressed a kiss to Amy's cheek, relieved when Amy didn't pull away. Was that a sign she was starting to adjust to her new home, to her "new" mommy and daddy? Or was Amy simply too tired to react?

"Tomorrow we'll go up in the attic and bring down a dresser for your clothes," Becca said softly. "And maybe we'll go shopping for some new curtains. Would you like that?''

But Amy had already drifted off to sleep.

Becca smiled. She turned off the light, leaving the door ajar and the hall light on. As she proceeded slowly downstairs, her contentment faded, step by step.

Now she would finally be alone with Ryan, for the first time since he'd made his shocking revelation this afternoon. Well, shocking to Becca. Probably most people wouldn't blame him a bit for seeking comfort, maybe even happiness, in the arms of another woman after his wife had walked out on him.

Still, picturing Ryan making love to someone else was like a blow from a two-by-four that left Becca reeling, vaguely nauseous. She couldn't help feeling betrayed, even though she was the one who had betrayed Ryan by running away from him in the first place.

You have no one to blame but yourself. So just stay cool, all right? Don't let him know how much it hurts.

She entered the living room cautiously, relieved in spite of herself not to find him. She forced herself to walk down the hall to the back room Ryan used as an office. Here Becca had spent many hours doing the bookkeeping for his construction business. With a tiny prickle of curiosity, she wondered who'd been doing his books since she'd left.

It had never occurred to her to wonder before. Now she wondered if his new bookkeeper might also be his new—

Stop it! You've got no right to be jealous.

But that didn't stop her.

Ryan wasn't in his office, either. Becca checked in the kitchen, found the back door open. She cupped a hand to her eyes and peered through the screen into the deepening dusk.

"It's safe to come out." Ryan's voice drifted lazily across the lawn. "The big bad reporters have apparently all gone home to bed."

Becca pushed open the screen door and stepped out. Ryan was sprawled in a wooden Adirondack chair, resting a drink can on one of the broad, flat arms. At his feet, Southpaw lifted his head and whined a greeting.

"Where's Amy?" Ryan asked. The gathering darkness made it difficult for Becca to make out his face.

She lowered herself into a matching chair. "Asleep."

"Already?" He sounded surprised, disappointed.

"She conked out pretty suddenly. She's had quite a day."

"I'll go up and kiss her good-night before I turn in."

"Mmm."

The silence stretched out between them, broken only by the steady hum of crickets and the dog's gentle panting. The lingering heat of the day seeped upward from the ground. Down in the Sacramento Valley the heat would still be oppressive, but up here in the crystal-clear mountain air the evening was balmy and pleasant.

A disturbing sense of déjà vu settled over Becca—a feeling that she'd lived this night before, or a thousand others just like it. She had to fight an instinctive urge to stroll over and stand behind Ryan's chair, to massage his shoulders while he made exaggerated groans of contentment, to lean over while he tilted his head back for an upside-down kiss...

A seductive sensation...a dangerous urge. Becca cleared her throat. "Nice out here," she said, trying to clear her mind of best-forgotten memories.

"Nicer than being stuck inside hiding out from the press, that's for sure."

"Do you think they'll be back tomorrow?"

Ryan took a swallow of his drink. "Not as many, probably. In a few days most of them will have given up."

"I hope you're right."

Restlessly, Becca kicked off her shoes, scrunched her toes through the long grass. The heady perfume of roses swirled around her. The overgrown bushes along the back of the house were drooping with their heavy burden of flowers and needed cutting back. The lawn needed mowing, as well. She'd noted other signs of mild neglect around the place—the loose front step, light bulbs that needed replacing, faucets that leaked a little.

Ryan had always been so conscientious about keeping their home shipshape. But that was before... before a lot of things.

"How's work?" Becca asked, steering her mind away from dangerous areas. She lifted her hair with both hands to let the faint breeze cool the back of her neck.

"Can't complain. Business is booming." Ryan reached down and scratched the dog's head. "Right now I'm building a big addition for a house out on Whisper Ridge."

Becca brought her knees up to her chin, propping her bare feet on the edge of the chair. "Amy and I will be all right here by ourselves, if you need to get back to the construction site tomorrow."

"Nah." Ryan tilted his head back to drain the last of his drink. "I've got a good assistant working for me now—remember Tommy Hansen? He can handle things at the site for a few days. I told him to call me if he ran into any problems."

Becca's lips twitched in amusement. "That might be kind of difficult, considering that you unplugged the phone this morning."

"Oh, yeah. I did, didn't I?" Through the darkness she heard the grin in his voice. "Well, Tommy's pretty resourceful. He'll manage somehow."

Becca's smile died away. She flattened her hand, skimming her palm along the arm of her chair. "I'm trying to decide if I should call my mother."

Pause. Then, cautiously, "How *is* Elaine?"

Becca worried a tiny crack in the wood with her thumbnail. "Still in Texas. Still married."

"Still drinking?"

She glanced up sharply. "I...don't know." She shrugged. "Probably. It's not exactly something you get into with a Christmas card."

"That the only contact you've had with her?"

"I used to call her once in a while. I'd get so lonely—" Becca sucked in a quick breath. "Well, never mind." She flipped up her palm. "Usually her husband would answer, and claim Mother was 'indisposed' at the moment."

"Guess you could figure out what that meant, huh?"

She gave a short laugh, drummed a rapid, nervous tattoo with her fingers. "Yeah. Indisposed. Inebriated. Passed out."

Ryan reached across the gap between their chairs and grasped her fidgety hand. "Honey, I'm sorry."

"I suppose it shouldn't still bother me. Heaven knows, I've had enough time to get used to it. All those years after my father died...worrying about her...being too embarrassed to bring friends home from school for fear Mother would be in one of her 'moods.'"

Ryan stroked the back of her hand with his thumb. "It's tough growing up with only one parent."

"Especially when that one parent isn't even really there for you."

"Yeah. That's where I was lucky. I mean, even after my dad ran out on us and my mom had to go to work full-time, she always managed to make time for me. Just to shoot the breeze about little day-to-day stuff, you know...school, football..."

"Girlfriends," Becca teased. Then she remembered what he'd told her that afternoon, and the subject of his girlfriends didn't seem so funny anymore.

"I wish Mom had lived long enough to see us married," Ryan said softly. "To meet Amy." He drew Becca's hand toward his mouth and kissed her knuckles.

Little shivers of delight skittered up and down her spine. He turned her hand over, pressing a kiss into her palm.

Heat flowed along Becca's arm, radiating through her other limbs with languid pleasure. She splayed her hand against the side of Ryan's face, tangling her fingers in his hair. The faint stubble on his cheeks rasped deliciously against her skin as his reminiscing drew her back into the past...to the day of their wedding...to the day their precious child had been born.

In the darkness she used her fingertips as a Braille reader would, feeling the growing pulse beat of his desire, tracing his eyebrows, sensing the magnitude of his self-restraint in the tense, quivering muscle along his jaw. His eyes were deeper, darker pools within the shadows, beckoning her, luring her closer and closer until she could feel his breath on her face, his hands in her hair, his lips—

Becca twisted away and launched herself from her chair like a slingshot. Her heart was pounding against her ribs hard as a sledgehammer, her knees wobbling like old table legs in desperate need of repair. She had to remember that this *wasn't* the past, they *weren't* the same two people.

Out of the night came the sound of Ryan's harsh breathing, and then his low voice. "Damn it, Becca, quit shutting me out like this. If you and I are going to be married—"

She whirled around. "I haven't said I'd marry you again, Ryan."

He took two steps toward her, then stopped, clenching his fists as if he were restraining himself on a very short leash. "Haven't you paid any attention to what we've just been talking about? We both know all too well how tough it is to grow up in a single-parent household. Don't you want what's best for—"

"Amy wouldn't have only one parent—she'd have both of us, even if we don't remarry."

"You think it's the same thing, shuttling back and forth between two households?"

"I already agreed to move back in here."

"But for how long, Becca? Until it's too inconvenient to keep maintaining our separate lives under one roof? Until it's too difficult to keep punishing yourself by turning me away, when we both know you want me as much as I want you?"

"*Punishing* myself?" She slapped a hand against her chest. "Is that what you think I'm doing, just because I refuse to hop into bed with you? You must think you're pretty hot stuff, Ryan Slater." A bitter laugh erupted from her throat. "Maybe other women can't resist you, but that doesn't mean that *I*—"

"What the hell is that supposed to mean?"

Becca hesitated, then charged ahead. "Don't play Mr. Innocent with me. You've made it perfectly clear that you haven't lacked for female companionship since I went away."

Talk about a shot in the dark. Becca wasn't sure what she'd said, but it had certainly hit home. After a long pause, Ryan's voice reverberated with an awkward, almost sheepish note.

"Um, look, about this afternoon..."

"Forget it. I don't need to hear the details of your love life." The last thing Becca wanted was to listen to Ryan's confession. As long as she didn't have a name or a face to attach to her jealousy, she could handle it. Barely.

Ryan ran his hands through his hair. "No, you don't understand. I—"

"And another thing." Becca rushed on, trying to ward off any more painful revelations. "I really resent the way you're using Amy to get me back in your bed."

His whole body stiffened. "You're way out of line, Becca."

"Am I? What do you call it, then, dredging up our own unhappy childhoods, parading the past in front of me like some warning sign—" she sketched an imaginary banner in the air "—Don't Let History Repeat Itself!"

"*You* were the one who brought up the subject of your mother!" he roared.

"Shh! Keep your voice down. The neighbors—"

"I don't give a gnat's eyelash about the neighbors." Ryan paced back and forth across the lawn with Southpaw slinking after him, whimpering in puzzled agitation. "Is it so terrible to want Amy to have the loving, secure childhood we both missed out on? Is it so awful to want my child to grow up in a home with two parents instead of one?"

"Of course not." Becca tossed her head with impatience. "What's despicable is the way you're using Amy to manipulate me into marrying you."

"Becca, I'm warning you . . ."

"Every time the subject comes up, you play Amy like a trump card. 'Do it for Amy's sake, Becca.'"

Ryan practically choked with exasperation. "I thought that was the whole point."

Was it? Maybe the idea of remarriage had started out that way. Amy needed both her parents, and nothing mattered more than that. But now, just once, Becca wanted to hear Ryan say that he needed her, too.

Might as well wish for the moon. "You make it sound like some kind of grand sacrifice on your part," she went on, spreading her arms in a dramatic gesture. "As if your only interest in me is due to the fact that I'm your child's mother."

"Hey, wait a minute." Ryan wagged a stern finger at her. "*You're* the one who's dragging your feet on the whole subject of our remarriage."

She could hardly argue with his logic. But somewhere during the twists and turns of this conversation, Becca had left logic in the dust. Jealousy and hurt and wounded pride had surged ahead. "Maybe you're the one who should reconsider, Ryan." She gave an imitation of a casual shrug. "After all, marriage is bound to cut into your social life."

Once again, a somewhat embarrassed hesitation before he replied. "Look, there's something we've got to get straight—"

"Get *this* straight, Ryan." Becca was too revved up now to let Ryan get a word in edgewise. "If you and I *do* remarry, I have no intention of turning a blind eye to your extramarital shenanigans."

"Becca, for God's sake—"

"Even if we're living as husband and wife in name only, don't expect me to be a good sport about your girlfriends."

"That's what I'm trying to tell you. I don't *have* any—"

This time it was Southpaw who interrupted with a wild barrage of barking. He ran back and forth between Becca and Ryan, tail swishing furiously, as if pleading with them to call a truce.

"Shh! Simmer down, boy." Ryan grabbed for his collar and missed. "For cryin' out loud—Becca, come back!"

But she was already halfway across the yard, propelled by a maelstrom of emotions that swirled inside her, shifting patterns, changing shape. Jealousy, anger, regret... and a few others she didn't dare name.

She was shocked to realize how quickly a seemingly innocent trip down memory lane had degenerated into a shouting match. Too late, she'd remembered her vow to keep a tight lid on her emotions.

The screen door swung shut behind her with a bang.

Problem was, the longer she lived under the same roof with Ryan, the harder it was for Becca to keep her feelings for him safely locked up in the emotional attic where they belonged.

And what really worried her was the strong suspicion that if they did get married again, ignoring her feelings for Ryan would be darn near impossible.

"Take that—"
Bang!

"—and that—"
Bang!
"—and that!"
Bang!

Ryan paused, wiping a film of sweat from his forehead with the rolled-up cuff of his shirtsleeve. He'd thought a session with the hammer might provide an outlet for the pent-up frustration that had itched at him for the last couple days like a bad case of poison oak.

No such luck. He plucked another nail from between his lips and pounded it into the front step. Usually he enjoyed carpentry—the neat way everything fit together after you measured and calculated, the sense of satisfaction on seeing the finished useful result.

But no matter how carefully he measured and calculated, he couldn't figure out how to get through to Becca. And he was far from satisfied with the results of his efforts.

He leaned back against the porch post and studied the peeling paint overhead. Ever since their argument in the backyard the other night, Becca had taken great pains to avoid being alone with him. She never let Amy out of her sight, and most of the time she encouraged the dog to hang around for extra protection.

Ryan was desperate to set the record straight, to explain that maybe he'd given her the wrong idea by implying there'd been other women in his life—okay, that he'd done it on purpose out of some petty need for revenge.

But how could he come clean when Becca wouldn't even give him a chance? She insisted on treating him with a cool, polite detachment that made Ryan want to grab her and kiss her until the old spark came back into her eyes—even if it was a spark of anger.

But Becca couldn't have broadcast the Hands Off message any more clearly if she'd been wearing a sign around her neck.

Not exactly the cold-shoulder treatment, but she refused to discuss anything more personal than decorating Amy's room or what they were going to have for dinner.

On the infrequent occasions when she accidentally smiled at him, the smile didn't touch her eyes. And once in a while, when she didn't know Ryan was watching, her face took on a sad, faraway expression.

It was driving him nuts.

"You look like Humphrey Bogart."

The sound of a car door slamming jarred Ryan from his miserable musings. Tyler was coming up the walk with a spring in his stride and a grin on his face.

Ryan scratched his head. "Bogart?"

"Yeah, you know." Tyler pointed. "With a cigarette dangling from your lips."

"Huh? Oh." Ryan removed the last nail from his mouth, examined it without interest, then tossed it into his toolbox.

"Becca got you making some repairs around the place, huh?"

"Yeah. Sorta."

Tyler lowered himself onto the porch step next to Ryan. "Need any help?"

"Nah."

"Now you sound more like Gary Cooper. 'Yep.' 'Nope.'"

"Sorry."

"See what I mean?"

Ryan cracked half a grin in spite of himself. "Last time I let you help, you wound up in the emergency room, remember?"

"Hey, how was I supposed to know that drill would start whipping around so fast? It wasn't even plugged in."

"That's why it's called a cordless drill."

"Whatever." Tyler dismissed the unfortunate mishap with a wave of his hand. "Say, I figured I'd have to fight my way through a mob of news media. Where'd they all go?"

Ryan closed his toolbox with a shrug. "Guess we're old news. They found some new story to chase, someone more interesting to harass."

"Boy, Becca must be relieved. I remember when Amy first, uh, disappeared, how they hounded poor Becca. Well, you, too, of course, but I'll never forget how Becca looked every time some reporter caught her on camera." Tyler shook his head in remembered sympathy. "Terrified. Like a cornered wild animal."

"She thought people were accusing her, blaming her for Amy's kidnapping." The minute the words were out, Ryan felt vaguely traitorous. Becca's personal anguish was something private, a kind of sacred trust between them.

Tyler gaped in astonishment. "She thought people blamed *her?* Geez, how could she think that?"

Ryan shifted uncomfortably. He and Tyler were as close as brothers, but that didn't give Ryan the right to discuss Becca's emotional turmoil with him. "She felt guilty because she left Amy alone. Look, could we, uh, change the subject?"

"Sure," Tyler said slowly, understanding dawning in his eyes. "Hey, how's Amy doing?"

Ryan perked up immediately. "She's terrific. Still a little quiet, but I really think she's getting used to us again."

"That's great." Tyler slapped his knee. "Poor little tyke. Must be rough on her, all this—"

"Ryan? I thought I heard voices— Oh, Tyler it's you." When she recognized a familiar, friendly face, Becca opened the door all the way and ventured onto the porch. "How are you?"

"Pretty good, so they tell me." He winked lasciviously as he scrambled to his feet.

Ryan muffled a groan, stealing a glance in Becca's direction to see how she'd react to Tyler's teasing. Figured. Ryan got a dirty look flung his way while Tyler, that charming old devil, received a fond smile.

"You'd better not let Gretchen hear you talk like that," Becca scolded. "She's liable to come after you with a frying pan."

"Come on, Becs, you know I'm just kidding." He jerked a thumb at Ryan. "Though if you ever decide to dump this bum, I might just be tempted."

Oops! Now even Tyler realized he might have gone too far, trod just a little too close to certain sensitive areas. To cover his inadvertent blunder, he said hastily, "Gretchen sent me over here to invite you to a barbecue at our house tonight."

Caution filtered into Becca's eyes, replacing her embarrassment. "Gee, I don't know..."

"It'll just be the four of us and the three of you," Tyler said in a cajoling tone, obviously comprehending the reason behind Becca's reluctance. "Gretchen thought it'd be fun, and Sarah and Christopher have been asking when Amy can come over and play again."

"Well..."

Ryan kept silent, knowing if he cast a vote in favor of going, Becca would be only more determined to stay home.

"Okay," she said at last. "Does Gretchen want me to bring anything? Potato salad? Paper plates?"

Tyler looked stricken. "Good grief, I don't know. Maybe you'd better call her and find out."

"Maybe I should." She ducked inside. "Nice seeing you, Tyler." Then she closed the door behind her.

"Whew!" Tyler raked a hand through his shaggy dark hair and shot Ryan a guilty look. "Sorry about that, old buddy. Guess I got a little too close to a sore subject, huh?"

"If you'd waded any deeper into that particular region of quicksand, you'd have missed the barbecue for sure." Ryan levered himself to his feet and hoisted his toolbox.

"Er, look, if I'm being too nosy just say so, but I thought you and Becca were, uh, getting back together." Tyler followed Ryan around the side of the house to the garage.

Ryan sighed. "Frankly, I don't know what the hell is going on."

Tyler winced. "That bad, huh?"

"That bad." Ryan walked past his truck and through the door in the back of the garage that led to his workshop. "Truth is, I did something really stupid."

"No! You?" Tyler swayed in mock amazement.

Ryan took a halfhearted swing at him. "Very funny." He set the toolbox on the shelf. "I sort of, uh, hinted that after Becca left me, I, uh, well . . . that I wasn't exactly living like a monk all the years she was gone."

Tyler whistled through his teeth. "Man, that *was* stupid."

"Yeah." Ryan propped himself against his workbench, crossing one foot over the other. "Now she won't even let me explain."

"Explain what? That you're a loudmouth jerk?"

"I knew you'd understand."

Tyler whistled again. Then his eyebrows bunched together. "You, uh, *were* lying when you said that to Becca, weren't you?"

"Of course I was!" Ryan flung his hands in the air in disgust. "You know how it's been for me, Tyler. Chasing women hasn't just been low on my list of priorities the last few years—it hasn't even been *on* my list."

"So why'd you tell Becca something so idiotic, anyway?"

"Geez, Tyler, I knew I could count on you to make me feel better."

"What are best friends for?" He buffed his nails on his shirt. "So, speak up. Let's hear it."

Ryan moved restlessly around the workshop, picking up tools, setting them down again. "I was . . . mad, I guess."

"Mad...like insane?"

"That, too." He jabbed a screwdriver into a scrap of wood so hard it remained upright when he let go. "She just...we were just—aw, hell." He dragged his fingers down both sides of his face. "We were fooling around, and I thought things were going great, and then Becca had to pour cold water over everything by claiming we just got carried away because it had been so long since either of us had, uh, made love."

"Aha!" Tyler's face lit up. "So you decided to prove her wrong by making it sound like it hadn't been all that long for *you.*"

"You got it."

Tyler shook his head sadly. "Boy, are you a jerk."

"Thanks for your support."

"You gotta fess up, pal."

"That's what I've been *trying* to do for days, but she won't listen!" Ryan punched a sack of concrete. "Ouch!" Now he had a fistful of skinned knuckles to add to his woes. Shaking his stinging hand, he went on, "She makes sure Amy's always in the room with us, and if I manage to catch her alone after Amy's gone to bed, she hightails it in the opposite direction before I can get two words out."

"Hmm." Tyler propped his chin on his fist. Then he snapped his fingers. "I've got it."

"What?"

"The amazing Tyler McCoy comes to the rescue again."

"Knock off the self-promotion and just tell me what's going through that pea-size brain of yours."

"This evening during the barbecue, while Amy's off playing with Sarah and Christopher, I'll clue Gretchen in, and..." He made a rolling see-what-I'm-getting-at motion with his hand.

"And while the two of you do a disappearing act, I'll get Becca aside and tell her the truth," Ryan finished. "You know, it just might work."

It had better work. Because Ryan had a feeling if he let this misunderstanding drag on much longer, he just might lose Becca forever.

He'd already lost her once. He wasn't about to let it happen again.

Tyler was shaking his head. "Boy, you really blew it," he said.

Chapter Seven

"Oh, I'm so stuffed I can't eat another bite." Gretchen surveyed the remains of their meal, then stretched across the picnic table and nabbed another of the chocolate brownies Becca had brought. "Well, maybe just *one* more bite. Mmm!" She licked her fingers and chewed enthusiastically. "These are delicious," she pronounced with her mouth full.

"Amy and I baked them this afternoon." Becca switched her gaze to the other side of the big backyard, where Amy and the two McCoy children were taking turns swinging in an old tire hung by a rope from the limb of a gnarled apple tree.

"Did you?" Gretchen drew her sneaker-clad feet up onto the picnic bench and sat sideways with her arms wrapped around her knees. "That's great. A nice mother-daughter activity. Sounds like the two of you are making good progress getting reacquainted."

Becca made little plinking sounds with the ring opener of her soft drink can. "It's so strange, having to get to know my own child all over again." She sighed, watching as little Christopher McCoy threw a stick for Southpaw to fetch. "I have to admit, I was disappointed when Amy didn't remember Ryan or me. That was something I never stopped to consider all those years she was gone."

"Because the only important thing was getting her back."

"Yes." Becca swallowed a lump in her throat. "Compared to that, nothing else should matter, I guess."

Gretchen touched her friend's arm. "Don't shortchange yourself in the emotional department, kiddo. You deserve to feel angry about what happened, to feel cheated out of the time you lost with Amy. You just have to keep it in perspective, that's all."

Becca leaned back against the edge of the redwood table, bracing her elbows behind her. "Sometimes I feel so ungrateful, when I let minor things bother me." Her glance drifted over to the barbecue grill, where Ryan and Tyler were communing with a couple of beers while they hashed out the 49ers' chances for next season.

Gretchen craned her neck to check the direction of Becca's gaze. "Minor things, huh?" She turned her head back to focus her sharp, perceptive eyes on Becca. "Care to elaborate?"

Becca didn't answer. Despite the danger to her peace of mind, she couldn't help admiring Ryan's handsome, animated profile as he argued with Tyler. Muscles rippled beneath his T-shirt when he flung his arms wide to emphasize a point. A lock of wheat brown hair slipped across his forehead, and his teeth gleamed white when he threw back his head and laughed at Tyler's rejoinder.

He lifted his beer to his mouth, and when his lips closed around the neck of the bottle, Becca shivered in spite of the warm evening. How well she remembered studying Ryan from afar like this, when he was a big-shot high school senior, star of the football team, and she herself was a lowly sophomore trying out for the cheerleading squad.

"Boy, you've still got it bad for him, haven't you?" Gretchen's voice disrupted Becca's woolgathering, the comment hitting uncomfortably close to target.

"Hmm? Who? What are you talking about?" Becca jumped to her feet and bustled around the table, gathering up paper plates, screwing tops back onto jars of mustard and relish.

Gretchen watched this sudden burst of activity with amusement. "Don't play innocent with me," she warned. "I can read you just as well as I could in high school, when you first got a crush on Ryan and spent all your time mooning over him when you were supposed to be studying."

"I did not *moon* over him." Becca banged a serving spoon against the bowl of potato salad.

"Oh, no? What would you call this, then?" Gretchen clasped her hands together, batted her eyes wildly and donned a goofy, lovesick expression.

Becca giggled in spite of herself. "That was a long time ago."

"Okay, maybe you don't drool over your trigonometry homework anymore, but don't kid yourself." Gretchen wagged a scolding finger. "You're even more goo-goo-eyed over Ryan now than when we were teenagers."

"Goo-goo-eyed?" Becca scoffed. "Is that the psychological term for it? Where'd you learn that, one of those daytime talk shows?"

"Don't change the subject." Gretchen cupped her hand to the side of her mouth and called, "Hey, kids, don't eat any more of those apples, okay? They're not ripe yet."

"'Kay, Mommy," Sarah called back.

Becca's heart gave a painful little lurch. What she wouldn't give to hear Amy call her Mommy.

A smoky whiff of hickory and hamburgers from the cooling barbecue wafted by, bringing tears to Becca's eyes—or so she told herself. She quickly dabbed her eyes with a paper napkin, then took her time covering the remaining brownies with aluminum foil.

"Quit fussing with those leftovers, will you?" Gretchen drummed her fingers on the red-and-white checked tablecloth. "It's Tyler's turn for cleanup tonight. I don't want him getting off too easy."

Becca sat back down on the picnic bench with a bump. "You're so lucky," she said, sneaking another glance at the two men. "I mean, you and Tyler. The way you get along together. You make marriage look so easy, like . . . like it's fun!"

"Ha!" Gretchen rolled her eyes. "Easy? That's a good one. You ought to hear us arguing over whose turn it is to do the dishes, or whether we can really afford to buy a new car, or where we're going on vacation this year."

"But that's what I mean." Becca spread her hands, searching for the words to describe exactly what it was she admired about the McCoys' marriage. "You and Tyler are partners, you share responsibilities and take turns, you have this wonderful give-and-take that Ryan and I—well, I envy you, that's all." Absently she began tearing her napkin into little pieces.

Gretchen's eyes darted toward the two men, and the sight of her husband softened her features, brought a wistful smile to her lips. For a minute she looked as lovestruck as she claimed Becca did. "Tyler's pretty nice to have around, I must admit. *Most* of the time." She swung her attention back to Becca. "But you and Ryan are great together, too."

"No." Becca shook her head as the pile of little napkin pieces continued to grow in front of her. "Maybe it seemed that way once, but after Amy . . ." She took a long, quavering breath. "Things just fell apart after Amy disappeared. If we'd had a strong marriage, if we were really right for each other, our relationship wouldn't have crumbled the way it did."

Gretchen responded with something curt and unprintable.

Becca's jaw dropped. "Why, Gretchen McCoy, I don't believe I've ever heard you use that word before." She set her mouth into a stern line. "If your mother were here, she'd wash your mouth out with soap."

"If my mother were here, she'd say the same thing I just did." Gretchen reached over and gently shook Becca by the shoulders. "You and Ryan went through a terrible tragedy capable of destroying *people*, let alone marriages." She drew back, suddenly hesitant. "I know you and I never really talked that openly about what you were going through, but—"

"Gretchen, I'm so sorry I shut you out like that, but I was going out of my mind, I didn't realize what I—"

"Shh." Gretchen held up her palm as if she were a crossing guard. "Never mind. That's all in the past. Anyone could see the terrible pressure you and Ryan were both under. It's no wonder your marriage suffered, but that doesn't mean the two of you don't belong together."

Becca's hair streamed from side to side as she shook her head. "I wasn't there for him, Gretchen. I wasn't strong enough. Ryan deserves more than that—he deserves someone who can stand by him when the going gets tough, someone good enough and loyal enough and brave enough to be an equal partner."

Mindful that the two men were within eavesdropping distance, Becca tried to gulp back the rising agitation in her voice. "Ryan deserves someone who loves him enough not to let him down," she finished in a nearly inaudible voice.

"Stop it." Gretchen slapped her palm on the table, scattering little napkin pieces in all directions. "You're being way too hard on yourself." She tucked her dark hair behind her ears, leaning forward to stare earnestly into Becca's eyes. "I won't argue that Ryan deserves the best," she said, "but *you're* who's best for him, Becca. No one who's seen the two of you together could have any doubt about that. You two are meant for each other." She banged the table again. "So knock off this ridiculous nonsense about not being good enough for him."

Becca studied her fingernails. "It's too late, anyway," she muttered. "I think Ryan's already found someone else."

"What?" At Gretchen's incredulous yelp, Ryan and Tyler both swiveled their heads around.

"It's okay," Becca called, panic providing quick inspiration. "I just told her Ted Danson wears a toupee."

The two men laughed and resumed their conversation.

Gretchen was not amused. "What do you mean, Ryan's found someone else?" she sputtered in an indignant whisper. "Where'd you get a crazy idea like that?"

Becca looked away. "From something Ryan said."

"You must have misunderstood him."

"Gretchen, I really don't want to get into this."

"You can't just drop a bombshell like that and not explain!"

Just then Southpaw bounded over, panting and wagging his tail. He dropped a stick into Becca's lap, then sat back on his haunches, waiting expectantly. Becca picked up the damp, chewed-on stick and flung it across the yard. Southpaw galloped off in eager pursuit.

"Ryan told me he's made love to other women since our divorce," Becca said quietly.

Gretchen's eyes grew as big and round as paper plates. "I don't believe it."

Becca spoke through gritted teeth. "It's true. He told me."

"Whoa." Gretchen held up her palm again. "Something weird is going on here."

"I know I have no one to blame but myself, of course—"

"No, Becca, I mean that you're wrong about Ryan. Completely wrong." She shook her head emphatically. "I swear to you, if Ryan has even so much as looked at another woman since you left, I'd be amazed."

"Gretchen, he *told* me—"

"I don't care what he told you, or why he said it." She slanted a look behind her to make sure no males were within earshot. "Take it from me," she went on in a low voice, "since you moved away, Ryan could have been living alone on a desert island as far as women are concerned."

For the first time, doubt began to nibble away at Becca's unhappy conviction. "How can you be so sure?"

"Come on, Becs, Pine Creek ain't exactly the big city. If Ryan so much as took a woman to the movies, it'd be all over town before they even finished buying their popcorn."

What Gretchen said was true. The Pine Creek grapevine was one of the wonders of modern communication technology. Instantaneous, widespread... if not entirely accurate at all times.

"Maybe she's not from Pine Creek," Becca said slowly, unwilling to let this tiny bud of hope blossom. "It could be someone who lives out of town—Sacramento, maybe."

"Forget it." Gretchen dismissed the idea with a flick of her hand. "Believe me, Ryan's been too busy with work to have time for any long-distance romance. Morning, noon and night, seven days a week. Ever since you left, he's thrown himself into his work like a man possessed."

"Well... it wouldn't necessarily have to involve what you'd call *dating*," Becca said, examining the lock of blond hair she'd twisted around her finger. "It could have been a one-night stand. Or *stands,* plural."

"Get real." Gretchen pulled a scornful face. "I shouldn't bother to dignify that with an answer." But she did, anyway. "You know Ryan even better than I do. He's not the one-night-stand type. He's too classy, for one thing—not to mention too much of a romantic for anything that...that—"

"Sleazy?"

"I was going to say shallow."

"But then why would he tell me...?"

Gretchen hoisted her shoulders in an exaggerated shrug. "Men. Who can understand the way they act sometimes?" She made a noise like *humph*. "And they say *women* are irrational."

Doubt and confusion swirled around Becca like a cloud of gnats. Could Gretchen possibly be right? But then, why would Ryan have said...?

She thought back to their argument, to that horrible moment when he'd blurted out those words. He'd been angry when she'd tried to play down the significance of that hungry embrace, those eager kisses...angry enough to strike back with a deliberate, hurtful lie?

That didn't sound like Ryan, either. Ryan was patient, honest, even-tempered...not the kind to let strong passions get the best of him. He must have been deeply affected—*wounded,* even—by her insistence that those kisses meant nothing.

On the other hand, maybe Gretchen was wrong. Maybe Ryan *had* been with another woman. Still...it definitely wasn't like him to practically brag about it, to fling it in Becca's face like an insult.

She knew it shouldn't hurt her, the thought that he'd made love to somebody else. After all, *she'd* been the one to walk away, practically shoving him into someone else's arms. Yet she couldn't staunch the flow of relief that now seeped through her, finding little cracks in the emotional barricade she'd tried so hard to throw up against him.

Maybe Ryan *had* made it all up. Maybe he *hadn't* been un-faithful to her.

Not that you could be unfaithful, exactly, to someone you weren't married to anymore. For the first time, Becca considered what it might feel like to be involved with an-other man, to kiss another man, to feel another man's hands on her body....

She shuddered with distaste. Even though she was no longer married to Ryan, it still felt like betrayal. It still felt wrong. But it hadn't felt wrong when Ryan had kissed her, had taken her in his arms.

Becca cupped her hand to her forehead, feeling feverish with confusion and desire. Dear God, what was she going to do?

"Whaddaya say I help you carry all this stuff inside, Toots?" Tyler swatted his wife playfully on the bottom.

Gretchen turned slowly around, rubbing her backside and pinning a ferocious glare on him. "What's this *you* help *me* business? This is *your* night to clean up, remember?"

"*My* night?" Tyler clapped his hand over his heart. "Who cooked the burgers?"

"Who made the potato salad? And cooked the corn on the cob? And set the table?" With each question, Gretchen jabbed him in the chest, driving him back step by step.

Tyler held up his hands in surrender. "Okay, okay, I give up! You're right!" He whipped off the checkered chef's apron emblazoned with the words Genius At Work. "Let me rephrase that. Would you mind helping *me* carry all this stuff inside, honeybunch? Darling? Sweetie-pie?" He kept twitching his head toward the house, bobbing his eye-brows up and down like Groucho Marx.

Gretchen grabbed the apron and swatted him with it. "Don't you sweetie-pie me, you...you—*oh*." Instantly her face was transformed by a bright smile. "Why, of course

Use These Stamps
to Complete Your
"MATCH 3" Game

Simply detach this page & see how many matches you can find for your "MATCH 3" Game. Then take the matching stamps and stick them on the Game. Three-of-a-kind matches in rows 1 through 3 qualify you for a chance to win a Big Money Prize—up to a Million-$$$ ...

...THREE-OF-A-KIND-MATCHES IN ROWS 4 & 5 GETS YOU FREE BOOKS & A NICE SURPRISE GIFT AS WELL! PLAYING IS FREE - FUN - EASY & THE WAY YOU COULD WIN!

PLAY TODAY!

PRE-FOLD & SEPARATE PAGE OF STAMPS ALONG DOTTED LINES. PLAY "MATCH 3" & RETURN GAME PIECE IN REPLY

I'll help you clean up, honeybunch." She started snatching up dishes with both hands.

Becca moved forward. "Here, I can carry some of that."

"No, no." Gretchen practically shoved her aside with her hip. "You and Ryan are our guests. Tyler and I can manage just fine, thanks."

Becca was starting to suspect some kind of conspiracy. She didn't dare look at Ryan, but she felt him hovering near her shoulder.

Gretchen motioned with her elbows as she balanced containers of leftovers in her arms. "Sit down, both of you. Have another beer. Enjoy the evening." She backed into the house behind Tyler and disappeared.

Ryan blew a disgusted stream of air through his lips. "Well, that wasn't *too* obvious, was it?"

Reluctantly, Becca turned to face him. "Mind telling me what this is all about?"

Ryan set down his beer bottle, scuffing his boot on the ground. "Look, I'm sorry for manipulating things like this, but it was the only way I could get you alone."

Becca edged away from him, seeking refuge by the big camellia bush on one side of the yard. "You still haven't answered my question."

Ryan followed her, positioning himself uncomfortably close behind her. He brought up his hands, then dropped them before touching her shoulders. "I—I wanted to apologize for something, Becca. Something I said. Something stupid and unforgivable."

He smelled pleasantly of wood smoke and sounded miserable. Becca's heart lifted.

"The other day, when I said that stuff about, well, about being with some other woman..." He shifted his weight from one foot to the other and cleared his throat. "It wasn't true. I lied. I haven't been with anyone since you, Becca. I just said it to make you jealous because I was mad."

Becca plucked a waxy green leaf off the bush. "Why were you mad?" she asked softly, stroking the leaf between her fingers.

"Why was I mad? Because... because, uh..." She felt him fidgeting behind her and took pity on him. Ryan had never been all that comfortable expressing his feelings with words. He preferred to use more... physical means.

The leaf fluttered to the ground. Becca turned and looked up at him. "It's all right," she said. "I think I understand."

"You do?" His brown eyes glimmered with a succession of emotions—relief, surprise, puzzlement. "But how... I mean, don't you want me to explain?"

All at once Becca was tired of explanations, tired of games and excuses and foolish hopes that things could ever be as they once had been. A great weariness sank into her limbs, filling her with despair, with bleak regret for what they both had lost.

She blinked to keep back the tears. "Why do we keep doing this, Ryan? Why do we keep doing things to hurt each other?"

His brow furrowed. "What do you mean, honey? *I* was the one who—"

She pressed her hand lightly to his mouth. "I hurt you by walking out on our marriage, by running away when you needed me most." She swallowed, closed her eyes. "Just like I wasn't there when Amy needed me."

Ryan gripped her fingers tightly, kissed her knuckles. "No, Becca. I won't listen to talk like that. You've got to stop blaming yourself for every bad thing that's ever happened to us."

"It all started with my mistake. If I hadn't been careless enough to leave Amy alone, you and I would still be together. We'd still be a family. We'd probably have other children by now..." To Becca's horror, her throat closed up, choking off her words.

Ryan looked grief-stricken. He pulled her into his arms, buried his face in her hair. "It's not too late, Becca." His voice was muffled, but there was no mistaking the desperate plea in his words. "We've got a second chance. We *can* be a family again."

"It's too late," she said, but her voice was so clogged with unshed tears, she didn't know whether he'd heard her or not. For a moment she allowed herself the luxury of leaning into him, seeking comfort in the reassuring strength of his embrace, savoring the tender closeness she didn't dare allow herself too often. She was so afraid—afraid of hurting Ryan again. Afraid of being hurt herself.

Amy... Amy had to be the center of Becca's universe from now on. She couldn't risk any distractions that might lead to another terrible mistake. There was only room for one person in Becca's bruised, battered heart, and that one person was her child.

Across the yard Southpaw erupted in a frenzy of barking. Becca's eyelids fluttered open. Over Ryan's shoulder she had a clear view of the apple tree where the children had been playing. As the scene registered on her brain, icy terror spilled through her bloodstream. "No!" she cried, wrenching free of Ryan with a paroxysm of fear.

"Becca, please!" As she broke out of his embrace, Ryan's spirits plummeted toward the center of the earth. Once again she'd pulled away from him, just when he'd begun to hope that—

Then he saw the cause of her panic, the reason for the dog's excited barking.

Across the yard, a stranger with a video camera was talking to the children, doing a crazy sort of dance as he kicked out his foot every so often to keep Southpaw at bay. Even so, he managed to keep the camera pointed right at Amy.

Something broke loose inside Ryan, something he'd carefully bolted shut years ago. Here, finally, was a living,

breathing threat to his child, not some mysterious, hypo-
thetical kidnapper he'd never seen and had no way to fight.
He'd been helpless to save Amy once before, but by God,
he wasn't helpless this time.

Outrage boiled up inside him, and in that moment Ryan
realized with an awesome, eye-opening jolt just exactly how
far he would go to protect his child. He would kill for Amy
if he had to.

He charged across the yard faster than he'd ever moved
during his football days. At the last moment he passed
Becca, scooped Amy up into his arms and handed her to
her wild-eyed mother.

Calm. He had to stay calm. He didn't want to upset the
children.

"Southpaw, sit! Quiet!" Ryan snapped his fingers and
pointed. The setter finally obeyed, but his twitching tail, his
bared teeth, said as clearly as words, "Let me at him!"

Ryan knew just how the dog felt. Every cell in his body
was sizzling with anger, vibrating with the urge to hoist this
character by the collar and toss him off the property.

He stepped directly in front of the intruder, planting his
feet in a wide-apart, aggressive stance to shield Becca and
the kids behind him. "Who the hell are you?" he demanded in a low, dangerous growl.

The guy continued to let the camera run, aiming it at
Ryan now. Ryan knocked it aside. "I said, who are you?
What do you think you're doing?"

"Hey, watch it! This here's an expensive piece of equipment." The guy was in his twenties, with red hair and a
boiled-lobster complexion. As he checked his precious
camera for any signs of damage, he chomped on a huge
wad of gum wedged in his cheek like chewing tobacco.
"Name's O'Leary," he said between chomps. "I'm with
one of the independent stations in Sacramento."

A reporter. He should have known. Behind him, Ryan
heard Becca's soft gasp of alarm. Fury all out of propor-

tion to the situation surged up inside him again. He knotted his fists, then jammed them across his chest and under his armpits to keep from thrashing the guy. "So that gives you the right to trespass on private property? Ambush little kids?"

The reporter squinted at him. "Hey, the public's got a right to know." He smacked his gum with infuriating calm. "Besides, those kids didn't mind talking to me."

"He gave us candy," Sarah piped up.

A scarlet haze filtered over Ryan's vision. He stepped forward and held out his hand. "Give me the camera," he said in a deadly still tone.

O'Leary jerked it back. "No way, man. This is going on the eleven o'clock news. Finally I got the scoop that'll land me that weekend anchor job." Smack, smack went his gum.

Ryan had to battle an impulse to wrap his fingers around the guy's skinny little neck and throttle him till he dropped the camera. But he didn't want to do it in front of the kids. "I'm going to ask you one more time," he warned through gritted teeth. "Give me that camera."

"Hey, ever hear of freedom of the press?" The guy sounded indignant, almost insulted.

"Ever hear of traction?" With one swift lunge, Ryan grabbed the camera.

"Hey!"

They struggled, but O'Leary was no match for Ryan. Damn it, how did the catch on this thing...there! He flipped out the videocassette, dropped it on the ground and crushed it with the heel of his boot.

"Hey, you can't do that!" O'Leary screeched. He stared at the ground openmouthed, as if Ryan had just squashed a helpless sparrow.

"Want to watch me do it to the camera, too?" Ryan hauled back, ready to pitch the camera over the hedge and into the trees.

"Ryan, no!" Becca cried.

He caught himself just in time. *What the hell am I doing?* he thought. This creep would probably stir up even more trouble if Ryan destroyed his camera. Besides, he wasn't setting a very good example in front of the kids. He was overreacting, flying completely off the handle for some reason he didn't have time to analyze.

He clawed his way back under control, lobbed the camera at O'Leary instead of hurling it toward destruction. The reporter caught it against his stomach with a soft *oomph.* "You'll be sorry for this," he said breathlessly, his face even redder than before. "I'll sue!"

"And I'll sue you right back for trespassing, harassment and invasion of privacy." Ryan stepped toward him.

O'Leary started to protest, but saw something in Ryan's face that made him back up instead. Ryan seized him by the collar and thrust him toward the narrow opening in the hedge where he'd apparently sneaked into the yard. "Now beat it before I do something *you'll* be sorry for."

"Hey, watch it! There's thorns in here. Ouch!"

Southpaw finally used up his last ration of restraint and dashed to the gap in the hedge. He stood there barking wildly even after the reporter had disappeared.

Dusting his hands with satisfaction, Ryan turned around to find all three children watching him in rapt fascination, their eyes big as silver dollars.

Becca's face was drained of color, her features pinched with shock and tension. She was staring at Ryan as if she'd never seen him before.

When Amy started wiggling in her arms, Becca lowered her reluctantly to the ground and knelt in front of her. "Sweetie, what did that man say to you?"

On the surface Becca's voice was calm and gentle, but as she stroked Amy's tousled curls, Ryan noticed her fingers were trembling. She was doing a good job of hiding it, but Ryan could tell she was profoundly shaken by what had just happened. He wondered which had disturbed her more—

the reporter's intrusion, or his own violent overreaction to it.

Amy hooked her finger over her lower lip and answered shyly, "He asked me my name, and how old I was."

"Then what?" Ryan crouched down beside them, making a forcible effort to slow his hammering pulse. He draped a fatherly arm around Christopher, who was looking a little scared by all the fuss.

Amy stared down at her shoes and mumbled, "He asked me how I liked being back with my mommy and daddy."

Becca froze as if paralyzed by a bolt of lightning. Ryan felt a renewed onrush of anger. Now he wished he'd given in to the urge to pound that interfering little weasel into a pulp.

Amy dropped her finger from her mouth, switching her puzzled, wide-eyed stare back and forth between Becca and Ryan. "How come he said that?"

Becca exchanged a quick look of anguish with Ryan. "I think he just wanted to know if you liked living with us, sweetie." The tendons in her throat contracted in a brief spasm. "Because we're going to be your mommy and daddy from now on, remember?"

"Oh." Doubt flashed briefly across her face. Then she lifted one small shoulder and said, "Living with you's all right, I guess."

Becca made a sound that was half sob, half laughter. "Well, Ryan and I are sure happy you're living with us now, pumpkin." She brushed Amy's cheek with her fingertips. "'Cause we love you a whole bunch."

"Can we go back to playing now?" Amy asked.

"Sure," Becca responded with a wistful smile. "But just for a little while longer, okay? We have to go home pretty soon."

She pushed herself to her feet, sending a troubled look in Ryan's direction. Then Ryan remembered something Sarah had said. "Did that man give all of you candy?"

Sarah bobbed her head and proudly held out a fistful of jellybeans. "Amy? Christopher?" Both children reached into their pockets and produced more of the same.

Ryan quickly confiscated the goodies before there could be any protest. "Sarah and Christopher, I'll bet your parents have told you not to take presents from strangers, haven't they?"

The two McCoy children exchanged guilty glances.

"My grandma told me that, too," Amy said.

Ryan's eyes found Becca's, and he saw that the bitter irony of this statement wasn't lost on her, either. He ruffled Amy's hair as he rose to his feet. "Your grandma was right," he said, even though the words tasted like acid. "Don't ever take anything from a stranger unless Becca or I say it's okay."

"We don't want to scare you, sweetie," Becca said, bending over and propping her hands on her knees, "but it's very important not to talk to strangers or ever go anywhere with them. Do you understand?"

Amy nodded solemnly.

"That goes for all three of you," Ryan added.

"Are we gonna get in trouble?" Sarah's chin was quivering.

Ryan tugged on one of her pigtails. "No. Just remember next time, okay?"

"If that bad man comes back, I'm gonna tell Southpaw to bite him," Christopher said ferociously.

The setter barked in agreement.

Becca looked worried.

The back screen door banged open. "Hey, what was all that ruckus out here?" Tyler asked.

Chapter Eight

"Coming, Becca?" Ryan paused in the doorway after kissing Amy good-night.

"I'll be down soon."

"Okay. Night-night, princess."

"G'night," Amy replied sleepily.

Ryan closed the door partway behind him, leaving the room in shadows. Becca knew she would have to face him alone sooner or later, but later suited her just fine, thank you. Today had been such an emotional roller coaster, she was still dizzy from all the ups and downs.

First, there had been the undeniable relief of learning that Ryan hadn't made love to someone else, after all. Then the terror of spotting a stranger accosting Amy. And finally, the shock of witnessing Ryan so angry, so out of control.

Becca had been upset by the encounter, too, naturally, but she couldn't imagine what could have prompted Ryan to react as strongly as he had. For a minute there, she'd thought he was going to stomp on the reporter the same way he'd stomped on his videotape.

Ryan had always been sort of the strong, silent type, but today he'd behaved more like the Terminator. Destroying video equipment, threatening people, tossing them around... maybe this new side of his personality was another aftereffect of the way Becca had hurt him.

Who could measure the emotional trauma he must have suffered, considering the circumstances in which she'd left him? According to Gretchen, Ryan had thrown himself into his work as a means of coping with the tragic loss of first his child, then his wife. He'd always been one to keep his innermost feelings to himself. Was it any wonder the pressure built up until some stressful incident lit the fuse and he exploded like a keg of dynamite?

Chalk up one more item for her guilt list.

Becca sighed. The agitated creak, creak, creak of the rocking chair disturbed the otherwise silent room. She forced herself to slow down, to relax, to turn her thoughts in other directions.

She glanced around the darkened room at the frilly new curtains, the whimsical wallpaper and white wicker furnishings. During the past several days they'd managed to sneak Amy out for some shopping, redecorating her room as well as replenishing her wardrobe.

Becca had decided to give Amy's babyhood possessions that were stored up in the attic to a thrift shop. For some reason it seemed important to make a fresh start, to sweep away all the old cobwebs of the past.

Next to Becca's chair, Amy stirred on her pillow. "Aren't you asleep yet?" Becca whispered. She leaned over and stroked Amy's forehead. "I thought you'd be all tuckered out after playing with Sarah and Christopher all evening."

Amy rubbed her eyes, thrashed around beneath the covers a little. "I can't sleep," she said in a small, plaintive voice.

"What's the matter, sweetie?" Tonight, for the first time, Amy hadn't insisted on having Jessica tucked into bed with her. The doll sat nearby, propped up on the new white wicker dresser. Maybe that explained Amy's restlessness. "Is something bothering you?" Becca asked softly.

Amy hesitated, then shook her head.

"You're not still worried about that man with the camera, are you?"

"No."

"Well...you had fun playing with Sarah and Christopher, didn't you?"

Amy nodded. "And Southpaw."

"Oh, of course." Becca smiled.

Amy plucked at the bed covers. "Sarah said..." Her voice trailed off.

"What, sweetie? What did Sarah say?"

Amy's eyes were deep, round smudges in the darkness. "She said that you don't really live here. That I'll probably have to go with you and live someplace else."

Her words slashed through Becca's heart like a knife. "Oh, Amy..." She bit her lip, not knowing what to say. Here she and Ryan had done everything they could to make Amy feel loved and secure...yet just when Amy was starting to adjust to her new home, her new life, this new monster reared its head to frighten her.

Becca knelt next to the bed and cuddled Amy in her arms. Carefully, she asked, "Do you like living here, sweetheart?"

For once Amy seemed content to snuggle against her mother. "Well, I like my room...and Southpaw...and Sarah and Christopher..."

Becca held her breath.

"And you and Ryan."

Becca hugged her. "We love you, too," she said, her shaky voice muffled against her daughter's sweet-smelling skin. She drew back. "This is your home, Amy. For as long as you want it to be."

"Does that mean I don't have to move away?"

"That's what it means, all right." Becca smoothed Amy's silky-fine hair back from her temples.

"But...what about you? Are you going back to where *you* live?"

Becca thought of her rented place in Sacramento—the house that had never been a home. She thought of her bookkeeping business, and realized that she had only clients, no friends in Sacramento. It seemed a lifetime ago that she'd fled to the anonymity of the big city, where no one would know her tragic past or guilty secret—that she'd left her baby unguarded long enough for someone to snatch her.

Only now her baby was home, thanks to an incredible miracle. Maybe it was time for Becca to come home, too.

"I'm staying right here with you and Ryan," she promised Amy. "Forever and ever. The three of us are going to be a family from now on." And as she spoke the words, Becca realized she wanted them to be true with her whole heart and soul.

"For keeps?" Amy asked.

"For keeps."

Amy rolled onto her side, tucked her hands beneath her cheek. "I think I'll go to sleep now," she announced with a big yawn.

Becca kissed her. "Sweet dreams." She switched on Amy's new night-light, then paused in the doorway for one last look at her soon-to-be-sleeping child.

In her heart, Becca had just made a commitment—perhaps the most important commitment of her life. But when she'd realized how much it meant to Amy, her decision had been a surprisingly easy one. Somehow she and Ryan would have to come to a truce, work out some kind of arrangement that would allow them to live together as a family.

Becca had failed her little girl once before—with devastating consequences. Tonight she'd assured Amy that this was their home from now on—home for all three of them. And this was one promise Becca intended to keep.

Even if it meant living a lie.

Bolstered with new resolve, Becca closed the door of her daughter's bedroom and went in search of her ex-husband.

Ryan leaned against the doorframe, staring moodily out into the backyard. He couldn't see a thing, of course, except for the insects that kept banging into the screen, attracted by the light in the kitchen behind him.

Man, he'd made a mess of things. First he'd told Becca that stupid lie about being with another woman, then he'd offered her some lame apology, then he'd completely lost his temper and practically slugged someone right in front of her.

With each stupid misstep, he could sense Becca withdrawing from him, could see her doubts about him increase. Every time they started to get close, Ryan blew it.

Who knows? Maybe subconsciously he was doing it on purpose. Maybe deep down inside, he didn't *want* to get too close to Becca, for fear she would leave him again. That was definitely a nightmare he didn't care to repeat.

He took a sip of his Scotch and told himself he should be grateful things had turned out the way they had. And he *was* grateful, damn it! When he considered how astronomical the odds had been of ever getting Amy back, of ever seeing his little girl again...

Hastily Ryan took another sip to loosen the tightness that clamped around his chest like bands of steel. He was a lucky man, all right. Luckier than he deserved. And if the only reason Becca was back in his life was because of Amy, well, he shouldn't complain. If this happy ending wasn't one hundred percent perfect, so what? He had his darling daughter back, and that should be enough.

Then why wasn't it?

"There you are." The unexpected sound of Becca's voice nearly made Ryan spill his drink.

He made an effort to rearrange his brooding features into a more neutral expression before he turned around.

The sight of her sent a shaft of near-painful longing through his belly. God, she was beautiful! In just the week or so since Amy's return, the gray hollows beneath Becca's cheekbones had faded and the haunted look was gone from her sapphire eyes. Her hair shimmered in the pale light like spun gold.

She'd been eating three nutritious meals a day—Ryan had seen to that, so that the contours of her body had lost their undernourished look. As her face and figure gradually filled out, she came to resemble once again that healthy, bouncing, glowing cheerleader Ryan had fallen in love with so long ago.

A vertical line creased the space between her eyebrows. "What are you staring at?" she asked.

Ryan raised his glass as if for a toast. "At a vision of loveliness."

Becca's cheeks bloomed like roses. "Oh, stop it."

"It's true." He swirled the liquid around in his glass. "I was just thinking how young and pretty you look. I'll bet if we dug out one of our high school yearbooks, you wouldn't look much different now than you did back then."

"Heavens, I should hope so." She rolled her eyes. "I was a pretty gawky adolescent, not to mention all that long, straggly hair that was always hanging in my eyes."

"You? Gawky?" Ryan dropped his jaw. "You must be kidding. You were gorgeous, Becca. Still are." He lifted his glass to his mouth.

Disbelief mingled with pleased embarrassment in her eyes. "Well...thanks." She moved to the refrigerator, pulled out an opened jug of white wine and poured herself a glass. She wet her lips with it, that was about all. "Ryan, there's something I want to talk to you about."

"I know, I know." He set his Scotch down unfinished.

"You do?"

"It's about today, right? The way I overreacted to that slimeball reporter."

"Um, actually, that wasn't what I mea—"

"Honey, I owe you an apology for the way I behaved." Ryan hooked his thumbs through his belt loops, shrugging his shoulders. "I can't explain exactly what got into me. It was sort of like . . . something just snapped."

Becca touched her glass to her mouth, regarding Ryan over its rim. "You were just trying to protect Amy, that's all."

"It was more than that." He dragged a chair out from beneath the table and propped his boot on it. "I—I just lost it, somehow." He rubbed his jaw. "You have no idea how close I came to beating the tar out of that guy—that eager young kid who was just trying to do his job, after all."

Becca set her glass down with a loud clink. "Ryan, he snuck into the yard through a hole in the hedge, bribed the children with candy and refused to leave when you told him to! I don't blame you a bit for getting mad."

"It went way beyond mad." Ryan slashed his hand through the air. "When I first caught sight of that guy . . . a total stranger, looming over Amy like that . . . an intruder we'd taken every precaution to avoid . . ."

He gripped the back of the chair till his knuckles were white as bone. "It brought it all back, Becca. All the horror of Amy's kidnapping. All those sleepless nights we spent torturing ourselves, trying to imagine what could have happened to our baby, trying to picture what the person who must have taken her looked like."

A chill blew through Becca's eyes, turning them wide and bleak as an Arctic landscape. "Oh, Ryan . . ."

He plowed both hands through his hair. "I felt so damn *helpless* back then, Becca. I was used to fixing things when they went wrong, to taking charge of a situation. But there I was, unable to do anything besides pace back and forth next to the phone till I practically wore a hole in the carpet. Just waiting, waiting, *waiting!*" He shoved the chair aside. It tipped over and hit the floor with a clatter.

Becca flattened her palms against ice-pale cheeks. "I know," she whispered. "That's how I felt, too."

Ryan was breathing hard now—great gulps of air tore in and out of his lungs. "Call me old-fashioned, but I felt it was my duty, my responsibility, to take care of you and Amy. Amy was my child, my little baby girl, for God's sake, and I could do nothing to help her—*nothing!*" He slammed his fist on the table.

The muscles in Becca's face went rigid with sorrow and despair. Her eyes shone with tears. "Oh, Ryan, it wasn't your fault—there was nothing you could have done, nothing *anyone* could have done."

"I know that." He locked his jaws together in a viselike grip, a last-ditch effort to maintain a hold on his teetering self-control. "But knowing only made it worse. I wanted to go after the person who stole her, I wanted to hunt him down and *destroy* him!"

Becca flinched at the barely repressed rage in his voice.

Ryan's words tumbled over each other faster and faster, clenched jaw or no clenched jaw. "But there was no trail to follow—not the slightest clue as to what had happened. It was like clutching at fistfuls of air—" He made a quick, violent grab at nothing. "It was like trying to catch hold of a ghost, for God's sake!"

Tears were trickling down Becca's cheeks now. "Ryan, please don't do this to yourself." She extended a hand like a trembling supplicant. "It wasn't your fault! It . . . it was mine!"

Ryan stormed on, as the years of pent-up anguish and frustration that he'd tried to submerge in his work, to hide behind a stoic facade, came pouring out in an unstoppable flood. "I swore that if we ever found out who kidnapped Amy, I'd hunt that person down to the ends of the earth if necessary to get my revenge." Every muscle, every tendon in his body was vibrating like a high-tension wire about to rupture in a burst of sizzling sparks. "I'd make that person pay for what they put us through, for what they did to our little girl!"

With one vicious swipe of his hand he accidentally knocked over his half-filled glass. Scotch spilled across the table, began to drip onto the floor, unnoticed.

"And then ... *then!*" Ryan shook both fists at the ceiling. "Lo and behold, our baby comes back to us, but guess what! There still isn't anyone to punish, no one to even the score with, because the woman's dead! She didn't just steal our child, destroy our marriage and rob us of four years of our lives—she even managed to cheat us out of our revenge!"

Becca's shoulders jerked with sobs, like a marionette dangling from strings. She pressed her fingers to her mouth and simply shook her head, too choked up to speak anymore.

Ryan seized her upper arms and brought her tear-streaked face close to his. "That's why—when I saw that guy today—I just went crazy. Here at last was a real, live, flesh-and-blood menace! Here was someone I could go after, someone who dared threaten my little girl." He gave Becca a little shake. "And by God, I was going to make him pay for it!"

Becca's ashen features were contorted in a haggard mask of misery. "Ryan, I'm so sorry for what I did," she managed to choke out. "It ... it was all my fault!"

He dug his fingers into her soft flesh and gave her an exasperated shake as if he could jolt some sense into her. "I'm tired of sounding like a broken record," he told her roughly. "For the last time, Amy's kidnapping was not your fault, Becca. The woman who stole her—*she's* to blame, not you."

"If I'd been a better mother... if I hadn't walked away and left her all alone...." Her words were barely decipherable through her near-hysterical sobs.

Ryan abruptly dropped his hands from her shoulders and pivoted away from her. It killed him to see Becca punish herself like this. And a dreadful truth hit him now with brutal clarity, as if all the breast-beating and soul-baring had swept the mists away.

Until Becca could forgive herself, could stop punishing herself and allow herself to be happy, she would never be able to love Ryan again. How could you love someone else, when you hated yourself?

He wanted to shake her till her teeth rattled, to holler until he was blue in the face that one tragic accident, a few fateful seconds, shouldn't condemn them both to a lifetime of loneliness and guilt.

Hopeless despair settled onto Ryan's shoulders like a sack of cement. If only there were some way to get through to her, some way to convince her that she wasn't to blame...

"You want to talk about guilt, Becca?" He advanced on her, brandishing his forefinger. "I'll tell you a thing or two about guilt." He shouldn't get into this now. He should shut up and walk away before he said things he could never take back.

But he might as well have tried to stop a runaway train. "After Amy disappeared... there were times..." It was a struggle to squeeze the words out past the anvil that had settled on top of his chest. "There were times... when I didn't think I could stand it anymore." Beads of sweat broke out across his forehead. "The helplessness... the hopelessness... the uncertainty of not knowing..."

Ryan dragged a ragged chunk of air into his lungs. "Round and round I'd go, picturing all the terrible things that could have happened to Amy, till I was so crazy with grief I thought I would die." He held out his hands in a beseeching gesture. "It was the uncertainty that was the worst, wasn't it, Becca? Day after day of not knowing what had happened to our baby, where she was or even whether she was alive or... dead." His face contorted with pain on the last word.

Becca managed one convulsive nod of her head. Her arms were wrapped tightly around her quaking body, hugging herself as if she wanted to curl up and die. Her eyes were swollen and sticky with tears.

Now Ryan started breathing rapidly again, almost gasping. "Sometimes, Becca, sometimes..." He squeezed his eyes shut. "God help me, there were times I even thought hearing our baby was dead would be better than not knowing." He seized her by the shoulders. "How's that for guilt, Becca? How would you like to live with the knowledge that you'd rather hear your own child was *dead* than go on being tortured by uncertainty?"

She looked at him helplessly, sobbing, limp as a dishrag in his arms.

Ryan's skin felt strangely feverish. He touched his hand to his face, discovered it was wet. That was when he realized he was crying.

With a low groan of anguish he hauled Becca into his arms, buried his face in her hair. They clung to each other, finally seeking comfort where they had been unable to find any after the devastating loss of their child.

Becca hugged her arms around Ryan's middle and felt the shudders that racked his body. Even in the midst of her own uncontrollable weeping, a small detached corner of her mind was taken aback by this overflow of emotion. She'd never seen Ryan cry before.

Somehow the need to comfort him eased her own wretchedness, and she found herself stroking his back and murmuring soothing, meaningless noises into his ear. She felt fiercely protective—not a feeling she'd ever associated with Ryan before. In all the years she'd known him, he'd always been the strong one. Or so she'd thought.

Even in the immediate aftermath of Amy's kidnapping, Ryan had never once broken down—at least, not in Becca's presence. He'd maintained a determinedly optimistic facade, had tried his best to reassure and comfort Becca, even though by then she'd already thrown up the emotional barriers that had effectively shut him out.

Tonight, at long last, Becca finally understood how much Ryan's effort to be strong for her sake must have cost him.

"Shh," she whispered. "It's all right, darling...everything will be all right...."

On one level Becca had realized, of course, that Ryan had to have been as devastated by Amy's disappearance as she was. But now she was forced to admit that, deep down inside, she'd never really comprehended that Ryan's grief and despair had been as soul-shattering as her own.

Perhaps if she hadn't turned away and crawled alone into her self-made prison of grief and guilt, she would have realized how deeply he suffered.

Why, oh, why, hadn't they been able to share the burden of their tragedy, to seek comfort in each other's arms the way they finally could tonight?

The answer, Becca knew, was that she'd been too wrapped up in her own agony to worry much about Ryan. And that was something she would have to live with for the rest of her life.

She tangled her fingers through the sweat-dampened hair at the nape of his neck, tried to absorb some of his pain into herself. Gradually his heaving shoulders stilled and the rusty sounds emerging from his chest died away.

When at last he lifted his head and drew back, his eyes were wet and red-rimmed. She brushed at his tears with her fingertips. "Oh, Ryan," she whispered. "How on earth could I have thought that enduring the nightmare alone would be easier than enduring it together?"

He captured her fingers and brought them to his lips. "You did what you had to, to survive." His voice was hoarse, as if his vocal cords had been strained by unaccustomed use.

Becca splayed her other hand across his chest, felt the unsteady thumping of his heart. "But it was so unfair to you." His warm mouth caressed her fingers, sending little spikes of pleasure along her skin.

Ryan hugged her closer. "We have to learn to put the past behind us, honey." His warm breath tickled her ear, making her shiver. Somehow he'd trapped her hands between them with his body, and now his mouth was making a slow progression along her neck, her trembling jaw, her cheekbones.

Becca swallowed. For her, the past would always be her cross to bear—a punishing reminder of all she had lost because of the terrible mistakes she'd made. But she knew Ryan would never accept that. And right now, she didn't exactly feel like arguing with him.

His lips traveled across her eyelids, followed the delicate tracery of her brows. There was something she was supposed to remember, some reason why they shouldn't be doing this, but Ryan's tender kisses drove all rational thought from her mind.

"Becca..." Her name hovered in the tiny gap between their lips. Then Ryan cupped the back of her head with his strong, capable hand, brought his face down and seized her mouth with his.

Becca's arms instinctively flew around his neck—a fortunate reaction, it turned out, because almost at once her knees turned to jelly and the room began to swirl around her. When she swayed and nearly lost her balance, Ryan slid his arm around her waist and held her securely against him.

Becca couldn't tell if the helpless sounds emerging from her throat were meant as urging or warning. The possessive heat of Ryan's kiss was achingly familiar, but the intensity surprised her. Ryan had always been a tender, sensitive lover, but Becca hardly recognized this reckless stranger who plundered her mouth with his tongue like a man dying of thirst in the desert.

With one hand tangled in her hair, he held her head locked in position so that she couldn't have turned away from him if she'd tried. "Becca...my love...my only love..." His muttered endearments gave her her only chance to breathe.

He swept his hand to her breast, eliciting a startled moan of pleasure from low in Becca's throat as he kneaded the soft flesh with increasing urgency. Sheer pleasure spiraled through her. This was crazy...she shouldn't allow this to continue...and yet her own hunger matched the desperate level of his own.

It was as if their recent emotional outpouring had stripped away their outer defenses, leaving behind the naked core of desire they still felt for each other. Like twin eternal flames, the passion they'd once shared had never been extinguished...not by unspeakable tragedy, not by divorce, not by three long years of separation.

"Becca...let me make love to you." Ryan finally put into words what they'd both been thinking.

Becca tasted desperation along with the faint flavor of liquor on his tongue. It would be so easy to say yes...to let herself sink into the flames of desire that consumed her...to blame whatever consequences followed on the relentless force of passion.

But all at once the thought of surrendering control scared her. She needed to keep her wits about her, to resist any distractions that might endanger the purpose to which she'd sworn to devote her life from now on.

She had to focus her emotional energies solely on Amy. And Becca knew that what Ryan demanded of her went far beyond physical surrender. She would have to lower her emotional defenses, as well, and risk letting him back into her heart as well as her bed.

She couldn't do it. Not now, not ever. She'd let a terrible thing happen, and this was the price she would have to pay for it.

She tried to tear her mouth from his, to escape the plundering kisses that now seemed more like a weapon than an instrument of pleasure. "Ryan..." Her unspoken plea was crushed beneath his lips.

From head to toe their bodies were pressed together, straining, as if struggling to occupy the same physical space. His hard arousal nudged against her, reminding her with a shock that she must put a stop to this madness *now*.

Wedging her hands between them, Becca shoved against Ryan's chest with all the feeble strength her watery limbs could muster. He held her tighter, deliberately misinterpreting her message. His hand dropped from her breast, and for an instant she breathed a sigh of relief. But then he slid it down to cup her bottom, to pull her abdomen even more snugly, more insistently, against his.

The powerful, responsive surge of desire that welled up inside Becca dismayed her, gave her the strength to wrench her mouth from his and cry out, "Ryan, no!"

He froze, motionless and unyielding as a granite statue. Then a second later he released her so suddenly she almost collapsed to the floor.

Becca's sharp gasp was a mixture of surprise, relief and disappointment. But she couldn't waste time sorting it all out. Now she needed to focus all her concentration on breathing.

Ryan, too, was panting—his dark brown eyes wild, his lips shiny with moisture. He dragged the back of his wrist slowly across his mouth. "This is ridiculous," he said.

The implied criticism stung. "You started it," Becca retorted indignantly, wincing at how childish the words sounded. But it was too late to retrieve them.

Ryan lifted his hand in a weary, dismissive gesture, as if her accusation didn't dignify a response. "We're not teenagers, Becca. We're two consenting adults. We were once married to each other—we've had a *child* together, for Christ's sake." His eyes were smoldering now like banked embers. "Don't you think all this virginal resistance on your part is a bit unnecessary?"

Becca's chin jutted up. "It's only necessary because you keep thrusting your unwelcome attentions on me."

He gave a harsh bark of laughter. "Don't try to pretend with me, Becca. I know you too well." He stepped forward to hover over her in a vaguely intimidating manner, but she held her ground. He brought one knuckle to her jaw and tilted her head back. "You want me as badly as I want you. So stop trying to kid yourself, and don't think for a second that you've got me fooled, either."

Anger and humiliation raced through her. She jerked her chin away. "You're fooling *yourself* if you think we can just go back to the way things once were. Just because I've agreed to share your house again doesn't mean I have any intention of sharing your bed."

"How long do you think we can go on this way?" Exasperation edged his ruggedly carved features. "What's the point of constantly having to squelch our desires, of pretending they don't even exist? It's not healthy, Becca." A glimmer of amusement crossed his face. "Sooner or later, something's going to explode."

She ignored his crude double entendre. "Take a cold shower, then." She folded her arms. "I made it perfectly clear when I moved back in here that this was how things had to be. You agreed. Don't blame me because you're finding it difficult to live up to our agreement."

"I never agreed to the sick kind of game you're playing, Becca."

"*Sick?* What are you—"

"I'm talking about the way you're punishing yourself by denying yourself something that could bring you great joy."

"And I suppose this great joy I'm denying myself is the thrill of your fabulous naked body?"

"Don't change the subject." Ryan gripped the back of a chair as if it were an anchor that kept him from flying at her. "You can't change the past by depriving us of a future, Becca. This orgy of breast-beating and mea culpas you're so determined to indulge in is *sick.*"

He leaned forward. "Because there's nothing to feel guilty about. Nothing to punish yourself for." He tipped the chair back and forth, pounding the legs against the floor for emphasis. "Because *you* ... weren't ... to blame ... for what ... happened ... to ... Amy." He let go of the chair with one final bang. "Or to us," he said with a sigh.

He was wrong. But Becca would never be able to convince him of that. She straightened her spine. "I'm going to bed."

"You can run away from me, Becca. Maybe you can even run away from your own feelings." Ryan's voice reached after her, held her motionless in the doorway. "But you can't run away from the truth."

Becca didn't know what the truth was anymore. She was operating on sheer instinct here...the instinct to protect her child, to make Amy the overriding priority in her life.

A vision of Amy's worried brown eyes rose up in front of her, those wide-awake, heartbreaking eyes brimming with anxiety about the future. All at once Becca recalled her reason for seeking out Ryan in the first place.

She braced a hand against the doorframe, let her head droop forward with exhaustion.

"What is it?" The undercurrent of dread in Ryan's voice certainly spoke volumes for the way Becca had hurt him in the past.

She hunched her shoulders as if a heavy cross had indeed been laid upon them. Slowly she turned. "This is going to sound ridiculous, after all—" her hands fluttered helplessly "—after all that's just happened."

"Tell me." Ryan's mouth yanked into a tight line, like a cable stretched to the breaking point.

"I came down here to tell you . . . that after thinking it over, I've decided . . ."

Ryan's entire body tensed. In a dazzling burst of clarity, Becca realized he was afraid she was going to leave him again.

"I decided you were right," she said quickly. "About what's best for Amy. She does need two parents, living together, being a family. At least, pretending to be family." She swallowed, her throat suddenly as dry as the Sahara. What if Ryan told her he'd changed his mind, that he took back his proposal?

"We can't let . . . *this* happen again," Becca went on, swirling her hands through the air as if to encompass their recent emotional outburst, the explosive passions that had very nearly swept them toward disaster. "But if you'll agree to those terms, what I came to tell you was . . ."

She drew in a deep, shaky breath and took the plunge. "I'll marry you, Ryan."

Chapter Nine

Ryan fiddled with his tie, cursed, finally unknotted it and started all over again. He was as nervous as a groom on his wedding day.

Which, in fact, he was.

But having been through this routine once before, he figured he should be an old pro at it by now. Especially since he was marrying the same woman again.

As he fidgeted in front of his bedroom mirror, though, Ryan admitted that a few things were going to be different this time around. Like the fact that he and his bride wouldn't be sharing the same bed tonight.

Like the fact that this wedding didn't mark the beginning of a bright new shining future together, but rather the start of an uneasy truce.

And this time they wouldn't be getting married in a church filled with flowers and music and pews crowded with beaming friends and relatives. No white lace gown or bevy of giggling bridesmaids for Becca the second time around. She'd insisted on a quick, private, no-frills ceremony in judge's chambers at the county courthouse.

"What about Gretchen and Tyler?" Ryan had asked several days ago when they'd first sat down to plan things. He'd still been dazed by Becca's unexpected acceptance of his proposal.

Becca had shaken her head. "I don't want to make a big deal out of this, Ryan. It's a simple formality, not a major production."

"I hardly think that having our best friends stand up for us constitutes a—"

"Gretchen already agreed to watch Amy while we're at the courthouse."

"You mean you don't even want *Amy* there?"

"The whole point of getting married is to reassure Amy that the three of us are a normal family, that her parents are just like everyone else's."

That hadn't been the whole point as far as Ryan was concerned, but he hadn't felt it wise to interrupt.

"How many other kids are present at their own parents' wedding?" Becca had continued. "I don't want Amy getting curious about why we had to go through another ceremony."

"You make it sound about as enjoyable as root canal," Ryan had grumbled. But he'd also dropped the subject. He could tell from the determined slant of Becca's mouth that she had no intention of getting into the festive spirit of things.

If she wanted to turn their wedding into nothing but a formality, a legal ritual that had to be endured, so be it. At least she'd finally consented to go through with it at all.

Ryan gave one final, frustrated tug on his tie and called it good enough. Why should he get all worked up about his appearance, when he'd practically had to browbeat Becca into even buying a new dress for the occasion?

Her strategy was obvious. She was desperately trying to minimize the significance of their remarriage by pretending today was nothing special.

Maybe Ryan should follow her example. Maybe the reason his palms were clammy, his feet cold and his stomach full of butterflies—the giant, tropical variety—was that he was afraid.

Afraid of committing himself to a woman who'd once walked out on him. Afraid of letting his sore heart get trampled again. Afraid he was setting himself up for another round of the searing, gut-wrenching pain he'd sworn never to go through again.

His face in the mirror looked like the reflection of a man about to walk the plank—in white shirt and charcoal gray pin-striped trousers.

A few days ago he'd accused Becca of trying to run away from the truth. Now Ryan himself had to confront the truth that Becca was the only woman he'd ever loved. Somewhere along the way, his love for her had gotten tangled up with a battleground of other emotions—grief, anger, guilt. Maybe he and Becca could never again have the kind of marriage they'd once shared, full of dreams and laughter and passion.

But Ryan was an optimist by nature. Amy's miraculous return had proved that happy endings weren't just the stuff of fairy tales. Even though he wasn't exactly stepping into wedded bliss with an enthusiastic bride at his side, Ryan intended to give this marriage his best shot.

For all their sakes.

He whipped a comb through his hair, shrugged on his suit jacket and winked at his reflection.

When he left the bedroom he was whistling a few bars of "Get Me to the Church on Time."

It was impossible for Becca not to relive her first wedding day as she and Ryan stood in front of the black-robed judge, listening to the words that would once again make them husband and wife.

Well, Becca wasn't *listening* to the words, exactly. She had tried to concentrate at the beginning, but the sentimental memories and emotions that swirled around her with dizzying persistence had proved too much of a distraction.

She slanted a sideways peek at Ryan, tall and handsome in the dark gray suit he'd bought for Amy's christening ceremony six years ago. Gretchen and Tyler had become the new baby's godparents that day. Now Becca was troubled by a vague sense of regret that they weren't here to witness this ceremony, as well.

She knew Ryan had wanted them here, that he was disappointed by Becca's attempts to play down the importance of their wedding.

But for her own peace of mind, she couldn't allow herself to become caught up in the symbolic trappings of what should have been a joyful occasion. She glanced down at the small bouquet of perfect white rosebuds that Ryan had surprised her with just before they'd left for the courthouse.

The delicate baby's breath stems quivered as Becca's eyes misted with tears. Tender affection welled up inside her chest, making it hard to breathe. How like Ryan to be so thoughtful, even when she didn't deserve it!

As the judge's words droned through her at a subconscious level, Becca swallowed her emotions, forced herself to remember that what she and Ryan were entering into was more of a business partnership than a real marriage.

If she let herself be swept away by romantic delusions, how on earth was she going to keep Ryan at arm's length where he belonged?

She'd been so close the other evening . . . so close to surrendering to those heart-pounding desires and the promise of ecstasy. To admit that this wedding had any emotional significance to her would only weaken Becca's resolve to avoid a repeat of that frantic, foolhardy embrace.

"Do you, Rebecca, take Ryan . . ."

The familiar lines tugged Becca's attention back to the role she was supposed to play. She mouthed the appropriate "I do," but she could barely hear her own response through the rushing in her ears. She couldn't believe she was actually standing here next to Ryan, about to rejoin her life with his. She still found it nearly impossible to comprehend the amazing changes that had swept through her life in the past few weeks, starting with that blessed, miraculous phone call that had informed her Amy had finally been found.

Ryan gazed deep into her eyes and murmured, "I do."

He could have stood there staring at his gorgeous bride all day long. Becca looked more breathtakingly beautiful today than she had as a blushing twenty-year-old. Her new dress was a pale grayish blue shade that turned her eyes to glittering cobalt jewels and clung to her body in all the right places.

For the moment, at least, that haunted look that occasionally still drifted across her face was gone, leaving her glowing with an inner serenity that belied the nervous twitching of her bouquet and the rapid pulse beat that fluttered just below her dainty earlobe.

Ryan ached to make love to her, to make Becca truly his with a fierce intensity that set every cell in his body on fire.

"Do you have the ring?" The judge turned toward Ryan, expectant and inquiring.

Becca jerked as if someone had bumped into her. Her long-lashed eyes opened wide, filled with startled embarrassment as she glanced up at Ryan. They hadn't discussed rings.

Ryan reached into an inside pocket and produced one. Surprise flitted across Becca's face, followed quickly by relief, then shock as she recognized the simple gold band.

It was her original wedding ring, the one she'd stubbornly, laughingly, refused to remove during all the time they'd been married.

Until the day she'd taken it off and placed it on the living room mantel next to the note telling Ryan she was leaving him.

Countless times during the past three years Ryan had told himself he should hock it, throw it away, get rid of it somehow—that even knowing it was tucked away in the back of a drawer was a constant painful reminder of everything he'd lost.

Perhaps he hadn't been able to get rid of it because the ring had come to symbolize hope—hope that someday the two people he loved most in the world would find their way home to him.

Now, miraculously, they had.

He couldn't think of a more fitting token to slip onto Becca's finger.

Her hand was cool and trembly in his, her eyes flaring suspiciously wide, as if she were trying to conceal the fact there were tears in them.

"I now pronounce you husband and wife." The judge closed the book he'd been reading from and beamed at them both. "Well, go on," he said with impatient amusement when Ryan and Becca continued to stare at each other. "Kiss her!" he instructed Ryan in a stage whisper.

So Ryan did.

Maybe it wasn't much of a kiss by his usual standards—after all, he wasn't about to demonstrate his technique in front of a smiling stranger. Yet something moved him deeply as his lips touched Becca's, and when she drew back with self-conscious haste, he could tell by the confusion and turmoil in those vulnerable blue eyes that she'd been powerfully affected by their quick, awkward kiss, as well.

"We've suffered more than our share of heartache during the past few years," Ryan said gently. He brushed a stray wisp of silky blond hair back from her temple. "Don't you think we've earned the right to be happy?"

Becca gazed back at him, her eyes luminous with wistful regret and unshed tears. "I—I'll do my best to make you happy, Ryan. I'll try to be a good wife to you. But..." A shadow clouded her pretty features. "Don't expect too much from me, all right?" She withdrew her hand from his. "I couldn't bear to let you down again."

"Becca...honey..."

But she'd already wrenched open her door and was halfway out of the car. "I'll go get Amy."

Becca's new pumps clicked rapidly up the front walk of the McCoys' ranch-style home. Behind her she could hear the car door slam as Ryan got out to follow her. She resisted the urge to break into a run. But if she had to take another look at his handsome, anxious face just now, she might very well break into tears. He was trying so hard to make this day perfect for her—the fancy car, the lovely bouquet, the wedding ring...

She didn't deserve his thoughtfulness, his tender concern. And with every considerate little surprise he produced, Becca was finding it more and more difficult to harden her heart against him.

She was the luckiest woman in the world to have a husband like Ryan, to have her long-lost child home at last.

So why didn't she feel all that happy?

The front door swung open as she raised her hand to knock. "There you are! Oh, Becca, you look beautiful, doesn't she, Tyler?" Gretchen threw her arms around her friend and whispered, "Congratulations."

Grinning from ear to ear, Tyler moved forward to shake hands with Ryan. "So you actually talked her into marrying you again, huh?"

"Tyler!" Gretchen jabbed him in the ribs with her elbow and scowled at him in warning. Then she turned a dazzling smile on the newlyweds. "Come on out back for a minute, why don't you?"

"We really just stopped by to pick up Amy..."

"Oh, come on, Becs, be a sport." Gretchen linked her arm through Becca's and practically dragged her through the house and outside onto the patio.

"I can't thank you enough for watching Amy while—"

"Surprise!" Gretchen clapped her hands while the three children bounced up and down with glee.

Becca stepped forward, stunned. The backyard was decorated with clusters of peach and lavender balloons. Crepe paper streamers festooned the shrubbery and even dangled from the trees. The picnic table was laden with a mouth-watering array of food and drink. "What...what is all this?"

"It's a party, silly." Gretchen propped her hands on her hips. "Don't tell me you've never seen one before, because I know better."

"It's for your avinursery!" Christopher shouted, barely able to contain his excitement.

Gretchen leaned over and whispered, "I told them it was to celebrate your anniversary, since you wanted to keep the wedding a secret."

Tyler leaned past Becca and plucked an hors d'oeuvre from a silver tray. "Besides, today *will* be your anniversary from now on, right?"

"Tyler McCoy, put that back! Don't you have any better manners than to start munching away before—no, for heaven's sake, don't put it back now that you've touched it!"

His eyebrows flew toward the sky—Mister Innocence. "But honeybunch, you told me to—"

Gretchen threw up her hands. "Honestly. *Men!*" She shook her fist at her husband, who popped the tidbit into his mouth and smacked his lips appreciatively. Then he leaned over and smacked his wife appreciatively on the cheek. "Oh, you," she muttered, pleased.

"Can we have something to eat, too?" Sarah asked. "I'm starving!"

Amy rubbed her tummy. "Me, too."

"Now see what you've started?" Gretchen asked her husband.

"Gretchen, you shouldn't have gone to all this trouble," Becca murmured.

"Trouble? What trouble? Look, we're even using paper plates." Gretchen picked one up and waved it through the air. It was edged in peach and lavender, and in the center were two interlocked wedding rings.

Becca's heart gave a strange little lurch. "But all this food..."

"It's not that much. Just some crab salad—"

"Yuk!" Christopher made a face.

Gretchen grabbed him with an affectionate armlock around the neck and pretended to rap him on top of his skull with her knuckles. "And peanut-butter-and-jelly sandwiches for the kids, of course."

"But the cake..." Becca gestured weakly at the white-frosted sheet cake, bordered with icing roses, the message Congratulations Becca And Ryan scrolled across the center. "It's beautiful!"

"Do you like it?" Gretchen beamed proudly. "I baked it myself. Even did the decorating."

"That's why the lettering's a little crooked here," Tyler said, pointing.

"Tyler!" Gretchen slapped his hand.

He slid his arms around her waist from behind and nuzzled her neck. "Just teasing, love muffin." Then he grabbed a bottle of champagne from the ice bucket and suggested, "How about a little liquid refreshment?"

With a flurry of plastic cups, the adults were quickly supplied with champagne, the children with lemonade. "A toast!" Tyler lifted his glass overhead as if it were the Olympic torch.

"We're having toast?" Christopher wrinkled his nose in puzzlement. "At a party?"

The adults broke into gales of laughter. Sarah rolled her eyes. "Not *that* kind of toast," she told her brother in disgust. Amy giggled.

Becca pinned on a wobbly smile as she surveyed the smiling circle of faces. Dear old friends . . . her precious little girl all decked out in a borrowed party dress . . . her handsome, considerate, wonderful husband.

Her heart began to patter rapidly against her ribs, and all at once she felt so strange inside—all fizzy and floaty, as if the champagne were already rushing through her bloodstream.

Ryan grinned at her with a flash of white teeth and a sunburst of crinkles around his twinkling dark eyes. The easy familiarity of his smile, his secret wink, made Becca even more light-headed. With all the personal history that lay between them, even an exchange of glances across a picnic table was as intimate as a caress.

Her stomach dipped in a roller-coaster swoop.

"Let's try that again," Tyler said with a chuckle as he raised his glass. "A toast!"

Gretchen and the children responded with another round of giggles.

This peculiar lightness inside Becca seemed to expand, to press outward against her skin till she thought she would float away like a helium balloon. Could this be happiness? Or maybe even . . . love?

"To Becca and Ryan," Tyler went on, ignoring his smirking, unruly audience. "Who have so much to celebrate." He dropped an affectionate smile on Amy, swallowed hard and had to pause for a second before he could continue. ''May this be the first of many, many more celebrations to come.''

''Here, here!'' Gretchen hoisted her glass high in the air. The three kids mimicked her.

Becca carefully set her glass on the picnic table. Her hand shook, her lips felt numb. ''Thank you all very much for the wonderful surprise party,'' she said. She swung her head slowly around to gaze in turn at the faces of the people who meant so much to her—happy faces brimming with warmth and love and good wishes.

Then she excused herself and stumbled into the house, where she locked herself in the guest bathroom and proceeded to cry her eyes out.

''And then I lay awake all night long because those rowdy teenagers next door were blasting that nasty rock-and-roll music till all hours. Honestly, it's almost more than a body can stand.''

Becca pinched the bridge of her nose as she spoke into the phone. ''Why don't you talk to their parents about it, Mother?''

''Good heavens, the parents are as bad as their kids. Besides, the last time I complained about their dog digging up my petunias, *someone* went out in the alley and tipped over all my garbage cans, and I'm almost sure it was them.''

Becca stifled a sigh. ''Call the police the next time they make too much noise, then.''

''The *police?* Fat lot of good that'll do. Why, the woman who does my hair down at the beauty parlor was telling me just the other day how *she* called the police when her neighbors' party got too loud the other night, and they as much as told her they had more important things to do than...''

Becca tuned out her mother's voice. For the past fifteen minutes her ears had been assaulted with a whining litany of her mother's problems—her husband, the neighbors, her aching back and swollen feet...

Becca hadn't spoken to her mother since shortly after Amy's return, when she'd phoned her in Texas to tell her the news. But the fact was, Becca's mother had moved away from Pine Creek long before Amy was born and hadn't been back for a visit since. Maybe it was no surprise she wasn't all that interested in a grandchild she'd never seen.

Tonight Becca had been moved by an impulse she couldn't explain to let her mother know that she and Ryan had gotten married today. Now she was regretting that impulse. After a rather ho-hum acknowledgment, her mother had launched into the tirade of complaints that usually passed for conversation between them.

Of course, it could have been worse, Becca had to admit. For once her mother didn't sound drunk.

"Mother? Listen, I really have to go now," she lied. "It was nice talking to you. I'll call you again soon, all right?" After another five minutes she was finally able to disentangle herself from her mother's self-pitying tales of woe.

She hung up the phone on the kitchen wall, pressing her forehead to its smooth plastic surface. Her mother's example only served to strengthen Becca's resolution to be a different kind of mother to her own child—one who put her child's needs and concerns first, not her own.

Becca still had her hand on the receiver when it rang shrilly, nearly startling her out of her skin. "Hello?" she answered cautiously. They hadn't been pestered by the news media since the day Ryan had destroyed that reporter's videotape, but you couldn't be too careful.

"Mrs. Slater?" inquired a brisk voice. "My name is Nancy Woods. I'm with the Sacramento chapter of the Missing Children Foundation."

Becca recognized the organization's name, even though she herself had never sought support from any kind of group. The idea of sharing her pain, of revealing her own role in her daughter's disappearance to a bunch of strangers had appalled her.

"First, let me tell you how thrilled all of us were to hear about Amy," the woman continued. "It's the sort of outcome we all pray for desperately, of course, but so terribly, terribly few cases turn out so happily."

A cold lump of dread congealed in Becca's stomach. She murmured some inane response.

"The reason I'm calling, Mrs. Slater, is to ask if you would consider coming to one of our support group meetings. I'm sure your insights and experiences would be very valuable to some of the parents, and frankly, I think you could be a great source of inspiration and hope."

"No!" Becca replied more abruptly than she'd intended. She curved a hand around her clammy forehead. "I mean, I—I don't think that will be possible."

The woman let a few seconds of silence pass. "I understand you're probably devoting most of your time to Amy right now," she said, "but it would mean so much to our group. Perhaps you could spare just one afternoon?"

"I'm sorry. I can't." Becca had so narrowly, miraculously escaped from that nightmare herself—the nightmare of despair and uncertainty and futile hopes, of sleepless nights and endless days and false leads that didn't pan out. How could she plunge herself back into that maelstrom of anguish again?

Guilt and fear rose up in her throat to nearly choke her. "Please. I just can't." She banged down the receiver, clapped her hand over her mouth and sank limply into the nearest chair.

What kind of terrible person was she, to turn her back on a plea for help, to ignore the fact that there were other parents still suffering out there, other parents tormented by grief and loss, other parents who weren't as lucky as she and Ryan had been?

She couldn't help them. She wasn't strong enough. Just the memory of that long, dark tunnel of misery she'd had to travel through made Becca break out in a cold sweat.

After a while she felt calm enough to go into the living room, where Ryan and Amy had retreated after supper to watch a videotape of a Disney movie.

Ryan's face brightened at the sight of her. He scooted over to make room for her, patting the couch beside him. Amy was sitting cross-legged on the floor in front of the TV, totally caught up in the adventures of the animated forest creatures. Southpaw was curled around her, his tail flicking lazily in welcome when Becca sat down.

"Feeling better?" Ryan whispered.

Becca stiffened in alarm. Had he overheard that phone call, witnessed her pitiful, selfish reaction?

Then she realized he was referring to her ridiculous crying jag at the McCoys' earlier. "I'm sorry I spoiled the party," she replied in a low voice. "I feel terrible, after all the work Gretchen went to."

"She understood." Ryan passed Becca the bowl of popcorn. "After all, it's traditional for brides to cry on their wedding day, isn't it?" he teased.

Maybe so, but Becca could hardly be called a traditional bride. This wasn't exactly a traditional wedding day. And it certainly wasn't going to be a traditional wedding night.

Suddenly her palms started sweating again.

She chewed on some popcorn, turned her eyes toward the television screen, but her thoughts were far away from the antics of the frolicking cartoon animals.

Ryan's voice made her jump. "Now that our situation has sort of... settled down," he said, "I really should go back to work tomorrow."

"Of course." Becca swallowed a dry piece of popcorn that had become wedged in her throat. "It's wonderful that you were able to take all this time off, but I'm sure your work crew will be glad to have you back."

"Well, I'm not so sure about *that*," he said with a grin. "They probably enjoy not having the boss around."

"Oh, come on. Those guys think of you more as their friend than their boss."

"Yeah, they're a good bunch of guys." Ryan fished through the unpopped kernels for another morsel of pop-corn. "Anyway...what I was thinking was, maybe you and Amy and I could drive down to Lake Tahoe this week-end."

"Tahoe?"

"We could stay in one of those vacation cottages, like where we spent our honeymoon," he said casually. "Rent a boat, do some swimming, work on our suntans..."

She noticed he'd refrained from mentioning the main recreational activity that had consumed most of their hon-eymoon. From what little Becca remembered of their sur-roundings at the time, those cottages were awful small—*cozy,* as the tourist brochures would describe them. Pretty close quarters to share with someone you were trying to keep at a safe distance.

True, this time they would have Amy as a chaperon. Be-sides, Ryan had made a bargain with her, and Becca trusted him to keep his end of it.

The problem was, she wasn't sure she could trust her-self.

"I think a change of scenery might be good for all of us," she said before she had a chance to chicken out.

"Great. I'll call tomorrow and book a reservation for us." Ryan draped his arm along the back of the couch, be-hind Becca's shoulders. He wasn't exactly touching her, and his attention seemed focused on the TV screen, but his closeness did nothing to soothe her jagged nerve endings.

Images kept barging into her mind...images of other evenings like this spent in front of the television, after their infant daughter was asleep in her crib.

Evenings that had frequently ended with articles of clothing strewn on the floor around the couch, while the TV flickered on and on into the darkened room, completely ignored.

Goodness, it must be getting late! Becca attempted to check her watch without moving either her wrist or her head, so that Ryan wouldn't notice. Impossible. But the clock on the VCR told her that Amy's bedtime was fast approaching. The evening was drawing to a close, along with the movie.

Soon Becca would find herself alone with Ryan.

On their wedding night.

She didn't know why she was nervous, for heaven's sake. Tonight would be no different from any other night she'd spent in this house since her return.

Except that tonight they were married.

What was she so afraid of? That Ryan would try to seduce her? That he would be so overcome by her charms he would forget their agreement to sleep in separate bedrooms, to live together as husband and wife in name only?

Not very likely. For one thing, Becca didn't have all that much confidence in her ability to drive him wild with desire. For another, Ryan was too much of a gentleman to go back on his word.

For one instant Becca's guard slipped and allowed her to imagine what it would be like to spend the night in Ryan's bed, to make love with all the passionate enthusiasm they'd shared during their honeymoon. The heat and smell of his body, the exquisite feel of his mouth and hands on her bare flesh, the delicious pressure that built up inside her, driving her to cry out until—

Becca hastily slammed a mental door shut on those dangerous, seductive images. She was going to wind up a panting, frustrated, lust-crazed wreck if she didn't learn to channel her thoughts in safer directions.

She twisted her wedding ring as if she were trying to unscrew her finger, and mentally recited the multiplication tables.

Why was it time always seemed to whiz by in fast-forward when something you dreaded was approaching? All too soon, the movie ended, the doors were locked, the downstairs lights were shut off. Before Becca knew it, Amy was tucked in bed, sound asleep.

Ryan gingerly shut the door to her room so as not to wake her. Light still trickled into the dim hallway from his bedroom. When he turned to Becca, the resulting play of shadows cast his handsome features into bold relief and gave his eyes a mysterious, dark intensity that made her shiver.

This was the moment she'd dreaded—anticipated?—since the moment the judge had pronounced them husband and wife.

She held her breath as Ryan stepped closer, effectively trapping her against the wall. He moved with slow, deliberate assurance, as if he knew exactly what he wanted and wasn't about to be denied.

He braced his palms flat against the wall, on both sides of Becca's shoulders so that she couldn't escape. That bubbly, exhilarating rush began to churn through her bloodstream again. Ryan's face was so close that even in the dark Becca could make out every chiseled detail.

"I guess this is it," he said in a voice so quietly intimate that she wouldn't have heard him if they hadn't been standing practically toe-to-toe. The heat radiating from his body enveloped her, seduced her.

Her throat was dry as chalk. "I guess so," she managed to squeak out.

Ryan lowered his head a millimeter at a time, until his lips finally made contact with hers. Becca closed her eyes and let the fire he ignited spread throughout her limbs. There was no hesitation in his kiss, yet no urgency, either, as if he refused to entertain the possibility that Becca might turn away.

As if he knew they had all night long.

His mouth tasted like butter, with a tang of salt from the popcorn. Becca's heart began to trip over itself, beating faster and faster like a time bomb about to explode. Every cell in her body strained toward Ryan, as if her longing for him were physically pulling her forward.

Just as her knees began to buckle and she swayed into him, Ryan stepped back. His eyes were obscured by shadows, unreadable. "Good night, Becca," he said politely.

She watched in astonishment, propped against the wall for support, as Ryan disappeared into his bedroom and closed the door behind him with a soft but resolute click.

Chapter Ten

"Lookee, a violin!" Clutching the battered musical instrument by its neck, Amy held it in the air like a trophy. "Can I play it?"

"I think we need to fix the strings first, sweetie." Becca pressed a finger across her lips as she scanned the surrounding jumble of junk. "Oh, dear, here's the bow. Guess we need to have that repaired, too."

"*Then* can I play it?"

Becca studied her dirt-smudged, wide-eyed daughter. "Would you like to take violin lessons?" she asked, plucking a gossamer strand of cobweb from Amy's ponytail.

"Yeah! Can I?"

Becca smiled. Amy's enthusiasm was infectious. "Of course, you can. Just set the violin over there by the stairs, so we remember to take it down with us. I'll call and see about having it fixed."

"Goody!"

They were up in the attic, sorting through Amy's belongings from the time Becca was coming to think of as B.K.—Before Kidnapping.

At least, Becca was sorting through them. Amy had found more interesting treasures to rummage through than a bunch of old baby stuff—like the antique violin that had belonged to Ryan's grandfather.

During last night's endless round of tossing and turning, Becca had suddenly recalled that someone from the thrift shop was coming today to pick up all of Amy's possessions that Becca had decided to give away. She could no longer postpone the emotion-charged task she'd been avoiding.

The truth was, though, that sifting through Amy's old toys and clothes turned out to be a rather welcome distraction from the lustful thoughts and treacherous desires that had tormented Becca through the long, sleepless hours before dawn.

Some wedding night.

Each item she set aside for the thrift shop had a memory attached to it. The tiny sleeper Amy had worn home from the hospital as a newborn. The huge, stuffed hippopotamus Gretchen and Tyler had given her for her first birthday.

A smile danced across Becca's lips as she thought back to that first special birthday party she'd given Amy. So much fuss for a little girl who couldn't possibly understand what was going on! In addition to the balloons and crepe paper streamers and silly party hats, Becca had baked a cake and decorated it with frosted animal crackers. It even had a single candle in the middle, which Becca had lit while all the grown-ups stood around singing "Happy Birthday" to Amy.

Just as they'd started on the last chorus, Amy had reached out an exploratory finger and extinguished the tiny flame before Becca had had a chance to snatch her pudgy little hand back. Amy had looked surprised when the strange, flickering light had disappeared all of a sudden, but she hadn't burned herself.

Just another one of those narrowly averted disasters that plague every mother.

Unbidden, a picture slipped into Becca's mind of those other mothers that Nancy Woods had spoken about—those heartbroken parents of other missing children, for whom the ultimate disaster *had* occurred.

Becca quickly shoved the picture aside. She wasn't strong enough to shoulder their pain. Not yet, anyway.

"What's this?" Amy was poking through one of the cardboard cartons that Ryan had packed in obvious haste with some of her baby paraphernalia. She crinkled her pert little nose and held up a plastic speaker device for Becca's inspection.

"That's a baby monitor," she explained. "Look, here's the other part. You leave this part in the baby's room, and take the other part with you, and then you can hear if the baby starts to cry."

"You mean, kind of like a walkie-talkie?"

"Kind of."

"Wow. Can I keep it?"

Becca gnawed the inside of her cheek. She'd intended to get rid of all these painful reminders of Amy's babyhood, but Amy looked so enthralled by the gadget, she couldn't bring herself to say no. "Okay, peaches. You can keep it."

"Oh, boy!" Amy immediately busied herself trying to get the monitor to work. Becca made a mental note to buy new batteries for it.

She shoved a clump of sweat-dampened hair off her forehead. It was hot up here in the attic, and downright oppressive beneath the rafters slanting so close overhead. The air lay thick and still, and everything was coated with dust and draped in cobwebs.

And ghosts. There were plenty of ghosts up here, too.

One of these days, she would have to get this place organized. With a sigh, Becca flipped open the flaps of another cardboard box. She expelled a startled puff of air from her lungs.

Lying face up on top of the box's contents was Amy's old teddy bear—the bedraggled, one-eared favorite toy she'd had in the stroller with her the night she was kidnapped.

Becca stared down at its vacant glass eyes, her heart hammering double-time, her skin clammy with a flood of adrenaline. The unexpected glimpse of the stuffed bear had transported her back to that horrible night—dredged up all the desperation, the helplessness, the panic that had seized her in its jaws like a snarling wild animal.

Nausea roiled in Becca's stomach. Breathing rapidly through her mouth, she quickly closed the top of the box and pushed it aside. She'd intended to make a quick inventory of everything she was giving away, just to make sure there wasn't something she wanted to keep. Repressing a shudder, she decided the thrift shop could have whatever else was in that box.

With unsteady hands, Becca slid open the top drawer of Amy's dresser and began to paw through the pile of baby clothes stored inside.

Her mind fumbled around for something else to latch on to besides the teddy bear. She wondered what Ryan was doing right now, his first day back on the construction site. All of a sudden it was strange not having him around. Amazing how quickly she'd grown accustomed to his presence. Even to depend on it.

Maybe she could help Ryan out by taking over his bookkeeping again. The other day he'd mentioned that he'd done his own books since Becca had left. She could just imagine the mess they were in by now. Ryan didn't have a lot of patience for troublesome details like columns of numbers that didn't add up.

Bookkeeping would make Becca feel productive, and at the same time allow her to keep a close eye on Amy. Of course, once school started in September . . .

Becca shuddered. She couldn't imagine sending Amy off to school all by herself. Either she or Ryan would definitely have to drive her right up to the front gates, that's all there was to it. Maybe they should think about enrolling her in a private school, one with good security.

Of course, another option was for Becca to teach Amy at home, but she doubted whether Ryan would agree—

"This is *mine.*" Amy's declaration was firm yet somehow puzzled.

As Becca glanced over, her heart leapt into her throat. Amy was holding the moth-eaten teddy bear at arm's length, her face screwed up with intense concentration.

Becca's hand flew to her mouth. Could it be . . . ? Was it possible that the sight of her beloved, long-lost teddy bear had strummed a faint note of recognition in some remote, cobwebbed corner of Amy's memory?

Gently she pushed in the dresser drawer, wiping her palms on the front of her shorts. "Do you remember him?" she asked in a soft voice that sounded peculiar to her own ears.

"Ye-es . . ." Amy tilted her head to one side, narrowing her eyes. "Dodder!" she exclaimed, her face suddenly lighting up with pleasure.

Becca blinked rapidly. "That's right," she said, trying to keep her voice level. "His name was Dodger. Only you were so little, you couldn't quite say it, so you called him Dodder."

Amy tugged on her ponytail as uncertainty flitted across her face. "How come he's *here?*" she asked, scrunching up her cheeks.

With slow, deliberate movements, Becca lowered herself to the floor next to Amy. "You used to live in this house," she said carefully. "When you were just a baby."

"I *did?*" Amy's eyebrows puckered as she tried to assimilate this surprising new information.

"Before you went to live with your...grandma." Becca forced the words out, nearly choking on their bitterness.

Amy nibbled the end of her ponytail and considered this doubtfully. Then she shrugged. "He's awful beat up," she said matter-of-factly, handing the bear to Becca. "Guess we'd better give him away, huh?"

"Good idea." Becca placed Dodger back in the box as if he were made of spun glass.

Then, when Amy wasn't looking, she took him back out again and stashed him behind a pile of old camping equipment.

"Windsurfing is too dangerous."

Ryan adjusted his sunglasses, studied his wife's stubborn profile, and sighed. "That's what you've said about every other activity I've suggested so far."

"That's because every other activity you've suggested *is* dangerous."

"*Bicycling* is dangerous?"

"There's too much traffic around the lake. She could get hit by a car."

"What about a hot-air balloon ride? Not much traffic up there."

"I just read a news item the other day about one of those things crashing." Becca held up her hand to stem the tide of his protest. "And don't suggest water-skiing lessons again. Amy's only six years old, for heaven's sake!"

"I saw other kids her age out there."

"She could drown, or get hit by a powerboat or one of those Jet-ski things zipping around."

"I'm sure it's perfectly safe, or they wouldn't let children take lessons. Besides, Amy knows how to swim and she'd be wearing a life vest."

Behind Becca's dark glasses it was impossible to read her eyes, but the tight-lipped set of her mouth said it all. Surrendering, Ryan settled back in his beach chair, linked his fingers together on top of his bare chest and twiddled his thumbs.

This was their second day at Lake Tahoe, a sparkling cobalt jewel nestled in the spectacular setting of the Sierra Nevada. From a distance the granite peaks seemed to soar straight up from the water's edge, their pine-studded slopes providing a dramatic backdrop for the boaters and swimmers and hikers who flocked to the lake's shores during the summer tourist season.

It was the perfect spot for a honeymoon.

Unfortunately, what Ryan had intended to be sort of a second honeymoon had turned into more of a battle of wills. First there was this ongoing tug-of-war with Becca over what activities were safe for Amy to engage in.

Even more frustrating was Ryan's internal struggle to keep his hot-blooded desires and reckless urges submerged. They kept bobbing to the surface like treacherous underwater obstacles, disturbing the even emotional keel he'd vowed to maintain.

He'd known it wouldn't be easy to keep his hands off Becca, not while they were cozily ensconced in a small, one-room cottage at the memory-filled site of their first honeymoon. Even with Amy there, even though they slept in separate beds.

He'd fully expected it would be a struggle to keep from ogling Becca's smooth, long limbs and the tantalizing expanse of creamy flesh bared by her one-piece bathing suit.

What Ryan *hadn't* counted on was this maddening, low-level arousal that never gave him a moment's peace—like a nagging toothache or a persistent attack of prickly heat. His blood seemed to race through his veins, his skin to tingle as if in constant contact with a live electric wire. His pulse thundered in his ears, a relentless pounding, pounding,

pounding he sometimes thought would drive him right over the brink of sanity.

This morning when Becca had been in the bathroom, Ryan had switched the pillows from their beds so that tonight he would be able to inhale her sexy, familiar fragrance all night long. An incredibly foolish move considering the circumstances, but where Becca was concerned, Ryan couldn't seem to help himself.

Even now, when he was downright annoyed with her, the sight of her sleek, bare calves...the elegant slope of her neck...the seductive shadow between her breasts...pumped up the level of his desire till it finally flung him from the beach chair.

He yanked off his sunglasses and tossed them aside. "I'm going for a swim," he mumbled, uncomfortably aware of Becca's curious eyes boring into the rigid wall of his back. He hurried across the sandy stretch of private beach that separated their cottage from the water.

He splashed into the rippling waves, diving in headfirst when he judged it was deep enough. Tahoe was a very deep mountain lake, and even in the middle of summer the water had a chill to it. Just what Ryan needed to take the edge off his itch.

He surfaced near the end of the wooden dock. shaking his hair and dashing the cool water from his eyes. "Hiya, princess," he called. "Catch anything yet?"

Amy perched at the end of the dock, feet dangling in the water, a crude fishing pole propped between her knees. She shook her damp golden curls. "Nope. Not yet."

Ryan had warned her when he'd assembled the makeshift fishing pole that there wasn't much chance of catching anything this close to shore. He grated his teeth, wishing for the dozenth time that Becca would at least let him rent a motorboat so he could take Amy fishing properly.

But Amy seemed to be enjoying herself, anyway. Ryan grinned at the jaunty effect of the plastic sunglasses she'd persuaded them to buy her yesterday so she would look like the grown-ups.

She did, in fact, resemble a miniature version of her mother, who was still keeping a watchful eye focused on Amy from a shady patch of sand near the cottage.

Ryan bent his elbows and hoisted himself backward onto the dock, dripping water all over the weathered wooden boards. He scooted over to sit next to Amy. "Are you having fun here at the lake?"

"Oh, yes!" Amy beamed up at him with a smile that nearly melted his heart. "I wish we could live here all the time."

Ryan laughed. "Don't you think you'd get tired of it after a while?"

"Nope." She shook her head emphatically so that her sunglasses slid down to the tip of her nose. She pushed them back up with her finger. "Only thing is, I wish we coulda brought Southpaw."

"Me, too, kiddo. But most places around here don't allow pets."

"Then I'm glad we're just visiting." She gave a decisive bob of her head. "'Cause I wouldn't wanna live anyplace where they didn't allow Southpaw."

"Me neither." A wave of love hit Ryan just then, so powerful it nearly knocked him back off the dock. He practically ached to bundle Amy into his arms, to tickle her and smother her with kisses. But instinct warned him that his little girl probably wasn't ready for such a rambunctious display of fatherly affection yet.

He had to force himself to go slow with her. The same way he was trying to go slow with Becca.

Ryan pushed himself to his feet. "What do you feel like eating for lunch today, pumpkin?"

An expression of dismay shadowed Amy's face. "I thought we were gonna eat the fish I catch!"

Oops! Ryan snapped his fingers. "That's right. How could I forget?"

Amy looked relieved.

"But, er, just in case we get hungry before you catch any, what sounds good to eat?"

"Hot dogs," she replied promptly.

"Hot dogs?" he echoed in a teasing tone. "But we had hot dogs for lunch yesterday."

"That's okay. I like hot dogs."

Ryan fondly rustled her hair. "Hot dogs it is, then. Are you ready to go eat yet?"

"In a minute. I just wanna keep trying to catch a fish for a little while."

"Okay." He touched her cheek and walked slowly back up the dock toward the shore.

"What were you two talking about?" Becca drew her legs up and propped her chin on top of her knees as he approached.

"Just discussing lunch," Ryan answered amiably, stretching out on the beach chair. He jabbed his sunglasses partway on, then peered at Becca over the tops. "Don't worry, I wasn't promising her we could go bungee jumping or anything."

Becca stiffened, then looked embarrassed. "That wasn't what I meant."

"Was, too." Ryan arranged his limbs beneath the baking heat of the sun.

A few beats of silence passed. Then, "How can you blame me for wanting to keep her safe, after what we've been through?"

"I don't blame you at all, Becca." Ryan propped himself up on his elbows so he could look at her. "But you can't keep Amy all wrapped up in a steel cocoon. You have to let her take normal risks, to live like other kids do."

She flipped her hair impatiently over her shoulder. "If I'd been more careful and kept my eye on her, she wouldn't have been stolen from us."

"What are you planning to do, Becca? Follow Amy around every single second until she's an adult? Catch her every time she starts to fall? Teach her to be suspicious and afraid of everyone she meets on the street?"

Becca's cheeks were flushed, and not from sunburn. "You, of all people," she exclaimed, "should recognize the necessity of teaching children to be wary of strangers."

"Being careful is one thing. Shying away like a frightened rabbit whenever you come near someone you don't know is another."

"Amy doesn't do that."

"No, but *you* do." Ryan tried to bite back his exasperation. He'd hoped a new environment with pleasant rather than painful associations would allow Becca to relax a little bit around other people. But, if anything, being surrounded by hordes of vacationing strangers had only made her more uptight.

He swung his feet over the side of the chair and sat up. "Don't you realize what kind of subconscious message you're conveying? When we're walking down the street, every time someone passes us you drop your arm around Amy and pull her close to you, like you're trying to shield her from imminent attack."

Becca's lips compressed into a tight white line.

"And whenever someone exchanges a few words with us, whether it's a store clerk or a waitress in a restaurant, you glare at them like you're trying to memorize their features for a police sketch."

"That's ridiculous! I do no such—"

"Maybe you don't even realize you're doing it, but *I* notice it and, more important, so does Amy." Frustration gripped Ryan as he realized he might as well be talking to a wall. "If you don't knock it off, eventually Amy's going to become as paranoid as you are."

"Paranoid?" Every muscle in Becca's body went taut with outrage. She whipped off her sunglasses and glowered at him through narrowed eyes. "You listen to me, Ryan Slater. I'd much rather have Amy turn out *paranoid* as you call it, than to risk letting her come to any harm or...or be kidnapped again!"

Ryan jerked off his own sunglasses. "It's fine to want to protect her, Becca, but not at the cost of warping her emotional development."

"What are you talking about, warping?" She ticked off points of rebuttal on her fingers. "Amy doesn't have nightmares anymore. She's come out of her shell. She's adjusted to her new home..."

Ryan made soothing gestures with his hands. "We have a wonderful child, Becca. No doubt about that. She's bright, outgoing, resilient...and I want her to stay that way."

"You talk as if you think I'm...I'm *ruining* her." Dismay was beginning to overtake Becca's anger. "I'm only doing what I think is best for her, Ryan."

"I know that, honey." He felt like a heel for coming down on her so hard. After the terrible ordeal they'd endured, Becca's overprotectiveness was perfectly understandable. But for Amy's sake, her parents would both have to overcome that natural tendency.

"As difficult as it is," Ryan went on, "you have to let up a little. Let Amy live like a normal kid, even if it means she'll wind up with a few bumps and bruises."

Becca's face crumpled. "I—I just can't bear the thought of anything bad happening to her." Hastily she jammed her concealing dark glasses back on.

Ryan swallowed. "I can't stand the idea, either." He shifted his chair through the sand so he was close enough to fold his hands around Becca's. "But I don't want Amy to grow up afraid to try new experiences, afraid to meet new people."

"Why did it have to happen?" Becca burst out. "Why us, Ryan? Why did that horrible woman have to steal our baby?" She clapped her hand over her mouth, as if to stifle the hysterical note in her voice.

Ryan squeezed her other hand. "I don't know." How many times had those same useless questions swirled through his brain, taunting and tormenting him until he wanted to bash his head against the wall to silence them?

"There are no answers to those questions," he said, trying to quell the surge of rage and injustice her outburst had stirred up inside him. "No answers, and nothing to be gained by replaying the past over and over again. We've got to look ahead to the future now, and focus on how lucky we are to have our child back—not on how unfair it was that we lost her in the first place."

Becca gripped his hand like a lifeline. "You're right. About everything. I—I don't want Amy to grow up scared of her own shadow, either."

"I know you don't." Ryan stroked her arm reassuringly.

"I'll try, I really will, not to be so overprotective of her."

Ryan scooted his chair even closer, so he could wrap his arm around Becca's bare shoulders. To his surprise, she didn't resist.

"It'll take time, though," she said.

"You're a wonderful mother." He kissed her temple, brushed away the fine strands of hair that clung to his mouth. "I think your instincts will tell you what's best for Amy. Just give yourself a chance."

"Oh, Ryan." Becca turned to him, resting her head on his shoulder, splaying her fingers across his chest. Her touch was as sizzling to his skin as the sun's fiery rays.

He filled his lungs with the scent of shampoo and suntan lotion. As she absently twirled her fingers through the coils of his chest hair, the heat began to build inside him again. "Becca," he whispered. "Tonight, why don't we try sleeping in the same—"

A piercing cry from the direction of the dock launched them both to their feet before Ryan could complete his impulsive suggestion.

Tense, frozen, ready to spring into action, they posed like statues until their frantic, searching eyes found Amy.

She was dancing up and down at the end of the dock, squealing with glee. "Lookit!" she cried, holding up a small object dangling from a string. "Lookit what I got!" She raced down the length of the dock, pole dragging behind her, bare feet drumming an excited tattoo against the boards. Ryan squinted and finally figured out that the prize she was proudly holding up was a wiggling minnow about the size of his thumb.

Amy thrashed across the sand toward them, sunglasses nearly bouncing off her nose, a triumphant smile illuminating her adorable face. "Lookit, it's a fish!" she cried. "Mommy, Daddy, I caught a fish!"

Something sweet and tender snagged inside Ryan's chest with a jolt that took his breath away. Beside him, Becca let out a soft gasp and clutched her arms around her middle, hugging herself as if she were about to double over. Ryan clamped his hand on her shoulder partly to steady her, partly to steady himself.

"Ryan," she said in a choked whisper, "did you hear?"

He nodded, unable to speak just then. If there were two more beautiful words in the English language than mommy and daddy, he sure didn't know what they were.

Happiness spilled through him, infusing him with a warm glow that radiated outward to encompass his wife, his child—the whole darn world, in fact!

He crouched in the sand on shaky knees. "You sure did catch a fish, princess," he said as Amy skidded to a breathless halt in front of him. For some reason he was grinning like an idiot.

Becca leaned over for a closer view. "Amy, I'm so proud of you!" Her voice had an airy, high-pitched quality to it.

Amy pushed her tipsy sunglasses back up her nose and beamed at Becca. Then her excited smile faltered a little. "How come you're crying?"

Ryan glanced up sharply. From beneath Becca's dark glasses, a single tear trickled down her smooth cheek. She dashed it away with trembling fingertips.

"I'm just crying 'cause I'm so happy, that's all," she replied, cupping Amy's face in her hand.

"'Cause I caught a fish?"

"Yes!" The word came out half laugh, half sob.

"Oh." Amy swung her catch up before her eyes and studied it with a sudden flicker of doubt. "What are we gonna do with it now?"

"Hmm." Ryan propped his chin on his fist and said cautiously, "Well, he's kind of puny to eat, wouldn't you say?"

Amy nodded in agreement. "I don't think we could all eat him for lunch, do you?"

"Probably not."

She brightened. "Could I keep him for a pet?"

Becca tucked a damp streamer of hair behind Amy's ear and said, "Sweetie, he wouldn't be happy living with us, not when he's used to having a whole lake to swim around in."

Ryan levered himself to his feet. "Of course, we could always throw him back in the water..."

Amy thought about this. "Otherwise he'll die, won't he?"

"'Fraid so, pumpkin."

An expression of alarm filtered over her features. "I don't want him to die, Daddy! I didn't mean to kill him!"

"Okay, come on, then—let's go!" Ryan grabbed Amy's hand, then reached back and tugged Becca along, too.

The three of them raced across the sand, splashing into the water with a chorus of shouts, squeals and laughter.

They set the minnow free.

Chapter Eleven

After their trip to Lake Tahoe, it seemed to Becca that life in the Slater household actually started to resemble life in a normal family. She went for entire hours at a time without thinking about Amy's kidnapping, or worrying that it could happen again. She sent Ryan off to work every morning with a sack lunch and a peck on the cheek. Evenings, the three of them watched television or played board games or took Southpaw for a romp along one of the wooded mountain trails that wound through the outskirts of Pine Creek.

It was as if a framed portrait of their family life, brutally shattered in one dreadful blow, was gradually being restored piece by piece by that master craftsman called Time, until the cracks were barely visible and anyone who wasn't deliberately searching would never even notice they were there.

Even their house itself had a lovingly patched-up look to it these days. On weekends Ryan repainted and pounded down loose boards and attacked the yard with the hedge trimmer, till the old Victorian looked as proudly revitalized as a dowager with freshly coiffed hair and a fancy new dress to match.

Some days Becca could almost forget that their marriage wasn't like other people's.

But she never forgot it at night.

Nights she thrashed around, got tangled in the sheets, punched her pillow and then lay very still, imagining she could hear Ryan doing the same in his bedroom down the hall.

Pure fantasy, of course. Ryan had behaved like the perfect gentleman ever since their wedding ceremony three weeks ago—affectionate but not seductive, never crossing the line between them that Becca herself had drawn.

She wished he weren't quite so perfect.

Only once had she suspected that he might be finding this platonic arrangement as frustrating as she was. At Tahoe, there had been a moment when she'd sensed passion roiling just beneath his calm, controlled surface and had thought with a little quickstep of excitement that he was on the verge of calling a halt to this charade and demanding his husbandly rights.

Or something to that effect.

But the moment had passed as irretrievably as any other missed opportunity, and Becca couldn't bring herself to try to recreate it. She herself had posted that particular area of their marriage as off-limits. It wasn't fair to change the rules of the game just because she was having second thoughts. What if she and Ryan made love, and then she changed her mind again?

Better to leave things as they were, she decided.

But that decision did nothing to reduce the number of sleepless nights.

Becca did decide to take one big risk, though—one more step toward recovery from the long ordeal of Amy's kidnapping. Late one afternoon she took a deep breath and dialed the phone, halfway hoping no one would answer.

Someone did.

"I'm trying to reach Nancy Woods, please." Please, please, let her have gone home already....

"One moment, please."

While she waited, Becca wrapped the phone cord around and around her wrist, till it practically cut off her circulation.

"This is Nancy Woods. How may I help you?"

"Hi. Um, this is Becca Slater. I don't know if you remember me, but—"

"Mrs. Slater, of course! How are you?"

Terrified, Becca thought. "The reason I'm calling is, uh, I thought about what you asked before—about coming to one of your meetings and talking to some of the other parents with missing children." It sounded to Becca like someone had punched holes in her voice so that all the air was leaking out as she spoke.

Nancy Woods, however, didn't seem to notice. She was delighted to give Becca the time and location of their next support group meeting.

Becca was just replacing the receiver with shaky hands when someone pounded on the front door.

She jumped about a foot in the air.

"Tyler," she said in surprise a moment later, after she'd cautiously peeked through the front window.

"Hiya, Becs." He jingled his keys in his hand. "I'm here to pick up Amy."

"Amy?" Becca's forehead pleated in confusion. "I don't understand. Did Sarah and Christopher invite her over? I was just about to start dinner."

"Actually, I'm on a secret mission." He gave her one of those sly, charming winks that had gotten him his way most of his life. "Following orders, you see. From that hubby of yours."

The back door slammed.

"Ryan? But he didn't say anything to me... Are you sure he said—"

"Did I just hear my name mentioned? Oh, Tyler, good— you're here. Amy!" he called up the stairs. He kissed Becca on her still-pleated forehead. "Hi, honey. How was your day?"

"Ryan, what on earth is going on? Why is Tyler here to pick up Amy?"

"All in good time, my sweet."

"But—"

"Here I am." Amy bounced into the foyer. "Hi, Uncle Tyler."

"Hi, yourself, gorgeous. Ready to go?"

"Yup. I got my pajamas and everything."

"Hold it right there!" Becca cried. She lowered her outstretched hands slowly. "Would someone mind telling me just exactly what's going on, please?"

Ryan was all innocence. "Tyler's just taking Amy over to eat supper at their place, honey."

"But her pajamas... Ryan, I don't want her spending the night away from home," she said in a low aside.

"Don't worry, Tyler's going to bring her back later this evening. But it'll be past her normal bedtime, so I thought it would be easier if she put on her pajamas at their place."

"You thought...? Past her normal...? Ryan, you have exactly three seconds to explain what's going on." Becca glared at him, hands on hips.

"Oops, guess that's our signal to go," Tyler said. "Come on Amy, race you to the car."

"'Kay!" Amy took off like a rocket.

Tyler winked at Ryan. "Have fun."

"Fun?" Becca echoed. "Ryan, what's he talking about? Where's he taking Amy?"

He dropped his hands onto her shoulders. "Shh, it's okay, honey, I told you. He and Gretchen are going to watch Amy for us this evening. So you and I can be alone."

"You arranged all this? Why? You still haven't explained—*alone?*" Becca swallowed. "Um, why?"

Ryan peered at her curiously. "You don't remember what day this is, do you?"

"I remember." Becca's cheeks grew hot. She slid her gaze to one side. "It's our anniversary."

"Of the first time we got married."

"Yes." All day long she'd avoided looking at the calendar, but she knew. She looked down at her wedding ring, which Ryan had first placed on her finger exactly ten years ago today. Suddenly the sight of it blurred.

Ryan tilted her chin up. "I wanted to do something special, Becca. Something to celebrate. Because you and I do have plenty to celebrate, don't we?" All at once he looked uncertain.

"Yes!" Becca's voice was choked with emotion. She covered her mouth with her hand, closed her eyes and leaned forward into Ryan's embrace.

His arms came around her, his head rested on top of hers. "Remember what we had to eat for our first anniversary supper?" he asked softly.

"Pizza!" she replied in a voice laced with tears. "We couldn't afford anything fancy, because we were still struggling to get the construction business off the ground, so we went to that funny little Italian restaurant that isn't even there anymore." She drew her head back and looked up at Ryan with shining eyes. "Remember? There were candles stuck in empty Chianti bottles, and clusters of plastic grapes hanging from the ceiling, and that tinny-sounding jukebox that kept playing 'Arrivederci, Roma' over and over again." By now Becca's tears had turned to giggles.

"I kept shoving coins into it and pushing other selections, but the darn thing would only play that one song." Ryan's laughter warmed Becca from head to toe. He hugged her close. "I'm going upstairs to shower," he said. "Then when I come back, I want you to do something for me."

He wouldn't explain what, however, leaving Becca in a floor-pacing state of anticipation and anxiety. When he returned, damp hair clinging to the collar of his clean shirt, he was holding a red-checked bandanna. "Put this on like a blindfold," he said with a smile.

Becca stared at him dubiously. "No kinky stuff," she warned, deciding to be a good sport and go along with this crazy, mysterious scheme.

Ryan tied the bandanna behind her head, leaning over to growl in her ear, "Maybe you'll change your mind later."

A delicious thrill shivered up and down her spine. Then Ryan led her to the couch and planted her there while he went off to make strange noises in the kitchen. Becca heard the back door open and close a couple times, then someone rang the front doorbell.

"Don't worry, I'll get it," he called.

She heard a mumble-mumble of voices, but couldn't make out what was being said. The front door closed, and Ryan's footsteps thudded back to the kitchen.

"What are you doing?" she called.

"Patience, my darling," he called back. "All will be revealed in good time."

"Somehow that doesn't reassure me," she muttered.

After what seemed an eternity but was probably no longer than ten minutes, Ryan came back, took Becca's hand and helped her to her feet.

"Finally," she said. "This silly bandanna was starting to itch."

"Don't take it off yet," he said quickly. "Come with me, first."

Becca groaned. "I'm too old for blindman's bluff!"

"Not to worry, I'll help you. Come on, that's right. Watch out for the end table there...oops, here's the door..."

Becca crinkled her nose, then inhaled appreciatively. "Mmm, what's that heavenly smell?"

"Ta-dah!" With a flourish, Ryan whipped off her blindfold.

Becca blinked as the light hit her eyes. Then her mouth fell open and she gaped at the scene in front of her.

The heavenly smell was pizza, still in its cardboard delivery box. Dangling from cupboard handles, the refrigerator door and the light fixture overhead were bunches of plastic grapes. The table was set with the china they'd received long ago as a wedding present, and in the center was a bottle of Chianti in a raffia holder, its neck dripping with waxy red trails from a flaming candle.

Becca flattened her hand over her heart and tried to catch her breath. "Oh, Ryan..."

He punched a button on the tape deck sitting on the counter, and the familiar, cloying strains of "Arrivederci, Roma" drifted into the air.

Becca found herself laughing and crying and just trying to breathe, all at the same time.

"Look, we even have a red-checkered tablecloth." Ryan whisked the bandanna onto the table, quickly rearranging the plates and glasses and silverware. "How's that for atmosphere?"

Even if Becca's dazzled brain had been able to come up with a clever rejoinder, she doubted whether she would have been able to squeeze it out past the lump in her throat.

Ryan produced another bottle of Chianti, this one containing dry red wine instead of a red candle. He splashed wine into two crystal glasses and handed one to Becca.

She managed not to drop it, though the liquid swirled precariously close to the rim.

"Happy anniversary, Becca." Ryan's quiet voice carried just a trace of uncertainty, as if he were worried about her reaction to his elaborate preparations.

For his sake, she collected together the makings of a wobbly smile. "Happy anniversary," she managed to reply.

They clinked their glasses together.

As she brought the glass to her lips, her eyes met those of her wonderful, handsome, romantic husband. With an astonishing flash of soul-deep certainty, it occurred to Becca that she'd never loved Ryan Slater more than she did at this very moment.

Ryan pointed at another photograph. "Remember the snowman we built in the front yard that year we got so much snow?"

"Don't you mean snow*woman?*" Becca corrected with a nudge to his ribs. "As I recall, the minute we finished it you ran inside and brought out one of my maternity blouses for it to wear."

"Hey, why not? The two of you were about the same size. Look, here's a shot of you standing in front of the lodge the day we went skiing with Gretchen and Tyler. All bundled up just like a snow bunny."

"A fat, pregnant snow bunny. And *we* didn't go skiing. I had to sit in the lodge all day drinking hot chocolate while the three of you were having fun on the slopes."

"It wasn't fun, honest." Ryan made a crisscross motion over his heart. "Not without you there, honey."

"Humph. I'll bet." But a second later she shook with repressed laughter. The ends of her hair danced up and down, tickling Ryan's arm, which was draped along the top of the couch behind her shoulders.

The sensation was oddly erotic, sending an unexpected flood of heat through his loins. In one steadying gulp he drained the contents of his wineglass, then set it down as he leaned forward to turn the next page of the photo album spread open in front of them.

He'd choreographed every step of this evening so carefully—the romantic dinner, the photo album that just happened to be sitting on the coffee table when they came into the living room afterward to finish their wine, the old cassette tapes he'd dug out to provide a musical background of songs that dated back to their courtship days.

But what Ryan hadn't planned for were these conflicting emotions that kept yanking him back and forth in an internal tug-of-war.

His intentions had been simple, deliberate, with a clear-cut goal in mind. By surrounding Becca with all this evidence of their past happiness, Ryan had hoped to show her what a solid foundation they had on which to build a future.

By weaving reminders of the past into the present, he'd hoped to convince her that they could still recapture the magic, the passion of the love they'd once shared.

Aw, hell. Why not admit it? He'd intended to seduce her with memories, is what it boiled down to.

Not the most noble of schemes.

Maybe that was why he was having trouble making his move. It certainly wasn't due to any lack of cooperation from Becca. She hadn't resisted when he'd casually put his arm around her, didn't pull back whenever he found an excuse to bring his face close to hers.

In fact, she seemed to rather enjoy snuggling next to him on the couch. She was certainly in a mellower, more receptive mood than Ryan had seen her in for a long, long time.

Yeah, after you plied her with wine and nostalgia, he admonished himself with disgust.

Still . . . it should have been easy to turn up the heat a little, to increase the intimacy of their embrace, to woo her with words and tender caresses. . . .

Ryan yanked his arm from around Becca's shoulders and lurched to his feet. Geez, he was afraid to make a pass at his own wife!

"Ryan?"

"Tape's nearly over," he muttered, crossing the room to the stereo. "Thought I'd flip it over to the other side."

Fact of the matter was, now that his clever campaign of seduction was actually within range of succeeding, Ryan was starting to realize that just getting Becca into his bed wasn't going to be enough.

He couldn't be satisfied with just her body—though, God knows, that was a temptation hard to resist. He wanted her to be his *wife*, damn it, in every sense of the word. He wanted her heart, mind and soul.

He wanted her to love him. Wholeheartedly. Without barriers or reservations.

The way he loved her.

Problem was, he didn't believe Becca *could* love him like that. Not anymore. Not until she forgave herself, stopped trying to punish herself for all the imagined sins she'd committed in the past.

How could you love someone else, when you hated yourself?

What he and Becca had once shared was incredibly special—too important to replace with even a close imitation. It would be like debasing their love to settle for anything less.

He would just have to wait and hope that someday Becca's emotional wounds would heal, that she could learn to love again.

That she could learn to love *him* again.

Because Ryan had just decided he couldn't make love to her on any other terms.

With a sigh, he tugged the cassette out and switched on the radio instead. This trip down memory lane had reached a dead end.

"Ryan, what is it? What's the matter?"

The unexpected touch of Becca's hand on his shoulder made him flinch. He hadn't even heard her get off the couch.

"Nothing, I—I guess looking at all those old pictures just got to me, that's all."

She rubbed his back. "It's kind of sad, isn't it? I see all those smiling faces and I think, if only we'd known what was going to happen, what terrible tragedy was laying in wait for us."

"We couldn't have known, Becca. There wasn't anything we could have done to prevent it." Ryan's words came out sounding more impatient than he'd intended. He moved away from her, lifted the wine bottle and discovered it was empty. Just as well. It was starting to give him a headache.

Becca picked up their glasses. "I'll help you clean up in the kitchen."

"No, that's okay. I meant this evening to be a gift for you." He forced his features into a smile. "Cleaning up afterward is part of the deal." Truth was, he preferred to be alone for a while.

Becca wavered, then reluctantly handed him the glasses. "If you say so." The cozy mood of the evening had evaporated, and Becca obviously sensed it.

When Ryan took the glasses from her, she took hold of his wrist. "Please tell me what's wrong."

He shrugged. "I told you. Those old photos depressed me a little, that's all."

"It's more than that. I can tell."

He tried to back away, but she kept her fingers clamped firmly around his wrist. "We've been through it all before," he said with weary resignation. "I don't want to keep sounding like a broken record, going around and around...."

Becca's eyes flared with understanding. She knew him so well. He didn't need to spell out for her the reasons for his abrupt withdrawal.

As the tense silence stretched out, they both noticed at the same moment that the Beatles were singing "Yesterday" on the radio.

A song that dated from way before their courtship days, true, but one that Becca had always loved. She'd always dragged Ryan out on the dance floor whenever she heard it.

Now its words carried a special, bittersweet significance that was reflected in Becca's face, in the poignant expression in her eyes, in the painful tightening of her lips.

"Dance with me, Ryan," she whispered.

Moving in slow motion, he set down the glasses and took his wife in his arms. This was a stupid move, a bad mistake...

Her arms slid around his neck, her head came to rest on the shelf of his collarbone. The music swirled around them, circling them with invisible threads of shared memories, of long-lost love that seemed to draw tight and bind them together as strongly as chains of steel.

They moved together as one, carried back to yesterday, to those happier, more innocent times when the present was full of love and laughter and the future full of dreams.

Physical reality drew Ryan back to the here and now, to the vivid awareness of Becca's soft breasts pressing into his chest, her hips swaying with his as if they were joined together in a far more intimate union. He kissed her hair, pulled her even closer, all the while warning himself that he was sinking into quicksand here.

She was so warm, so soft, such a perfect fit against his body. His heart was thudding in his chest, pounding in his ears, sending wave after wave of desire pulsing through his bloodstream.

God, how he wanted her! She was the only woman he'd ever dreamed of, ever needed, ever loved.

The song ended. They stopped moving. Becca lifted her head from his shoulder.

Ryan kissed her.

He couldn't help himself. He'd learned how to be strong over the years, but to resist the allure of her bewitching blue eyes, her enchanting fragrance, her sleek, sexy curves would require a superhuman display of willpower that even Ryan didn't possess.

He plunged his fingers through her hair, savored the taste of her mouth, pulled her abdomen more snugly against him so she could feel how much he wanted her.

With a hiss of satisfaction, he noted her rampaging pulse, her quick, shallow breathing, the faint whimpers of pleasure that escaped her lips whenever he adjusted his mouth to kiss her more deeply, more thoroughly.

She filled his senses with her heat, her scent, her passionate response. Somewhere in a far corner of his mind Ryan remembered that he'd decided not to do this. There was some very good reason why he should unwind Becca's arms from around his neck, disengage his mouth and his hands from her body.

For the life of him he couldn't recall what it was. He was drunk on her essence, on his own desire. Senses reeling, better judgment suspended. The prospect of future regrets had no power to stop him.

He slid his hands beneath her blouse, spanning her ribs and brushing the lower curves of her breasts with his thumbs. Becca arched against him, gasped out his name.

Ryan buried his lips in the soft, sweet curve of her neck and prepared to peel off her clothes, to make her his once again right here on the floor of the living room.

Then they both heard the front door open.

The effect was comparable to a keg of dynamite exploding between them, hurling them apart at breakneck speed.

"Mommy, Daddy, where are you?"

Becca straightened her blouse, regret and embarrassment mingling in her strained features. She slanted Ryan an almost furtive look. "We're in the living room, Amy," she called. Her voice sounded rusty.

Ryan combed his fingers through his hair, making a valiant effort to erase any lingering traces of lust from his expression.

Amy, clad in pajamas, burst into the living room with Tyler following at a more sedate pace. "My tooth fell out!" she exclaimed, brandishing the object in question. "I was wiggling it, and it just came right out!"

Tyler took in the atmosphere of the room, Ryan and Becca's disheveled appearances, and grimaced in apology. "She insisted on coming right home. Gretchen and I tried to get her to stay a while longer, but she couldn't wait to show both of you her tooth."

"I had to come home so I could put it under my pillow," Amy explained with perfect logic. "Else, how was the tooth fairy gonna know where to find me?"

"It's all right, Tyler." Becca avoided his eyes as she bent over to examine Amy's tooth. "Oh, that's a good one. I bet it's worth fifty cents, at least."

"Goody!" Amy jumped up and down.

Becca's eyes glittered with moisture. "Look, Ryan, her very first baby tooth to come out."

Ryan gave the tooth a complete inspection. "You're sure this is yours?" he asked with mock suspicion.

"Look, it came from right here." Amy gave them a broad, jack-o'-lantern grin, pointing at the small gap in her lower row of teeth.

Becca hugged her. "I guess that proves it, doesn't it?"

"Good enough for me." Ryan handed the tooth back to Amy and kissed the top of her head. "You know where to leave it, don't you? Under the rug, so the tooth fairy can find it."

Amy rolled her eyes. "Dad-*dee*," she said in exasperation. "You're s'posed to leave it under your *pillow*."

Ryan snapped his fingers. "By golly, you're right."

"You're silly."

"And you're cute as a button, princess."

"Come on, Amy, let's go upstairs to bed." Becca took her hand.

"I'm gonna stay awake all night and watch for the tooth fairy."

"Oh, you are, are you? Didn't anyone ever tell you that the tooth fairy won't come as long as you're awake?"

"Like Santa?"

"Just like Santa."

"Hmm." Amy puckered her forehead in deep thought. "Then I'll *pretend* to be asleep. I'll close my eyes and lie real still, and when the tooth fairy comes I'll just peek out of one eye."

Becca's laughter trailed over her shoulder as they left the living room. "That sounds like a real good plan, sweetie. Especially the part about closing your eyes and lying real still."

Tyler shifted from foot to foot as he watched his friend. "Bad timing, huh?" he asked sheepishly.

Actually, his timing had been pretty good, Ryan thought. By showing up when he had, Tyler had saved Ryan from making a major, irreversible mistake. In a weak moment he'd almost taken advantage of Becca's vulnerability, had nearly forgotten his vow not to make love to her until she was capable of returning his love completely, with her heart and soul as well as her body.

It was still too soon.

"Yeah, bad timing," Ryan said aloud.

But he didn't mean it the same way Tyler had.

Midnight.

His bedroom curtains stirred in the warm breeze from the open window.

Ryan told himself he couldn't sleep because it was a hot night. Because the full moon was shining right in his eyes. Because he was listening for the tooth fairy to come.

All those excuses were equally lame.

The real reason Ryan couldn't sleep was that he was still too full of Becca, too aroused by the memory of his mouth exploring hers ... her breasts swelling beneath his hands ... the erotic pressure of her hips against the rock-hard evidence of his desire.

With a groan he rolled over and dragged the pillow over his head. Maybe the tooth fairy would find it there and leave him a quarter.

No good. He struggled with the bed covers, tossing them all to the floor except for one sheet. He was mashing the pillow into submission when he heard a noise.

A very faint noise. Like a footstep in the hallway.

Then ... nothing.

Ryan held his breath.

With a tiny creak, the door to his bedroom slowly inched open.

Outside the crickets whirred. Somewhere far away a dog barked. The curtains billowed gently on a puff of warm, pine-scented air.

Becca stood in the doorway ... her filmy nightgown, her smooth bare arms, her shimmering hair all silvered by moonlight.

Chapter Twelve

Becca locked the bedroom door with a quiet click and leaned back against it. She needed a solid prop just now, what with her wobbly knees on the verge of collapsing. In the silence of the room, the rapid-fire beat of her heart seemed deafening.

She'd never been so nervous in her life.

Terrified . . . grief-stricken . . . but never before this knee-knocking nervousness that simultaneously turned her palms damp and her mouth as dry as chalk.

What if he sent her away?

Dear Lord, what if he didn't?

Ryan swung his feet over the side of the bed and sat up. The sheet dropped away, baring the sculpted contours of his chest. The moonlight reflected off his dark eyes so that they glinted like diamonds. Or steel.

Becca stared directly into those unreadable depths, unable to move, unable to tear her gaze away. It was as if his eyes held her pinned to the door. Dimly she was aware that her lungs were pumping air in and out as if she'd just run a marathon.

Ryan waited, motionless as a Greek statue, silvery shadows casting the sharp planes and chiseled hollows of his face into even bolder relief.

Then the statue came to life. He stretched out one magnificently muscled arm, reaching for her.

"Come here," he said.

As if his voice had broken a spell, Becca found herself able to move forward. She placed one bare foot in front of the other, and in her turbulent state of mind it seemed like these few steps were the longest journey of her life.

She placed her hand in his.

Ryan drew her down to sit beside him on the edge of the bed. He turned her head so moonlight spilled across her face. He framed her face between his palms, studying her closely.

"Are you sure?" he asked in a tone that sent tingling vibrations along her nerve endings.

Was she sure? Well, that depended on which part of her anatomy Becca listened to. Her brain seemed to be yammering from someplace far away that she had no right to be here, that she was breaking her own rules and heading straight for trouble.

Her body, however, was sending an altogether different message. From the top of her head to the tips of her toes, every square inch of her skin was crying out for Ryan's touch. She ached with desire, longed to taste him and smell him and hear him whisper secret words in her ear while his hands and mouth set her on fire.

And her heart . . . oh, her heart, whispering that she and Ryan belonged together, that the joy and passion they'd once brought each other was a precious gift meant to be shared, over and over again. . . .

It appeared her brain was on one side, her body and heart on the other. Two against one. Majority rules.

Becca nodded.

"I'm sure," she murmured.

A great tension seemed to drain out of Ryan's body. The cords in his neck shifted as he swallowed. He lowered one hand from her face to cup her breast in his palm.

The heat of his skin seared through the flimsy fabric of her gown. Becca closed her eyes as a spasm of excitement rippled through her. His thumb found her nipple, began to circle it slowly. She tried to hold herself still, to capture the indescribable pleasure and hold it inside her, but it was impossible not to move, not to make a sound, not to respond to his touch.

Then his hand dropped away and she opened her eyes with vague disappointment. But he'd only paused to reach for the hem of her nightgown. Instinctively she shifted her weight so that he could skim it off over her head.

It fluttered to the floor, ghostlike in the pale glow from the window. Her panties followed.

Ryan grasped her shoulders, holding her at arm's length while he raked his hungry gaze up and down her body. "You're so beautiful in the moonlight," he told her in a voice containing equal parts awe and admiration. "Look at your skin, how it gleams like satin."

The undisguised lust glittering in his eyes made Becca bold. She slipped her fingers beneath the elastic band of his underwear, tugging downward. Ryan lifted his hips so that she could strip it off. He settled himself on the edge of the bed again, took Becca's hand and brought it down onto his lap.

He groaned as she began to stroke the hard, throbbing length of him, rediscovering the thrill of her own power to please him. He braced himself on his arms, letting his head drop back. "That feels good," he managed to rasp out.

Becca rubbed herself against him, reveling in the scratchy feel of his hairy skin. She'd forgotten how exhilarating it could be, this sharing of pleasure between two people who knew each other so well, who didn't need to play guessing games, who could measure and anticipate the other's response with each heightened level of excitement.

She bent her head, began to explore Ryan's earlobe with her tongue.

"That does it," he growled. With one swift move he grabbed her, pulled her down onto the mattress and imprisoned her beneath him. "So, you wanna play rough, huh?"

Becca smiled.

"I'll show you rough." Ryan brought his mouth down to hers, teasing her with his lips and tongue. "Take that. And that."

"Mmm, Ryan..."

He tasted like peppermint toothpaste. Becca eagerly kissed him back, craving more and more of him. She trailed her hands down the ridge of his spine, reacquainting herself with every bump, every indentation.

Ryan propped himself up on his elbows and sifted his fingers through her hair with all the greedy delight of a pirate sifting through a treasure chest of jewels. His eyes flashed like the blade of a cutlass, his mouth curving into the satisfied smirk of a buccaneer.

He pinned her wrists to the pillow, began to blaze a slow trail of burning pleasure down her body. He kissed her eyelids, her chin, the pulsating hollow of her neck.

Then her shoulders...her collarbone...the cleft between her breasts.

Becca arched into him. "Ryan, please," she gasped.

He raised his head long enough to send her a satisfied male grin. "Told you it was going to get rough." Then he took the tip of her breast into his mouth.

Molten pleasure spilled through Becca as he swirled his tongue around her hardened nipple. She dug her fingers into his shoulders, silently begging him to enter her, to fill the emptiness inside her, to quench the desire that raged through her till she thought she would fly apart at the seams.

Ryan repositioned himself and started to massage the sensitive juncture of her thighs with the heel of his hand.

Sheer, mindless ecstasy spiraled through her. Reduced to incoherent moans, Becca plucked at him, twining her fingers through his hair, urging him to bring this delicious, mind-numbing torture to its inevitable, explosive climax.

She pushed her hands along his ribs, dragged them across his well-muscled thighs, caressed his pulsing, rigid flesh.

A hoarse cry tore from Ryan's throat.

He levered himself upward, desperately seeking her mouth with his, parting her lips with his tongue. Then in one sure, solid stroke he thrust himself inside her.

A dazzling burst of fireworks exploded in front of Becca's eyes, blinding her, stealing her breath away. Despite the countless times in the past when they'd joined their bodies together as one, tonight their lovemaking had a startling new intensity to it, as if every touch, every breath, every heartbeat were laden with significance.

Perhaps it was the four years of abstinence and deprivation. Perhaps it was the excitement of rekindling and rediscovering the passion that was even stronger, more overpowering than what they'd felt as lovestruck teenagers.

Or perhaps tonight their lovemaking symbolized a celebration of life, a joyful new start to a family that had been destroyed and then miraculously reborn.

As Ryan moved back and forth inside her, his tender caresses, his potent strength carrying her closer and closer to the brink of a whole new frontier of ecstasy, Becca couldn't even begin to figure it all out.

All she was certain of, deep down to the very center of her being, was that she belonged here with Ryan.

A fuse ignited somewhere deep inside her, traveling rapidly, expanding outward, flinging her to the very edge of heart-stopping oblivion.

"Ryan," she breathed. "Darling, I—I—"

And then she was sailing out over the edge, whirled aloft by the most incredible upwelling of pleasure. Just as she thought she'd surely reached the pinnacle of rapture, a fierce shudder racked Ryan's body and he gave a muffled cry that sent her skyrocketing toward the heavens.

Seconds passed...minutes...hours, perhaps. For a timeless interlude they lay panting, collapsed in each other's arms amid a tangle of sheets.

Becca felt dazed, rocked to the core not only by the sublime physical sensations she and Ryan had just shared, but by this incredible, overwhelming sense of togetherness, of emotional union. It felt as if not just their bodies but also their hearts and minds had melded to become as one.

Heartbeats slowed, feverish skin cooled beneath the gentle caress of the night breeze coming through the window. Gradually Becca could hear the hum of crickets again. The old house creaked softly, settling comfortably onto its foundations as if it could finally relax now that everything inside its walls was back to the way it was meant to be.

Ryan hoisted himself up on one arm to gaze down at Becca. He skimmed his hand over the contours of her body as if he couldn't quite believe she was really there. Becca looked deep into his eyes, touched his kiss-swollen mouth with her fingertips, brushed back the sweat-dampened hair that clung to his forehead.

"I love you," Ryan said.

His words sent a flood of joy cascading through her, but it was joy diluted by uncertainty. She ought to say the same words back, but caution dammed them up in her throat. Once those words were out, there would be no going back. She would be committed to living with and loving Ryan the way a wife should.

But that wasn't their agreement! Hadn't they both decided to do what was best for Amy?

On the other hand, what could be better for Amy than living with parents who weren't afraid to express their love not only for her, but for each other...?

Becca was confused, tugged in different directions by conflicting loyalties. Or maybe they really didn't conflict at all.

She threw her arms around Ryan's neck, pulled him back down beside her. "Oh, Ryan..." Her voice was muffled against his shoulder. He was so warm, so generous, so loving. How could she continue to hold a part of herself aloof from him?

He nuzzled her neck, flicking his tongue across her earlobe so that she squirmed with delight. Maybe she should follow Scarlett O'Hara's example and worry about all this tomorrow.

For tonight, it was enough that she was nestled in her husband's arms—that, somehow, after the terrible years of tragedy and separation, they had managed to find each other again.

They snuggled together like spoons, sharing the same pillow. A delicious sleepiness stole over Becca. In the morning...tomorrow...she'd figure it all out. Surely there was some way to reconcile her debt and her duty to Amy with her love for Ryan, so that tonight would be only the first of many, many blissful nights to come.

Ryan's breath tickled her neck. Becca sighed happily.

"Honey," he murmured. "You asleep?"

"Mmm," she replied.

"Did you remember to leave money under Amy's pillow?"

Without opening her eyes, Becca nodded. She rolled over and entwined her limbs through Ryan's. When she drifted off to sleep, it was with a dreamy smile on her lips. Such a considerate father...such a wonderful husband...such a...tender...lover...

Ryan dropped a kiss onto her peaceful, contented brow. "Good night, tooth fairy," he whispered.

He emerged slowly from sleep, reluctant to let go of the dream he'd been enjoying. His senses kicked in one by one. First he noticed sunlight filtering through his closed eyelids, then he heard the blue jay's raucous chatter in the maple tree outside the window, then he felt the warmth, the softness of the woman who still lay cradled in his arms.

The corners of Ryan's mouth quirked lazily upward. So it hadn't been a dream, after all. He inhaled deeply of her sweetly familiar fragrance.

Becca.

With an incredibly delightful sense of well-being, Ryan gently disentangled one arm from around her body and stretched. His muscles felt as limber and capable as the workings of a finely tuned machine this morning. He straightened his legs beneath the partial covering of the sheet and curled his toes with pleasure.

He wondered if he would ever get used to waking up next to Becca again.

God, he hoped not! Not if it meant diminishing this sense of pure contentment, this conviction that he was the luckiest man in the world. Not to mention the tempting zip of excitement that put a speculative gleam of lust in his eye as he craned his neck toward the clock to see how late it was.

He licked his lower lip with satisfaction. Plenty of time.

He cupped one naked breast in his hand and began to nibble on Becca's ear.

She stirred, languidly opened her eyes, and smiled at him. "Good morning."

"It's certainly starting out that way." Ryan continued to knead the soft mound of her breast, relishing her quick intake of breath and the way her pupils dilated sharply in response to his touch.

She framed his face in her hands, touched her lips to his, flicking her tongue along the ridge of his teeth. Now he could feel his own pulse accelerate as desire uncurled deep in his belly.

In the space of a heartbeat he was ready for her, aching for her, longing to sink himself into the inviting folds of her body. She urged him on with her hands, her mouth, her writhing movements.

If last night had been an exquisitely slow, carefully choreographed ballet, then this morning was a quick, frantic tumble in the hay. Ryan arched himself above her, closing his eyes and gritting his teeth as he slid toward the heated core of her body. "Ah, Becca..."

They crescendoed rapidly together, their passion spent as quickly as it had erupted. Ryan lay sprawled on top of her. "I can't move," he groaned into the pillow. "Am I squashing you?"

"Definitely not," Becca replied. "I bet you can move, though."

He shook his head by moving it about a millimeter. "Nope. We may have to lie like this forever."

"Interesting possibility." She tiptoed her fingers across his ribs. "Let's see if you really mean it."

"Becca," he warned in a stern tone.

She completely disregarded it and tickled him, anyway.

"Hey! Cut that out!"

"See? I told you you could move."

"Pretty clever, aren't you? How'd you like a taste of your own medicine, huh?"

Becca giggled, trying unsuccessfully to wiggle out of reach. "Stop it! I mean it, Ryan, or...or—"

"Or what?" he demanded with a wolfish grin.

"Or...or I'll have to use my secret weapon, that's what," she informed him between giggles.

"Secret weapon, huh? And what, pray tell, would that be?"

Becca proceeded to show him. The tickling stopped.

Much later, Ryan roused himself awake with a jaw-cracking yawn. When he opened his eyes, his gaze landed on the bedside clock. "Yikes!"

He scrambled into a sitting position as Becca drowsily mumbled, "What—?"

Ryan brought the clock over to show her. Instantly she was wide-awake. "Oh, my goodness, I had no idea it was so late." She untangled her ankle from the knotted sheet, groping around on the floor for her nightgown.

Ryan slipped on his bathrobe, giving the belt a solid tug to cinch it around his waist. "I'm surprised we haven't heard the dog scratching at the back door to go out."

"I'll let him outside as soon as I look in on Amy." Becca hopped up and down on one foot as she hastily pulled on her panties.

When she moved to step past him, Ryan grabbed her shoulders, temporarily barring her hurried exit from the bedroom. He kissed her lightly on the mouth. "Last night was wonderful," he told her. Another kiss. "So was this morning."

The tiniest frown lines gathered between Becca's pretty blue eyes. She rested her palm against his chest, almost as if she were trying to widen the distance between them. "It *was* wonderful." It came out sounding almost like a question.

Ryan couldn't bear to have her draw away this time—he just couldn't.

He pulled her close against him, giving her a little shake. "I love you, Becca," he said, as if trying to drill the words into her heart.

Her lips parted slightly, but the response he longed to hear didn't emerge. Instead a shadow of uncertainty drifted over her face. He waited for that blasted shutter to slam shut in her eyes, to close him out once again.

Amazingly, it didn't happen. Okay, so maybe she didn't pledge her undying love, but at least she didn't push him away. Even though Becca's eyes were troubled when she unlocked the door and slipped out of the room, Ryan still chalked up the encounter as a minor triumph.

He was whistling when he turned on the water for his shower, encouraged by this sign of progress, happily replaying their lovemaking in his mind.

He was just about to take off his robe when an eerie noise penetrated the loud whoosh of rushing water. Frowning, he turned off the faucet and cocked his head to listen for a repeat of whatever it was he'd heard.

When the sound came again, it turned his blood to ice.

"Ryan!" Becca screamed as she pounded up the stairs.

Dear God, she couldn't go through this again.

This time she wouldn't survive the nightmare…it would close in around her, suffocate her, envelop her in spreading darkness until the pale flickering light of her sanity went out forever.

"Amy!" she cried. "Amy, where are you?"

Becca's mind seemed to jerk back and forth between past and present. One instant she was stumbling along the alley that ran behind their house, the next she was back at the fairgrounds on that terrible night, searching for her baby, the child she wouldn't see again for four long years.

The fear that had lain coiled in Becca's stomach like a hibernating snake ever since Amy's return had sprung forth with terrifying ferocity.

Amy was missing again.

Becca had gone into her daughter's room this morning, found an empty bed. A quick glance at the attic door had shown her it was still bolted from the outside, so Amy couldn't have crept up there to explore. She'd dashed downstairs, run frantically from room to room, checked the backyard, called her little girl's name.

No answer. No sign of her.

That was when Becca had started screaming for Ryan.

It had all happened less than fifteen minutes ago, but to Becca it seemed they'd been searching for fifteen hours. "You take the alley," Ryan had told her as he threw on his clothes. "I'll go up and down the street."

Becca had nodded, her vocal cords paralyzed with fear.

Ryan laid a reassuring hand on her shoulder. "I'm sure she's okay, honey. Probably just wandered off to play somewhere."

Becca pulled away from his touch.

Ryan's mouth tightened. "Southpaw's gone, too, so he's probably with Amy. He'll take care of her." But considering the grim set of Ryan's jaw and the worried look in his eyes, his comforting words hadn't fooled Becca one bit.

She barged through back gates, pounded on back doors. She'd taken great pains to avoid running into the neighbors ever since her return, but their startled surprise at seeing her on their back doorsteps quickly turned to concern as her anxious inquiries tumbled forth.

"Amy? Why, no, I haven't seen her this morning. 'Course, I might not even recognize her, to tell you the truth, but I'd have remembered seeing a little girl...."

"Southpaw? Haven't seen hide nor hair of him. If I do, I'll be sure to let you know...."

Visions of catastrophe leapt in front of Becca's eyes as she continued her frantic search through the neighborhood. Even if Amy hadn't been kidnapped again, she could have been hit by a car—she could be lying in a heap somewhere, injured and unconscious....

Pine Creek was an old gold-rush town. There were still abandoned mining tunnels running beneath the streets, probably long-forgotten mine shafts no one had bothered to close up, concealed in the brush like booby traps just waiting for some helpless child to fall into.

Pine Creek.

The creek!

Southpaw loved to go for walks down there. What if Amy had followed him, slipped on the mossy wet rocks alongside and fallen in? If she'd hit her head, she could easily drown in the shallow water.

Becca froze, then whirled around and charged off in the direction of the creek. Their house was on the outskirts of town. Amy could easily have skipped down to the creek without anyone seeing her. Just last week they'd all been down there taking the dog for a walk, and Amy had fussed a bit when it was time to leave.

Why, oh, why, hadn't she warned Amy not to go back there alone?

Becca's exhausted muscles screamed, her overworked lungs threatened to burst. She had to get to the creek . . . if Amy had fallen in, even seconds could be critical.

Oh, please, don't let me be too late . . . too late . . . too late. . . .

She didn't see or hear Ryan's pursuit until his hand seized her arm and dragged her to a halt.

"Let me go," she gasped, flailing in his grip. "I have to get to her!"

Ryan, too, was panting like mad. "Did you . . . find someone . . . who saw her?"

"No!"

"Then where . . . are you running . . . so fast?"

"The creek!" Finally she managed to wrench away from him.

Ryan took off after her. "How do you know . . . she's down there?"

"I just . . . know!" she called over her shoulder. "South-paw . . . last week . . ."

Ryan must have grasped what she was saying, because he immediately shifted into high gear and sprinted past her. Becca stumbled after him, down the hiking path, along the rock-strewn slope, beneath the concealing trees.

She heard him yelling before she reached the creek. "Amy! Southpaw! Here, boy! Where are you?"

Becca skidded to a halt beside him, nearly toppling into the creek herself when her foot landed on an unstable rock. Ryan grabbed her elbow and hauled her to safer ground.

"Did you hear—?" Before she could even finish the question, Ryan shook his head. Then he inserted two fingers into his mouth and emitted a piercing whistle that made Becca wince.

Silence. Except for their labored breathing, the rustle of leaves, the gurgling rush of water.

Then . . .

From somewhere far away, a dog barking.

Every overwrought muscle in Becca's body snapped to attention. "Is it—?"

"I don't know." Ryan made a shushing motion with his hand. The barking came again. "I think so. Yes! Yes, that's him, I'm sure of it." He grabbed Becca's hand and towed her behind him along the uneven bank of the creek, pushing aside the overhanging branches.

Becca twisted her ankle, but kept on going. The barks were getting louder now. Oh, God, don't let him be standing guard over her limp little body.

Then a break in the trees, a small, pebble-strewn strip of beach. Southpaw came bounding toward them, tongue hanging out, tail wagging furiously. Time switched into slow motion, and Becca could have sworn her heart actually stopped.

Ryan halted one step ahead of her, blocking her view. Oh, no . . . no . . . no . . . please . . .

"Daddy!"

Ryan let out a strangled sound. Then he moved forward so that Becca could see Amy—Amy, her darling, sweet, precious child, the light of her existence—splashing happily in the shallow water right below the creek bank.

Becca lurched forward, arms pinwheeling to keep her balance, and collapsed in a heap beside her daughter as her legs finally gave way. She grabbed Amy in her arms, plastered her face with kisses, held her pinioned against her chest till Amy began to squirm.

"Mommy, I can't breathe!"

Becca held her at arm's length, frantically scanning her child for any sign of injury. Amy was sopping wet from head to toe, but otherwise physically unscathed by her adventure.

Becca hugged her close again, rocking back and forth. "Amy, Amy, we were so worried."

Ryan knelt beside them. He stroked Amy's hair, exchanging a glance of infinite relief with Becca. "You had us pretty scared, princess."

Amy wriggled out of Becca's stranglehold and regarded him solemnly. "I didn't mean to, Daddy. Southpaw and me, we just went for a walk, that's all."

Ryan didn't answer right away, as if he were still trying to get a grip on himself. When at last he spoke, his voice was stern but gentle. "How come you left the house all by yourself, Amy? Didn't Mommy and I tell you not to go out of the yard unless one of us was with you?"

"But I didn't," she replied indignantly. A drop of water dripped from her bangs and plopped onto the tip of her nose. "Southpaw was with me."

Becca could tell Ryan was trying not to smile, but she didn't see anything funny about this narrowly averted disaster. "You should have told us you wanted to go outside, Amy." She smoothed her daughter's wet hair back from her forehead.

"I tried," Amy said, "but I couldn't find you when I got up."

A chill slithered down Becca's spine.

"I went to your room to show you what the tooth fairy left me." Amy beamed at both of them, displaying the gap where her tooth had been. "She gave me a whole dollar!"

Becca swallowed, unable to speak.

Ryan shot her a look of startled comprehension.

"Then I went to Daddy's room to show *him*, but the door was locked."

The truth slammed into Becca with sickening force. While she and Ryan had been making love, playing silly tickle games and otherwise indulging themselves, Amy had come looking for them.

And they hadn't been there for her.

They'd been too wrapped up in themselves, too busy reveling in their own selfish pleasures to spare a thought for their child.

Look what had nearly happened because of it.

Her guilt-ridden, self-recriminating thoughts must have telegraphed themselves to Ryan, because his face shifted into that exasperated, helpless expression he always wore whenever Becca started blaming herself for the past.

During the past few days, she'd almost started to believe that what Ryan had said all along was true. Maybe Amy's kidnapping hadn't been totally her fault. Maybe it *was* simply a case of being in the wrong place at the wrong time. Maybe it *had* been a cruel twist of fate rather than a crime of neglect.

They'd been getting along so well together, really interacting like a family. Amy accepted them as her parents now, and seemed happy to be living with them. Becca and Ryan had been growing closer, mending the huge rift that had separated them. Heavens, you had only to look at last night and this morning for proof of that.

Becca had actually dared to let herself be happy, to believe that maybe she wasn't going to be punished for the rest of her life for one tragic mistake.

But all that had changed now.

She had failed Amy once again. This time there was a happy ending, but the warning was unmistakable. She'd violated her own rules, allowed herself to be distracted by the seductive enticement of Ryan's lovemaking.

Amy had come looking for her. And Becca hadn't been there.

The results could easily have been tragic.

Becca's selfish needs had nearly cost her her child again.

Ryan was shooting her all kinds of meaningful looks, practically dancing up and down with frustration at his inability to speak his mind in Amy's presence.

But this time, Becca wasn't going to be swayed by persuasive words and sweet caresses. She'd vowed to protect Amy, to dedicate her life to making sure her child was safe and happy.

Once again, she'd screwed up big-time. But this was the last, the absolute last time she would let it happen.

Even though it meant that this morning had also been the last time she and Ryan would make love.

Ever again.

She levered herself to her feet, wincing as a stabbing pain shot up her leg from her twisted ankle.

"You all right?" Ryan asked. Becca knew he was inquiring about more than her physical well-being.

"I—I think I must have sprained my ankle." She hopped awkwardly on one foot.

"Here, lean on me." Ryan draped her arm around his neck and slung his arm around her waist. "You going to be able to make it back to the house?"

"I think so." Just an hour ago, Becca had lain in his arms, cherishing his warmth, his closeness, the sound of his breathing. Now, this clumsy embrace was like torture.

They slowly made their way back along the creek with Southpaw blazing the trail. Amy bombarded her mother with solemn looks and anxious inquiries about her progress.

"How's your foot now, Mommy? Does it feel any better yet?"

Becca smiled through gritted teeth. "I think it *is* starting to feel a little better, sweetie."

Her ankle was killing her.

But what Becca couldn't admit to Amy, or to Ryan, or even to herself, was that the pain splintering upward from her twisted ankle was a mere pinprick compared to the pain that lanced through her shattered heart.

Chapter Thirteen

"Becca, let me in there!"

Ryan was trying to keep his voice down, but it was impossible to keep the aggravation out of it. Ever since they'd found Amy down by the creek this morning, Becca had been giving him the cold-shoulder treatment.

He knew exactly the kind of crazy thoughts that were running rampant through that guilt-ridden brain of hers, and he was determined to banish the whole misguided lot of them before they took root.

"Becca! Open up!" He thumped on the guest room door again.

It opened a crack. "Ryan, it's late."

"It's nine-thirty, for cryin' out loud!"

"My ankle . . . I think I should sleep in my own bed tonight so I don't disturb—"

"I know what you think." Losing his patience, he curled his fingers around the edge of the door and pushed it open slowly but firmly so that Becca had no choice but to back up and let him in. "And you're wrong." He closed the door behind him.

Becca crossed her arms. "I'm not going to have an argument with you right now."

"No? Then when are we going to have it? All day you made sure you and I were never alone together. Would you prefer to argue in front of Amy?"

"I'd prefer not to argue at all."

"Becca . . ." Ryan ran his hands through his hair in frustration. "Come to bed. My bed. Our bed. We can talk about this in the morning."

"There's nothing to talk about." Her chin jerked slightly upward. "And it isn't *our* bed anymore. Last night was a mistake—a mistake I don't intend to repeat."

Even though he'd known what she was thinking, her words fell on Ryan like a rain of blows. "A mistake? How can you call what we shared a mistake?"

"Because it could have cost us Amy's life!" Becca blurted out. She clamped a hand over her mouth and flicked a glance toward the wall. Amy was sleeping just on the other side of it.

Ryan seized her by the elbows, hauling her roughly against him. "That's crazy, and you know it. Our making love didn't put Amy in danger."

"How can you say that?" Becca tore herself free and hobbled to the far side of the room. "We didn't hear her when she came looking for us, Ryan. We weren't there to watch out for her." A sob caught in her throat. "Dear God, we actually forgot about her," she whispered in horror.

"That's nonsense." Ryan made a slashing motion with his hand. "Amy is a constant presence in our lives. She's always there in our hearts. Just because we focused our attention on ourselves for a while instead of on our child doesn't mean we forgot her."

"We should have learned our lesson the first time." Becca seemed not to have heard him at all. "After what we've been through, how could we have been so careless?"

The only light in the room came from a small bedside reading lamp. Ryan could barely make out Becca's face in the shadows, but there was no mistaking the anguish, the conviction in her voice. "What happened today was a sign," she said.

Ryan's stomach took a sickening plunge. "No." He could feel her pulling away again, retreating, withdrawing into herself. He couldn't let it happen, couldn't let her shut him out, because this time he sensed it would be for good.

After they'd finally found their way back to each other, how could he stand to lose her again?

He took a deep breath, mustering every rational, reasonable argument he could think of. "Becca, children wander off sometimes," he said, trying to sound calm. "It's a normal childhood occurrence, not some kind of sign. It doesn't have anything to do with the fact that we made love together."

"Yes," she told him in a hushed voice, "it does."

"Honey, I was worried about Amy this morning, too, but that's just a normal part of being a parent." He gave a chuckle that sounded desperate even to his own ears. "Why, I'll bet there's not a parent alive who hasn't panicked over a lost child at one time or another."

"I *won't* let it happen again," Becca said, and the icy, steel edge to her voice chilled Ryan to the bone.

He was losing her. Damn it, he'd had her back for one glorious night, and now he was losing her again. He loved her. Didn't that count for something? Didn't it mean anything to her?

"So you actually believe Amy's little adventure today was the equivalent of some cosmic neon sign, huh? Warning, warning, warning?" Ryan opened and closed his fist to mimic a blinking sign. He'd meant to reason with her.

Now that he saw reasoning was useless, he decided to try sarcasm.

A mistake.

Becca stiffened her spine, knotting her fists at her sides. "I don't care whether you agree with me or not," she said, and the hostile finality in her voice told Ryan he'd lost her. She limped toward him, no longer on the defensive. "We struck a bargain, you and I. I'll admit that I'm the one who broke it last night, but that doesn't invalidate our agreement."

Her coldhearted summation hurt him more than he would have believed possible. "This is our *marriage* we're talking about, for God's sake, not some cold-blooded legal arrangement."

"That's exactly what it is," Becca said quietly. "A legal arrangement. A marriage in name only. That's what we both agreed to."

Something inside Ryan snapped. He yanked Becca into his arms, jammed his fingers through her hair and forced her head back so she had to look up at him. "Can you honestly tell me," he said in a low growl, grinding his body against hers in an obscene parody of their lovemaking, "that you're willing to give this up? That some ridiculous so-called omen is more important to you than this?" He closed his hand over her breast.

Becca flinched at his touch. The ghost of something he recognized as sorrow shimmered through her eyes and was gone. "Yes," she said.

Desperation exploded inside him. He bent his head and kissed her roughly, with no finesse, just sheer brutal determination, as if this assault could somehow breach that damnable wall she'd erected around her heart again.

Becca stood motionless, unresisting and unresponsive, enduring his kiss until his anger spent itself and drained away, leaving behind cold despair, and an empty ache in his chest.

He released her and backed toward the door, wiping his mouth with the back of his hand. "So we're back to square one, is that it?" To have come so far, only to lose her in the end . . . was it any wonder he sounded bitter?

Becca smoothed her hair, straightening her blouse with precise little movements that seemed calculated to give her time to recover before she spoke.

When she met Ryan's eyes, her face was arranged to convey both resignation and determination. "This isn't a chess game," she said. "This is our child's well-being we're talking about."

"You think Amy can be happy when both her parents are miserable?"

Becca's calm conviction seemed to waver for an instant before reasserting itself. "We'll just have to do the best we can," she replied softly.

She appeared as composed and serene as a Madonna when Ryan let himself out of her room, secure in her mother's heart that she'd done what was best for her child.

But as Ryan paused in the hallway to collect himself, still reeling from the devastating blow Becca had dealt him, he heard muffled sobbing from behind the door he'd just closed.

Becca stood at the kitchen window, watching Amy throw a stick for Southpaw in the backyard. She jumped, whirling around at the sudden noise behind her.

"Sorry," Ryan said, replacing the coffeepot on its burner. "Didn't mean to scare you."

She wiped her palms on the skirt of her new suit. "Guess I'm a little nervous, that's all."

"About talking to people at that meeting?" He lifted his coffee mug to his lips, quirking his eyebrows. "Or about leaving Amy here with me?"

"Don't be silly." Becca tugged the sleeves of her blouse so they peeked out from beneath the cuffs of her jacket.

"You're perfectly capable of taking care of Amy. I'm not worried about that."

"Gee, thanks." He sipped his coffee. Everything Ryan said to her these days seemed to have hidden undercurrents, second meanings that lurked beneath the surface of his casual comments.

Kind of like their entire relationship, now that she thought about it. Outwardly they were happily married, loving parents. But beneath the facade they presented to the world festered all kinds of resentments, regrets, recriminations.

Becca didn't blame Ryan for being angry with her. Oh, he'd behaved like a perfect gentleman ever since that last violent kiss a week ago, the night she'd told him that the physical part of their marriage was over for good.

But she couldn't help noticing his brooding glances, the little sarcastic digs that peppered the most innocuous conversation.

She'd turned the most decent, kind, thoughtful man in the world into a hard-edged cynic. Just one more crime she'd committed against the people she loved.

Only around Amy was Ryan his old self—affectionate, full of laughter, eager to go out of his way to surprise her with some special treat.

At least Becca hadn't destroyed the doting-father part of him.

"Shouldn't you get going?" Ryan asked.

Becca checked her watch. Yipes! It was later than she'd realized. Gretchen would be here any minute. She and her two kids were driving to Sacramento for a back-to-school shopping spree, and were going to drop Becca off at her old house so she could retrieve her own car.

Now that the day had actually come, Becca was plagued by second thoughts about agreeing to attend this meeting of the Missing Children Foundation. It felt funny to leave Amy, for one thing. What with a nearly two-hour drive in each direction, Becca would be gone most of the day. This would be the longest she'd been separated from Amy since her return.

But what worried Becca even more was the prospect of facing those grief-stricken parents, of listening to other tragic stories that would surely dredge up the horror of Becca's own experience.

She was one of the incredibly lucky ones. Her story had a happy ending. Her nightmare was over. And Becca wanted to bury it forever.

Ryan followed her into the backyard. "Down!" she scolded Southpaw as he was about to jump up and leave paw prints all over the sober dark outfit she'd bought for the occasion.

"Mommy, you look so different," Amy told her in wide-eyed amazement at Becca's transformation. "You look . . . taller."

Becca smiled. "It's just my high heels." She bent over and kissed the top of Amy's head. "You be a good girl while I'm gone, all right?"

Amy puffed up her chest. "I'm *always* a good girl."

Even as Becca laughed, her eyes misted with tears. That fierce, overpowering surge of love crashed into her again, nearly knocking her to her knees so she could fold Amy into her arms and smother her with kisses.

But a horn honked from out front on the street. "There's Gretchen," Becca said, contenting herself with one last squeeze of Amy's hand. "I'll see you late this afternoon, sweetie." She headed across the yard, her pointy heels sinking into the grass and making her progress a bit undignified.

"Bye, Mommy. I love you!"

"I love you, too," Becca replied, but she was passing by Ryan at the time, and her glance landed on him while she said it.

His eyes narrowed, or maybe he was only squinting into the morning sun. He didn't move, didn't make a sound, but Becca sensed him watching her with intent concentration as she made her wobbly way toward the street.

The back of her neck prickled. Ryan's gaze felt as intimate as a caress. Her skin tingled, her heart beat faster— almost as if she could feel his hands grazing her body. Heaven help her, she still wanted him so much!

All at once Becca was glad she was going to be a hundred miles away for a while.

The meeting was held in a converted storefront in a small, corner shopping mall. The walls of the reception area were plastered with posters of missing children, and volunteers manned the phones, stuffed envelopes and entered data into computers. The clickety-clack of a typewriter provided background noise.

Nancy Woods led Becca into a back room furnished with an overstuffed sofa, a dozen folding chairs and a table holding a pitcher of water, glasses and several boxes of tissues.

"Everyone, I'd like you to meet Becca Slater, the woman I mentioned at our last meeting. Her husband Ryan is home taking care of their little girl, Amy, but Becca has kindly consented to sit in on our meeting today and perhaps share some of her experiences with us."

A subdued murmur of greeting rose in response to Nancy's introduction. Most of the chairs were occupied, and Becca summoned a weak smile as she gingerly lowered herself onto one end of the sofa.

She felt like a fraud. What advice could she possibly give to these people? They were still searching, still suffering, still grieving for their lost children. Frankly, if she were in their place, she would probably resent the hell out of anyone lucky enough to have gotten her child back.

As the meeting got under way, however, Becca couldn't ignore the strange, sad bond between herself and these people. In their hushed voices, their pale faces, their stiff, mechanical movements, she recognized herself. These people were the walking wounded, and she'd been one of them. If they looked and acted like zombies at times, it was only because they were trying so very hard to keep a tight lid on their emotions—to keep from screaming, tearing their hair out, plunging into the abyss of hysteria.

Though Becca was trying very hard to block out the memory, she remembered all too well what it had felt like to be held prisoner in the grip of such a nightmare.

The atmosphere in the room was brittle with tension, as if they were all holding their breaths, waiting for the phone to ring or a policeman to appear in the doorway with news. Any news.

But at least they were going through the motions. They hadn't given up hope. And Becca found herself awestruck at their courage.

They went around in a circle, taking turns reporting on what, if any, progress had been made in the search for their children. Each update was greeted either by sympathetic sounds or hopeful encouragement from the others.

Just about everyone had spoken now, except for Becca and the woman who sat at the other end of the sofa from her. Becca grew increasingly uncomfortable. Was she expected to share her own story? Make a speech? Give some kind of pep talk that would make things better for them?

She couldn't. She simply couldn't. After Amy had disappeared, Becca had been unable to discuss her feelings with Ryan, let alone with a group of strangers. And she didn't think she could do it now. Her heart raced, her palms went clammy with fear.

She sank back into the sofa, weak with relief, when Nancy Woods said, "This is Jean's first meeting with our group. Do you have anything you'd like to share with us, Jean? If you'd rather not just now, that's fine, too.''

The woman at the opposite end of the sofa looked down into her lap, where she'd been twisting her handkerchief into a rope. She wore a faded cotton dress and appeared to be about Becca's age, though it was hard to tell, since her straw-colored ponytail and incredibly thin arms and legs brought to mind a skinny, young teenager.

She glanced nervously around the group with red-rimmed eyes that looked huge in her pale, undernourished face. ''I—I'm a single mother,'' she began. She took a deep, quavering breath, as if even this short statement had been too much for her.

She looked as if a good strong breeze would knock her right over, but she surprised Becca when she continued in a louder but still shaky voice.

''My husband died a few years ago, so I had to go back to work to support our daughter, Crystal.'' Her voice choked off and she pressed the knotted handkerchief to her mouth before continuing. ''I—I don't have much education, see. I got married right out of high school. So to make enough money to support us, I have—*had*—to work two jobs.''

The other members had shifted their chairs toward her now. But their faces were filled with compassion, not curiosity.

''I can't—couldn't—afford day care for Crystal, but I'm usually there when she gets home from school. I get off one job at three in the afternoon, then I have a little break until I start my evening job at five. So Crystal and me, we have a snack together, then my sister picks her up and takes her over to her house to play with her kids. My sister feeds her supper, puts her to bed, then I pick her up when my shift's over and take her on home.''

Becca noticed that Jean had stopped correcting herself when she spoke in present tense, as if she couldn't bear to face the significance of using the past tense.

"Then one afternoon, about a year ago, when Crystal was ten, I got held up at work. I didn't get home till after four, and Crystal—Crystal wasn't there." Jean's voice rose to a high pitch and choked off. Instinctively, Becca reached out a hand to her, but Jean nodded briefly as if to indicate she was all right.

"I thought...I thought my sister had already picked her up. I wasn't worried a bit. I had to rush around to get ready for my other job, see, so in a way I was glad Crystal had already left." Her words spilled over each other in a rapid torrent now. "I went to work, and right after I got there I got a call from my sister. 'Where's Crystal?' she asked. 'I went by to pick her up and she wasn't there.'"

Jean dabbed her streaming eyes. "See, my sister had had car trouble, and it took her a while to get to a phone. She hadn't picked Crystal up at all. So I called the school, but there was no one there. I told my boss I was sick, and he let me go so when I got out I drove over to the school and looked around for her. But she wasn't there! She wasn't anywhere!"

Jean's frail body shook with sobs. Becca slid over beside her and put an arm around her shoulders. She felt sick herself, sick with grief over what this poor woman had suffered, over what they'd all suffered. Sick with understanding.

"I called the police," Jean went on in a voice clogged with tears. "But they never found any trace of her. She just—disappeared! She's gone! My little girl's gone, and I'll never even know what happened to her!"

Half the people in the room were crying by now. Tears trickled down Becca's cheeks as she hugged Jean, wishing with all her heart she could think of something to say to comfort her, instead of just patting her helplessly on the shoulder.

"Why? Why? Why?" Jean pounded her fist on the arm of the sofa, sounding as if her jaw had been wired shut. "Why didn't I check earlier, to make sure she was really at my sister's? Maybe the police could have found something then, if I hadn't been so stupid, so careless."

"You had no reason to think anything was wrong," Becca said, trying to soothe her. "Anyone would have assumed the same—"

"I should have fixed it so I could pick her up at school every day," Jean went on, her eyes glazed with sorrow. "If only I was smart enough to get a decent job, if only I could have afforded to move us out of that crummy neighborhood where terrible things like that happen. It's my fault! I should have been there to protect her, to walk her home from school so that some creep couldn't—"

"Stop it!" Becca said, startling herself along with everyone else in the room. "Stop it right now." A blinding, razor-sharp emotion was rising inside her, and she was astonished to recognize it as anger.

She gave Jean a little shake. "It wasn't your fault. Parents can't guard their children twenty-four hours a day. You're a good mother—look at how hard you worked to provide for your child!"

Jean sniffed. "I should have watched her more closely, made sure she was safe."

"You did the best you could under the circumstances." Her own words reverberated inside Becca like an eerie echo. Wasn't this exactly what Ryan had tried to tell her from the beginning?

She focused intently on Jean's swollen, doubtful eyes, digging up every scrap of her persuasive ability to make the poor woman understand what Becca herself hadn't been able to. "No matter how watchful we are," she went on, "short of locking our kids in their rooms until they grow up, there's just no way we can protect them every single second."

From the corner of her eye, Becca noticed that the other group members were sitting up straighter, nodding in agreement.

"But I'm her mother," Jean said with a little gulp. "I was responsible for taking care of her."

"You're not responsible for what some lousy creep decides to do," Becca said. "Instead of blaming yourself, you should be blaming whoever took her."

Jean still looked unconvinced. Frustrated, Becca searched her heart for words that could make her see the truth. When she finally found them, she recognized the words as Ryan's.

"What happened to Crystal isn't your fault any more than if she'd been struck by lightning or hit by a car. It was a terrible, terrible tragedy, and I guess when something like that happens to someone we love, we have to find someone to blame." Becca squeezed Jean's hands. "But for God's sake, don't blame yourself. Don't turn all that pain and guilt and anger inward, because if you do, it'll destroy you and everyone who cares for you." She gave a bitter laugh. "Believe me, I know."

And then, amazingly, Becca found herself telling her own story to these kind, understanding strangers. It was a story full of despair and hope, full of terrible loss and great joy. But when she was finished, Becca realized it was also a story without an ending. Yet.

As long as she kept blaming herself, punishing herself the same way Jean was doing, the nightmare of Amy's kidnapping would never truly be over.

People came up to shake Becca's hand as the meeting broke up. Several, including Jean, asked for her phone number, wondered if Becca would mind if they called to talk sometime.

She gave out her number gladly, feeling excited and alive and pleased that she might be able to help. Inside she felt strangely buoyant, as if a great weight had been lifted from her heart. Somehow, through sharing her own torment and trying to stop others from falling into the same trap of guilt and self-hatred, Becca had finally exorcised her own demons.

She would always regret leaving Amy alone at the fairgrounds during those few fateful moments four years ago. But the guilt that had poisoned her soul, destroyed her marriage and tainted her happiness at Amy's miraculous return had finally loosened its grip, allowing her spirit to soar free and the boundless love she had tried to contain to blossom and expand inside her.

Ryan. He'd never stopped trying to convince Becca that her guilt was misplaced, that she deserved to be happy. He'd never given up on her, even when she'd pushed him away. He'd agreed to Becca's unreasonable terms of marriage when most men would have laughed in her face and walked away.

He must really love her.

Maybe even as much as she loved him.

Becca felt like a fool, remembering now how she'd insisted that Amy's disappearance last week was a sign, a warning to keep their emotional distance from each other.

Everything seemed so clear now that the dark, obscuring clouds of guilt had blown away. She and Ryan were meant for each other. How could she ever have doubted that for a second? The three of them were meant to live together as a family—a real family, not just three people living under the same roof.

Her love for Ryan was part and parcel of her love for Amy. It was wrong to try to separate the two, to store them away in separate compartments of her heart.

Even if she could anymore.

Suddenly Becca could hardly wait to get back to Pine Creek, to tell Ryan she finally understood what he'd been saying all along.

To tell him she loved him.

She was accelerating down the interstate on-ramp when an awful thought struck her. In her mind's eye she fast-forwarded through the past week—Ryan's aloof behavior, the little sarcastic barbs he tossed her way whenever they spoke, the disgusted, fed-up twist of his mouth.

Maybe she'd finally gone too far. Maybe her hysterical reaction to Amy's brief disappearance last week had finally convinced Ryan she was a lost cause.

Maybe she'd finally managed to destroy his love once and for all.

Becca's foot instinctively pressed down harder on the gas pedal. Her hands clenched the steering wheel in a white-knuckled grip as she headed up the freeway, back toward the mountains.

Toward home.

Hoping with all her heart that it wasn't too late.

Chapter Fourteen

Took Amy to the fair. Back before dinner. R.

Becca stared at the note she'd found stuck to the refrigerator with a magnet.

The county fair. Dear God, the same place she'd taken Amy the day she was kidnapped.

Her hand trembled as she laid the note on the kitchen table. Back before dinner, it said. She glanced at the clock. Gosh, it was after four already. They'd be back soon enough. There was really no need for her to go over to the fairgrounds and look for them.

The place would be jammed with people, anyway. And really, what was the rush? What she had to say to Ryan would keep.

"Oh, nuts," Becca said softly. Then she dashed upstairs to change her clothes.

She was so tired of being afraid, so tired of going through life looking back over her shoulder, checking under the bed, jumping when the phone rang.

Hadn't she decided on the drive home from Sacramento that today marked the start of a whole new life for her? For all of them?

And guilt, pain and fear had no place in this new life.

Sooner or later she was going to have to stop cowering, to stop avoiding certain people, certain places. And returning to the site of Amy's kidnapping, confronting those terrifying memories, was certainly a step in the right direction.

So why was her skin crawling with dread, as if she were on a roller coaster creeping up that first impossibly steep, death-defying stretch of track?

Becca drove to the fairgrounds, then sat in the parking lot taking deep breaths before she mustered the nerve to walk up and buy an admission ticket.

Once inside the gates, she was transported back in time with an abrupt jolt that nearly made her heart stop. Once again she was a young mother with a baby, pushing the stroller through the crowd of fair-goers, unaware that somewhere in that crowd lurked a disturbed woman who was about to change the course of her life forever with one tragic, impulsive—

"Stop it," Becca scolded herself, drawing a few strange looks from passersby. "Amy isn't a baby anymore. Four years have gone by. The important thing is that she's home again, that we're a real family again."

Or at least they were going to be, if it wasn't too late.

Becca headed deeper into the fairgrounds, swiveling her head from side to side for a glimpse of Ryan and Amy. This, too, reminded her of that horrible night, of her frantic, futile search....

And, oh, the smells! Popcorn, cotton candy, caramel apples. The smells evoked that fateful night with such vivid intensity that her stomach churned with nausea.

From the direction of the midway, people screamed. Becca's heart leapt into her throat. Then she realized it was only the enthusiastic riders on the roller coaster. She turned her footsteps in that direction.

The tinny waltz music from the whirling merry-go-round...the crack of toy rifles from the shooting arcade...the thumps and delighted squeals of kids driving bumper cars....

Becca began to walk faster and faster.

Then she spotted Ryan and Amy.

They were standing at the end of a long line for the Ferris wheel, right behind the McCoys. Gretchen spotted Becca first and nudged Ryan with her elbow.

He turned, his eyes widening in surprise as she approached. "Becca," he said slowly. "I didn't expect to see you here."

"Mommy, look! Daddy won this for me at the ring-toss!" Amy hugged an enormous purple giraffe.

"Did he?" Becca kissed her on the cheek, tasted sugar. "How wonderful! Are you having fun?"

"Oh, yes." Amy bobbed her golden curls emphatically. "I've never been to a fair before."

"Is that right?" Becca kept her smile carefully pinned in place. She ruffled Amy's hair. "Well, I'm glad you're having a good time."

She turned to Ryan, found him watching her closely. She swallowed, suddenly nervous. She had so much to say, but she hadn't really considered how to begin. "Could...could I talk to you for a minute?"

He lifted his eyebrows. "Right this second? We're about to go on the—"

Gretchen took one look at her friend's face and interrupted. "Amy can ride with one of us if you don't get back in time. Right, Tyler?"

"Why, sure! She can squeeze right in next to Christopher and me." He poked Amy's prized possession. "'Course, I'm not sure how we're gonna fit Mr. Giraffe in, too, but we'll manage."

"Thanks, Tyler." Becca shot him a grateful glance. Gretchen winked at her.

Ryan had a sinking feeling deep in his gut as he and Becca moved away from the line of people. Whatever Becca wanted to talk about, it must be pretty darn important to have brought her back to the place where Amy had been kidnapped.

He dreaded hearing what new conclusion she'd come to in that guilt-fogged brain of hers. First, it was separate beds. Then she'd changed her mind for one night. Then she'd called their lovemaking a terrible mistake that could never happen again.

What if she'd finally figured out a way to ensure there would be no repeat of that one magical night?

What if she'd decided to leave him?

His heart plummeted at the thought.

"I guess this isn't exactly the best place to have a private conversation," Becca said with a nervous laugh. The midway was thronged with fair-goers, and any discussion they had would likely be overheard by several dozen people.

Personally, Ryan himself wasn't all that eager to hear what Becca had to say. Might as well get this painful ordeal over with, though. "This way," he said, leading her off to one side.

Behind the Ferris wheel was a deserted area with giant cables snaking across the ground, winding through other assorted equipment belonging to the ride operators. It was noisy back here, but it would have to do.

"Okay, what's all this about?" he asked, dreading the answer.

Becca clasped her hands together, then unclasped them. Whatever motive had prompted her to rush to the fairgrounds seemed to have run out of steam. She murmured something Ryan didn't catch over the racket made by the rides.

He cupped his hand behind his ear. "You'll have to speak up, Becca."

Her skin was pale, stretched taut across her fine-boned features with tension. "I said, I didn't know this would be so difficult," she repeated at a louder volume.

Ryan's stomach took another sickening swoop. Damn it, she *was* leaving him! For the past week he'd felt like a fool for ever believing they could have a normal marriage again, that they could ever regain the love, the passion, the magic they'd once shared.

He'd been bitterly disappointed by Becca's irrational insistence otherwise. But the last week seemed like a stroll through paradise compared to the bleak, empty existence that awaited him if Becca left him for good.

Now the realization struck Ryan with full force that he would rather have half a marriage than no marriage at all. He would agree to any terms, strike any bargain to keep Becca in his life.

But if she'd made up her mind to go, Ryan knew he couldn't stop her. Any more than he'd been able to stop her the first time she'd left.

A steel fist clamped around his heart and squeezed painfully. "Tell me," he said in a strained voice.

The harsh slant of his features, his almost belligerent posture, struck Becca as ominous. He certainly didn't appear to be in a very receptive mood to hear what she had to tell him.

"I—" She twisted her hands together. What on earth had made her think this was going to be easy? "Ryan, there's something I have to— That is, there's so much I want to say...."

His hooded, dark eyes weren't giving anything away. Dear God, what if she told Ryan she loved him, only to have him look back at her with pity?

"I want to ask you to forgive me," she said.

Amazingly, she thought relief flashed across his face. His entire body seemed to relax slightly, as if some imminent danger had passed, but he remained on guard. "Becca, for Pete's sake, how many times do we have to—"

"No, no, it's not that," she said hastily.

"I understand that it's difficult for you to be here at the fairgrounds, to deal with all the unpleasant memories it dredges up—"

"Ryan, please!"

"—but to tell you the truth, I'm really not up to hearing you confess your imagined sins one more time." He sounded weary rather than irritated, but his eyes were watchful, expectant.

"You don't understand." Not that she blamed him. Good heavens, most men would have reached the end of their patient understanding long ago. "What I'm trying to tell you is that you were right all along. I see that now. Finally." Becca spread her hands in a pleading gesture. "I'm asking you to forgive me for taking so long to see the truth."

Ryan opened his mouth, then snapped it shut. He peered at her cautiously. "What do you mean, exactly?"

"I mean that I've finally accepted that Amy's kidnapping wasn't all my fault. That I can't keep punishing myself for what happened."

Ryan straightened in surprise, his sandy eyebrows spiking upward. "That must have been some meeting you went to today," he said, stroking his jaw.

Becca gave him a relieved smile. "Yes. It was."

All at once his expression turned stony again. "So someone there at the meeting was finally able to convince you of what I've been trying to for years."

"Yes! No!" Oh, dear, this wasn't going at all the way she'd planned. "I mean, it was *you* who convinced me, Ryan. I found myself trying to persuade another mother that she wasn't to blame, and I heard your words coming out of my mouth."

"I see." Instantly Ryan was ashamed. It was selfish to get all bent out of shape over the idea that a complete stranger had succeeded where he hadn't. He should be thankful that Becca had finally stopped being so hard on herself—no matter who had gotten through to her. "I'm pleased to hear it," he told her. "But don't you think we'd better get back to—"

"Ryan, wait." She put her hand on his arm.

Ryan's gaze dropped to her hand, which was trembling. He looked up at her face, at the way she was biting her lower lip to keep it from quivering, at those luminous blue eyes so full of anxiety and concern.

Whatever Becca was about to say, she was worried about how he would take the news.

Warning alarms clanged noisily inside his head, drowning out the sounds of the midway and the panicky pounding of his heart. She *was* going to leave him, after all!

Ryan gazed helplessly at his wife, whose hair shimmered with glints of gold in the sunshine, whose slender, delicate frame belied the incredible strength that had allowed her to survive so much tragedy.

She was the most beautiful woman in the world, and he'd adored her ever since he'd spotted her standing on the sidelines during high school football practice.

Now, she was about to tell him goodbye forever.

Ryan braced himself for the blow, though he knew nothing could lessen the crushing impact.

"What is it?" he said.

Becca had to read Ryan's lips to make out what he was saying. All of a sudden he'd gone very quiet and still. Why should he look so worried, unless he anticipated what she wanted to tell him and dreaded having to hurt her?

"I—I know now that it wasn't my fault our baby was stolen," she began haltingly. "And I . . . also realize that I can't protect Amy by cutting myself off from the other people I love."

Something ignited in Ryan's eyes at her choice of words. Then caution—or regret—quickly extinguished it. "Well, I'm happy you realize that now."

Becca gathered up all her courage. She and Ryan were standing only a couple of feet from each other, yet it felt like she was about to leap across the widest chasm she'd ever encountered in her life. "And you were right about something else. I *was* trying to punish myself by denying myself a chance at happiness, by denying—" she took a deep breath "—my feelings for you."

Ryan didn't move a muscle, yet somehow his entire body tensed. A popcorn-scented breeze rustled his hair. "Becca, what—" He cleared his throat, flicked a few strands of hair out of his eyes. "What exactly are you trying to say?"

And all at once it was easy. The easiest thing in the world.

"I love you, Ryan," she said simply.

He blinked. An entire spectrum of emotions shuffled rapidly across his handsome face—astonishment, relief... then, miraculously, love.

"Oh, Becca." His voice was hoarse as he pulled her into his arms.

She flung her arms around his waist, squeezing her eyes shut as Ryan held her tight against his chest. Beneath the cotton fabric of his shirt she could hear his heart thumping wildly.

"I thought you were going to tell me...I mean, I thought you meant...aw, never mind." His ragged voice was muffled by her hair. "Becca, honey...I love you. I love you so much."

Astonishingly, she thought she heard tears in his voice. She tightened her grip around him, snuggled even closer into the hard, familiar contours of his body. Happiness flooded through her like a healing balm, and at that moment, Becca knew she had finally come home.

"Mommy, Daddy, hurry up!"

There were probably hundreds of children all over the fairgrounds impatiently hollering at their parents. But this particular, precious voice was instantly recognizable.

Becca lifted her head from Ryan's chest, and they both turned toward the Ferris wheel. The McCoys and Amy had reached the head of the line.

Still holding Becca close, Ryan smoothed back her hair, then kissed her lightly on the mouth. "Guess we'd better hurry, huh?"

She smiled dreamily up at him, feeling nearly as shy and excited as a teenager on her first date. But as she looked deep into those dark brown eyes so full of love, of kindness, of patience and understanding, a tide of serene contentment rose up within Becca, filling all the empty spaces inside her.

She lifted her hand to touch the side of his face. "We have all the time in the world now."

"Mommy, Daddy... come *on!*"

Ryan rolled his eyes. "All the time in the world, you said?"

Becca laughed. "Oops! Come on, we'd better run."

Hand in hand, they arrived breathlessly just as the ride attendant was about to boost Amy onto the Ferris wheel next to Tyler and Christopher.

Then it was their turn to board. "Up you go, princess," Ryan said. Amy kicked her feet back and forth with excited glee as she settled in between her parents.

The ride slowly began to move. Ryan dropped his arm along the back of their seat, then made a face and repositioned the big purple giraffe so he had a clear view of Becca over the top of Amy's gleaming blond head.

I love you, he mouthed silently as they rose upward. "And as soon as we're back on good, solid ground," he said aloud with a wink, "I fully intend to prove it to you."

Becca's heart lifted toward the sky along with the Ferris wheel. Up, up, up they went till the people below shrank to tiny toy figures and she could see over the trees, past the nearest ridge to the pine-blanketed mountains beyond.

She was filled with exhilaration, buoyed up by happiness, ready to soar to the heavens now that she'd finally broken free of the chains of guilt that had shackled her to the dreary walls of her own private dungeon.

Now, at last, Becca was no longer afraid to open her heart to the only man she'd ever loved, the one man on earth who'd shared her greatest joys, her deepest tragedies.

"Whee!" Amy cried, her hair whipping about her head. "This is so fun, Daddy!"

Ryan threw back his head and laughed, and the warm, loving sound of it went straight to Becca's heart.

"Look how high up we are!" Amy's eyes were huge with wonder when she turned to look at Becca. "My stomach feels kind of funny, but kind of good, too." She tilted her head to one side, considering. "It feels like it's happy."

Becca hugged her, knowing that at last they'd come full circle. Through loss and heartbreak, through hope and despair, somehow they'd all survived to become a family once again.

Thanks to a miracle. Thanks to love.

Amy scissored her legs back and forth and aimed an eager, gap-toothed smile over her shoulder. "Mommy, have you ever felt this happy before?"

Becca glanced over the top of Amy's head, saw the twitch of Ryan's mouth, the twinkle in his eye and the love written all over his face. "No, sweetie," she replied, linking her fingers through her husband's. "I never have."

* * * * *

JINGLE BELLS, WEDDING BELLS:
Silhouette's Christmas Collection for 1994

Christmas Wish List

*To beat the crowds at the malls and get the perfect present for *everyone,* even that snoopy Mrs. Smith next door!

*To get through the holiday parties without running my panty hose.

*To bake cookies, decorate the house and serve the perfect Christmas dinner—just like the women in all those magazines.

*To sit down, curl up and read my Silhouette Christmas stories!

Join *New York Times* bestselling author Nora Roberts, along with popular writers Barbara Boswell, Myrna Temte and Elizabeth August, as we celebrate the joys of Christmas—and the magic of marriage—with

Silhouette's Christmas Collection for 1994.

MILLION DOLLAR SWEEPSTAKES (III)

No purchase necessary. To enter, follow the directions published. Method of entry may vary. For eligibility, entries must be received no later than March 31, 1996. No liability is assumed for printing errors, lost, late or misdirected entries. Odds of winning are determined by the number of eligible entries distributed and received. Prizewinners will be determined no later than June 30, 1996.

Sweepstakes open to residents of the U.S. (except Puerto Rico), Canada, Europe and Taiwan who are 18 years of age or older. All applicable laws and regulations apply. Sweepstakes offer void wherever prohibited by law. Values of all prizes are in U.S. currency. This sweepstakes is presented by Torstar Corp., its subsidiaries and affiliates, in conjunction with book, merchandise and/or product offerings. For a copy of the Official Rules send a self-addressed, stamped envelope (WA residents need not affix return postage) to: MILLION DOLLAR SWEEPSTAKES (III) Rules, P.O. Box 4573, Blair, NE 68009, USA.

EXTRA BONUS PRIZE DRAWING

No purchase necessary. The Extra Bonus Prize will be awarded in a random drawing to be conducted no later than 5/30/96 from among all entries received. To qualify, entries must be received by 3/31/96 and comply with published directions. Drawing open to residents of the U.S. (except Puerto Rico), Canada, Europe and Taiwan who are 18 years of age or older. All applicable laws and regulations apply; offer void wherever prohibited by law. Odds of winning are dependent upon number of eligibile entries received. Prize is valued in U.S. currency. The offer is presented by Torstar Corp., its subsidiaries and affiliates in conjunction with book, merchandise and/or product offering. For a copy of the Official Rules governing this sweepstakes, send a self-addressed, stamped envelope (WA residents need not affix return postage) to: Extra Bonus Prize Drawing Rules, P.O. Box 4590, Blair, NE 68009, USA.

SWP-S994

MONTANA
Mavericks

Stories that capture living and loving beneath the Big Sky, where legends live on...and the mystery is just beginning.

This October, discover more MONTANA MAVERICKS with

SLEEPING WITH THE ENEMY
by Myrna Temte

Seduced by his kiss, she almost forgot he was her enemy. *Almost.*

And don't miss a minute of the loving as the mystery continues with:

THE ONCE AND FUTURE WIFE
by Laurie Paige (November)
THE RANCHER TAKES A WIFE
by Jackie Merritt (December)
OUTLAW LOVERS
by Pat Warren (January)
and many more!

Wait, there's more! Win a trip to a Montana mountain resort. For details, look for this month's MONTANA MAVERICKS title at your favorite retail outlet.

Only from ❤ *Silhouette*® where passion lives.

BABIES ON BOARD
Gina Ferris
(SE #913, October)

As if being stranded in a jungle wasn't enough,
Kate Hennessy had been left to care for three helpless,
irresistible infants! And the sole person who could
help was know-it-all Matt Sullivan. He was definitely
trouble—and the only man who ever made Kate feel
like a natural woman....

**Don't miss BABIES ON BOARD,
by Gina Ferris, available in October!**

She's friend, wife, mother—she's you! And beside
each Special Woman stands a wonderfully
special man. It's a celebration of our heroines—
and the men who become part of their lives.

Don't miss **THAT SPECIAL WOMAN!** each month—
from some of your special authors! Only from
Silhouette Special Edition!

TSW1094

WHAT EVER HAPPENED TO...?

Have you been wondering when much-loved characters will finally get their own stories? Well, have we got a lineup for you! Silhouette Special Edition is proud to present a *Spin-off Spectacular!* Be sure to catch these exciting titles from some of your favorite authors:

A HOME FOR THE HUNTER (September, SE #908) Jack Roper was looking for wayward Olivia Larrabee...and then he discovers a Jones family secret, in the next JONES GANG tale from *Christine Rimmer*.

A RIVER TO CROSS (September, SE #910) Shane Macklin and Tina Henderson shared a forbidden passion which they can no longer deny, in the latest tale from *Laurie Paige*'s WILD RIVER series.

**Don't miss these wonderful titles, only for our readers—
only from Silhouette Special Edition!**

SPIN6

Maddening men...winsome women...and the untamed land
they live in—all add up to love!

A RIVER TO CROSS (SE #910)
Laurie Paige

Sheriff Shane Macklin knew there was more to "town outsider"
Tina Henderson than met the eye. What he saw was a generous
and selfless woman whose true colors held the promise of love....

Don't miss the latest Rogue River tale, A RIVER TO CROSS, available
in September from Silhouette Special Edition!

BABY'S CHOICE

Join Marie Ferrarella—and not one, but two, beautiful babies—as her "Baby's Choice" series concludes in October with *BABY TIMES TWO* (SR #1037)

She hadn't thought about Chase Randolph in ages, yet now Gina Delmonico couldn't get her ex-husband out of her mind. Then fate intervened, forcing them together again. Chase, too, seemed to remember their all-too-brief marriage—especially the honeymoon. And before long, these predestined parents discovered the happiness—and the family—that had always been meant to be.

It's "Baby's Choice" when angelic babies-in-waiting select their own delivery dates, only in

Silhouette ROMANCE™